THE ISLAND OF DR SADE

'Slow but steady, girls,' Philippa ordered. 'Take a lungful of air and *ration* it. But not too slow. There's a delicate balance to be struck and a possibility that Cock-breath, perverted as she is, will learn to take pleasure in being blown upon. That's it. Excellent. Now, carry on while we get Edwina ready for her waxing.'

Theodora bucked and rocked again, unable to prevent another snarl of frustration escaping her lips. Philippa had been right again, damn her: she *had* been beginning to take pleasure in the breath being blown across her left nipple, but now Jacky had lowered the rate at which she was blowing and the pleasure was no longer there. How cruel they were being to her. Bringing her to the point of orgasm, then dragging her back from the brink. But cruellest of all, chief tormentrix, Inquisitrix General, was Philippa, who was now speaking again.

'Ah, so there little Winnie's nipples are. *Look* at them, girls. How they glisten with Zoë's spittle! And they're *stiff* too, look. What an excitable little thing she is, to be sure. But we have a cure for that, in our hot wax. Light the candle again, darlings. But first, as I mentioned before, I need to renew my *salt* and Winnie, most considerately, has shed copious quantities of salted water on her cheeks. Here, let me lick them before we begin to drip hot wax on her nipples.'

THE ISLAND OF DR SADE

Wendy Swanscombe

This book is a work of fiction.
In real life, make sure you practise safe, sane and
consensual sex.

First published in 2007 by
Nexus
Thames Wharf Studios
Rainville Rd
London W6 9HA

A catalogue record for this book is available from the
British Library.

www.nexus-books.com

Typeset by TW Typesetting, Plymouth, Devon

ISBN 978 0 352 34112 9

Penguin Random House is committed to a sustainable future for
our business, our readers and our planet. This book is made from
Forest Stewardship Council® certified paper.

Printed and bound in Great Britain by Clays Ltd, St Ives plc

Though she received the male in three orifices she nevertheless berated Nature for not having pierced her breasts with larger holes, that she might contrive a new form of coition in that part of her body also.

The Empress Theodora described in Procopius's *Anecdota*, or *The Secret History*, Chapter IX (c. 550)

'Pray do not interrupt anything on my account, Signor,' I hastened to say to him, 'simply remember that she is not the one you contracted for.'

'And I am dreadfully sorry about it,' the rake replied, his words punctuated by gasps of pleasure. 'I am dreadfully – sorry – for her arse – the most beautiful arse in creation, the – tightest fitting – oh, with this there are – wonders to be achieved . . .'

The Marquis de Sade, *Juliette* (1797)

. . . une tasse pleine de cornichons et d'oignons au vinaigre, Boule de Suif, comme toutes les femmes, adorant les crudités . . .

Guy de Maupassant, *Boule de Suif* (1880)

As I opened the double door into the dining room, blow me if Boris, the new gardener, didn't pop up from behind some flower arrangement, playing out a length of flex to a wall-socket and explaining in that peculiar accent of his: 'Zis dropical daffodil cannot survive wizzout heat.'

The Best of 'Dear Bill': The Collected Letters of Denis Thatcher, Richard Ingrams and John Wells (1986)

One

Dear Diary,
It's Marie's birthday today (elle a dix-huit ans, cher journal!) *and the darling ship's cook has made an absolutely scrumptious cake for her. Where he got all the ingredients from nobody knows, but Philippa is determined to find out and I don't much fancy the kitchen-staff's chances of keeping the secret when she starts batting those big brown eyes of hers and playing all those other little tricks she has! I've seen men melt like butter when she starts, the minx, but,* comme Catherine dit, *she doesn't mind as . . .*

'Theodora!'

The cry came faint but clear through the cabin-wall behind her.

'Damn.'

She sighed, put down her pen and twisted in her seat, feeling sweat slide on her skin beneath her blouse.

'What is it?' she called back to the wall.

'We're waiting to eat the rest of the cake, Dorrie! Can't start without you!'

'All right! Just let me finish this line!'

She turned back and picked up her pen.

. . . long as they don't stay melted like butter.

Now to hide the diary again. She suspected – no, she *knew* – that Philippa or one of Philippa's spy-squad had been searching for it, eager for the raw ingredients of power it contained, and she was determined to keep it out of their hands as long as she could. Not that they would make much of it when they *did* get their hands on it: none of them would make head or tail of her personal shorthand. She smiled at the thought of it, still holding the book open as she pushed her chair back and stood up, feeling trickles of sweat begin to find new routes down her body. Damn this heat! But it was really the humidity that made it so trying. Ink didn't dry, for one thing, and neither did sweat, and *that* had greatly curtailed their freedom. They were under strict orders from Miss Callaghan not to go *anywhere* near the troop-deck. The sight of eighteen-year-old schoolgirls would be bad enough, but eighteen-year-old schoolgirls with clothes made semi-transparent by perspiration – oh, it didn't bear thinking about!

She smiled again, glancing down at her breasts and the faint pink smudge of nipple visible through the sweat-soaked cloth over each. No bra, you naughty girl, Dorrie! Think how provoking you would be to any young soldier who chanced to see you! But Miss Callaghan was in her lair, taking a class of the younger girls, so the older girls were safe for the next hour. Which would be quite enough time. There, that would baffle them for a little longer and she wouldn't have to close the pages, so the ink would have a chance to fully dry. She slid the diary into the cavity and stepped back, putting her head on one side, then the other, checking that the book was well aligned with the edge of the panelling, and nodded. Fine. Now for the rest of the birthday cake! She automatically wiped her hands on the back of her skirt at the thought of it, her face assuming an almost professional seriousness. Dry hands for a clean grip, Dorrie. Most important.

The corridor outside her cabin felt fractionally cooler, shielded as it was from the steamy breath of sea that had come through her open porthole, and she wanted to stay there longer. But the birthday cake called and she knocked softly on the door next to hers. *Tit-tit-tat tit-tit.* A suppressed giggle sounded in the cabin beyond, there was a rattle of key-in-lock and the door opened a crack through which she was surveyed by a pair of cool blue eyes that could only belong to Edwina.

'In,' came the whisper, and she whisked through the door as it was swung half-open for a moment. As Edwina closed and locked it again, Theodora took hold of her buttocks through her dress and squeezed, provoking a wriggle and squeak.

'I want to *swim* in your eyes, Winnie,' she murmured into the slender blonde's ear, then kissed it, savouring the impression of its whorls on her lips.

'Alas, her eyes are *mine*,' came Philippa's drawl from behind her, and she spun to face the rest of the cabin.

'Ears as sharp as ever, Philly,' she said coldly.

'Yes, dear. Now, if you two are quite finished?'

Edwina wriggled free of Theodora's grip, trotting back to one of the two empty chairs around the table. Theodora turned and was met by twelve pairs of eyes. She nodded, drew the air of the cabin into her nostrils for a moment, then released it with a satisfied sigh.

'I can smell the cake from here,' she said. '*And* all those *lovely* cocks!'

'Slut,' said Philippa. 'Get into your place.'

There were five girls sitting at the table now, including Edwina, and to the right of each, unzipped and blushingly erect, stood a young British soldier. Theodora walked to her place and sat down, running her eyes over the cock that quivered with extra excitement beside her, then lifting them to probe her soldier's face.

'Are your balls full, cocky?' she asked in her Australian accent, smiling as she watched the fresh skin flush a deeper red. Someone giggled, but Philippa tutted.

'Stop it, Theodora. *All* of their balls are full, as you well know. Now, the rules of the willy-race are as ever but I'll just run through them again for the benefit of two of our guests, who are meeting us for the first time. Using bare right hand only – nothing more, I'm afraid, boys – we girls will manipulate these six fine members to successive *paroxysm*.' (Theodora met Gwen's eyes for a moment, with an almost imperceptible quirk of her eyebrows.) 'You boys are asked to direct your *effusion* onto the cake that rests in the middle of the table.' (She watched Gwen pretend to examine her soldier's cock, hiding the laughter that spurted in her for a moment. Yes, the same thought was passing through her friend's head: Philly likes a big word as much as she likes a big cock.) 'The manipulator – the *manipulatrix* – of the last soldier to *effuse* will then have to eat the cake. Is that clear, corporal? Hmmm?'

Theodora heard one of the young soldiers swallow hard. He was a corporal? He looked as though he had barely started shaving but his cock was certainly impressive enough, making up in breadth what perhaps, from Theodora's seat, it lacked in length. Gwen certainly seemed satisfied with it, pouting unconsciously as she stroked it with her eyes.

'Er, yeah,' he said in a strangled voice. 'That's clear.'

'Can you just repeat those instructions in your words then, dear?'

The corporal ran his fingers around his already loosened collar, flushing deeper red under the gaze of six pairs of cool female eyes, but his thick cock jerked even higher and Theodora could see a thread of pre-ejaculate already beginning to trickle from the lips in the glans.

'Yes'm,' he said. 'Basically, you wank us, we come on the cake, young lady wanking the last one to come has to eat cake.'

4

'And come,' said one of the other soldiers in a dreamy voice. Jacky and Frances, his manipulatrix, laughed, but Theodora guessed what he was doing. His eyes were closed and he didn't dare open them, in case he woke up. Or was he trying to imagine that the girl about to 'manipulate' him was his favourite movie-star? A poor compliment for Frances, their dark-haired Eurasian beauty, but perhaps her breasts were too small. She was always complaining that she lagged behind the others by at least a year.

'An excellent summary,' said Philippa. 'We wank, you come, one of us has to eat cake-and-come. Very well, then, are we all ready? Yes?'

Theodora felt her heart begin to beat faster even as she reached for the cock that jutted beside her. But as she took hold of it she frowned and opened her mouth to speak. She didn't have a chance, though: Philippa's domineering voice drawled on, perhaps increasing in volume a little, as though she had anticipated an interruption.

'Then over to you, corp. On the count of three.'

Theodora mentally shrugged and felt her professionalism take over, seeming to flow into her arm from the feeling of solid, moist-skinned cock in her hand, and up her arm into her brain. Christmas, she was a practised *tart* already and two months ago she hadn't set *eye* to a full-grown cock, let alone hand and (she stirred a little in her chair at the thought of it) *mouth*. Mummy had watched over her too closely for that! But now Mummy was who-knew-where and she was in the middle of her very big adventure. The corporal was licking his lips and swallowing again.

'All right,' he said. 'Ready, fellers? One ... two ... three ...'

Theodora's hand was moving before she was aware of it, gripping the cock about halfway up its shaft and cycling up and down on a two-second rhythm. Her

5

tongue-tip appeared in the corner of her mouth, wriggling with concentration, but her inner tart – her inner whore – was sitting cool and collected in her brain, directing her flickering eyes around the table, reading the expressions in her competitors' faces. Edwina looked as though she were struggling a little: her wrist ached easily and Philippa, cunning as ever, seemed to have contrived to give her the boy with the thickest cock. Theodora's eyes lingered on it, noting how Edwina's slender, well-manicured fingers barely spanned two-thirds of its bulk.

Jacky's soldier was a big boy too, but that dark siren showed no trace of strain as she wanked briskly at his thick member. She had been the first and most enthusiastic masturbatrix amongst them, initiating the craze for cock that had run through their party once they and the young soldiers on the troop-deck discovered a way of meeting on the sly, and it was rumoured that she went *further* than masturbation when she had a soldier quite to herself. Those rose-bud lips and that butter-wouldn't-melt mouth . . . Theodora jumped in her seat: as though her competitor were perfectly aware of what was passing through Dorrie's mind, Jacky's eyes had swung to meet hers and her slender eyebrows had quirked ironically. That big boy of hers was not only big but eager, for a heavy shaft of seed was already spurting from his cockhead.

It landed on the table with a slap, splattering in all directions and missing the cake by a hand's-breadth, and Jacky frowned, gripping harder at his cock as she tugged it up and pointed it more accurately.

'Cake, not table, you big brute,' she said, expertly firing her disdain into the soldier's brain, knowing how it and the rough jerk on his cock would heighten his orgasm and the strength of his ejaculation. Yes, Theodora almost missed a stroke on her own cock in her concentration on Jacky's technique: the soldier groaned with spurred lust and his further six shafts of seed, all dropping perfectly atop the cake, were as copious as any Theodora had yet seen. And as often happened, Theodora had learnt, the sight of one boy coming triggered almost immediate orgasm in one of his 'mates': with a little grunt of satisfaction Frances acknowledged that her boy was ejaculating.

'Wonderful, dear,' she murmured into his grunts and gasps, for her boy had landed his first shaft perfectly on target. The cake was already soaked with semen as it landed, and Theodora knew that the losing girl would have to lick the table clean of all splatters too. Her stomach rolled at the thought of it and her inner whore panicked a little, beginning to pump harder at the cock in her hand. Sugar and salt – birthday-cake and the discharge of six sets of big boys' balls. Almost a cupful or maybe, considering what Jacky's thick-cocked swain had contributed, more than a cupful. The gasps of another masturbatee turned into a groan of orgasm: it was Gwen's corporal, and look, the cheating slut's hand had flashed into his trousers and she was plainly, in blatant violation of the rules, squeezing his balls, encouraging an even heavier discharge of seed.

Another soldier groaned and began to ejaculate even as the corporal's first shaft of seed splashed onto the birthday-cake: it was the one who had kept his eyes tightly closed, the one she thought was fantasising about a film-star, and hadn't he *said* something as he groaned? A female name? Theodora hadn't quite caught it, and her satisfaction at this partial confirmation of her theory was lost now in her rising panic. Only she and Edwina were left wanking now, and Edwina's boy, a suety-cheeked farm-hand, from the look of him, was already gnawing at his lower lip, trying to ride the rising pleasure in his cock and tightening balls. But now his mouth came open and he groaned; and there he was, spurting across the table onto the birthday cake, while she, Theodora, was still pumping at her boy's cock.

Last. Last. She had lost, and she would have to eat *all* the birthday-cake and lick the table clean. Her hand faltered in its pumping, but she kept her face neutral, knowing that Philippa would be gloating over her defeat. Oh, more than gloating: now came the final insult.

'Tits, girls,' she heard Philippa murmur, and round the table her companions were quickly unbuttoning their blouses, tugging them open, and neatly flipping down their sweat-soaked bras to expose their young breasts to the lagging soldier. But perhaps it was the scent of breast-sweat, fresh from stiffened nipples and shining areolae, as much as the sight of breast-flesh that triggered his orgasm. Certainly his nostrils flared and his mouth gaped, taut lips lifting away from his gums, and he drew air in with a sighing moan. She smoothly changed grip on his cock, slipping her thumb under the swollen glans and scratching delicately at the rein of the foreskin, encouraging the full emptying of his testicular vats.

There: at last he was coming, but what a disappointing show! The first spurt was weak and barely covered half the distance to the birthday-cake, and Theodora bit her lip in chagrin, resisting the impulse to thrust her left hand into his trousers and squeeze more out of his balls. Now came the second and third spurts, slightly stronger but still falling short of the cake, and a dying fourth and fifth, and then more dribble than spurt for the sixth . . . and that was it.

'Well done, Dorrie,' Philippa drawled through the subsiding gasps of the soldier. 'Got there in the end.'

Theodora's suspicions flared at the tinkle of laughter underlying the words and she glared across the table at her rival. Wide-eyed innocence met her gaze, but those full lips curved faintly at their corners and Theodora was suddenly convinced she had the truth.

'Cat,' she hissed. 'You've *arranged* this. He's . . .' she nodded sideways at her soldier, whose cock she was still

8

gently pumping, still unable to come to terms with her defeat 'been *nobbled.*'

Philippa pouted disdainfully.

'What on earth do you mean, you silly girl?'

'He's been nobbled,' Theodora repeated, feeling her temper rising and trying to hold it down. Philippa always did this to her: provoking her to anger and even tears, while remaining perfectly cool and collected herself.

'What is "nobbled"?' Philippa asked with a sniff, echoed twice around the table, Theodora heard, by her allies Jacky and Gwen.

'It's what criminals do to horses before a race,' Theodora said, knowing that she was speaking too fast. 'They, they feed them too much mash or drug them or something.'

'What, so you think we fed your boy too much mash or drugged him? Or maybe – I've heard they do this too – stuck an onion up his bum?'

Sniggers from Jacky and Gwen, and fickle Edwina too.

'No, you cat,' Theodora flung back. 'I think you *wanked* him off today before the race. Or you s—'

She snapped her own mouth shut, knowing she had been about to go too far. But Philippa, thinly smiling, eyes glittering icily despite the heat, was now acting out a rage of her own.

'What was *that*, Dorrie? I'll overlook that "wanked" crudity in view of your extreme youth, but you were adding something more. Either I "wanked" him . . .' she paused fractionally, giving Jacky and Gwen their cue to sniff 'or I did something else to him. To "nobble" him . . .' another pause, giving Jacky and Gwen their cue to snigger 'for the race. What was the other thing you are accusing me of possibly doing?'

'Nothing,' Theodora muttered, finally letting go of her soldier's cock. 'I am only saying you nobbled him, and that's more than en—'

9

But Jacky's cool voice cut across her words.

'It started with "s", Philly. Either you "wanked" him or you s-something'd him. To "nobble" him,' Gwen choked with laughter this time, 'for the race.'

Philippa grunted disdainfully.

'Nonsense,' she said.

Now Gwen, swallowing her laughter, joined the game.

'*I* think,' she said, flicking her chin at the semen-splattered table and semen-soaked plate of birthday-cake, 'that she's just looking for an excuse to avoid the loser's penalty, Philly. She's trying to pretend that it wasn't her own laziness and lack of skill that lost her the willy-race.'

'That too, of course, Gwen, dear,' said Philippa, 'but she won't escape the penalty and we're still trying to get to the bottom of her mystery verb. Either I "wanked" him or I s-something'd him. To "nobble" him for the race.'

Even Frances joined in the laughter this time, and Theodora felt tears beginning to sting her eyes. Philippa had won again, humiliating her in the willy-race, then using the accusation she made of malpractice to humiliate her even more.

'Well, perhaps the central figure can shed light on our puzzle,' Phillipa went on. 'You, soldier, did I or anyone else "wank" today? Or s-something you?'

Theodora's hand flashed back out to the cock she had wanked. It had softened considerably, drooping forward in a thick curve, and she felt her heart skip a beat as the soft contact of her hand provoked a strong twitch from it. She squeezed it, looking up at its owner, forcing a smile to her lips that suddenly strengthened and grew genuine as she felt it beginning to stiffen again.

'Did she, darling?' she asked him. The brown, proletarian eyes in the sweating face met hers and blinked.

'I . . .' he stammered, then looked up as Philippa cleared her throat and sniffed slightly. Theodora followed his gaze and was just in time to intercept a meaningful flicker of Philippa's right eyebrow.

'You *cat*,' she burst out. 'You *did* nobble him, and now you're threatening him with something. Or *promising* him something. To make sure he stays quiet.'

Philippa swung her eyes to meet her indignant accuser's.

'What are you blethering about, you silly little girl?' she said.

'You cleared your throat as he was about to tell the truth,' Theodora flung back, feeling new confidence flow into her as the cock in her hand continued to stiffen. 'And *sniffed*. And when he looked at you, you raised . . .'

Her voice trailed away. Philippa's contemptuous smile had got stronger and stronger as she spoke, and it was plain she was planning some devastating reply.

'I signalled to him, Dorrie? By clearing my throat? And *sniffing?* If only you could hear yourself as others are doing, Dorrie. You sound quite, quite mad. There's no threat I could *possibly* hold over this dear boy's head. What was that, Dorrie dear?'

'Or a promise,' Theodora muttered, letting go of the cock again. It was nearly fully erect, paying tribute to the skill with which she had masturbated it, but she knew final defeat was staring her in the face.

'Promise of what, child?'

'That he'd get something . . . nice if he kept quiet.'

Philippa's smile strengthened again.

'Kept quiet about my sticking an onion up his bum, dear?'

The whole table erupted with laughter, girls and soldiers both, and Theodora hung her head and felt tears beginning to trickle from her eyes.

'Well,' Philippa continued, and Theodora's tears began to flow faster as she heard the triumph in her enemy's voice, 'we're still to hear from the horse's mouth, as it were. Did I "nobble" you, dear?'

11

Theodora heard the soldier swallow and sensed him glance at her bowed head. Would he speak the truth after all? Describe how Philippa or one of her underlings had wanked it off before the willy-race? Or *sucked* him off? The soldier began to speak, his deep voice uneven with strain.

'No, miss. You didden nobble me, miss. It's jus' . . . I wurren on top of me form today, miss. No offence to the miss here, miss.'

'She's called Theodora, dear. Or Dorrie, if you prefer.'

'No offence to 'er, then, miss. No offence to lickle Dorrie. She wanked me luvly, like, but I was feelin' under the weather, like, an' me balls jus' wooden . . .'

'We understand, dear,' Philippa cut in. 'You were under the weather. No reflection on Dorrie's skill at all. Of course not. None whatsoever. But sadly, sadly, we make no provision in the rules for one of our boys "being under the weather". Last girl to succeed has to, well, has to suck seed.'

More laughter round the table. Theodora knuckled hard at her eyes and looked up, unexpected defiance flaring in her breast.

'If it's the rules you're talking about, Philly,' she said, 'what about Gwen squeezing her soldier's balls? *That's* against the rules and she should have lost then and th —'

Philippa had held up her hand, shaking her head sadly.

'Not at all,' she said. 'We had a meeting of the arbitration committee last night. Or', with a sly glance at Theodora's soldier, 'the Jockey Club, if you prefer, and we decided that the no ball-squeezing rule is *obviously* meant to apply *only* before the, ah, mount begins to *flow*. But squeezing his balls after that, to encourage a more copious flow, is quite within the rules. The whole committee agreed.'

'The whole committee is packed with your . . .'

Up went the hand again.

'Shut up, you silly little girl. Your evasions and excuses have gone on for far too long, wasting all our time. These boys will have to be back on their deck shortly, and they're all eager to watch you eat their offerings, Dorrie. And look: I've made it even easier for you.'

Sniggers and chuckles around the table that strengthened to roars of laughter. Theodora shook her head furiously, trying to blink away the prismatic curtain of her tears so that she could see what Philippa was holding up. A moment before it was thrown onto the semen-splattered table with a contemptuous flick of the elder girl's wrist she saw what it was. A slice of toasted bread with a pale shape on both sides – grinning, Philippa had turned it so that the whole table could see. And the shape was a letter – a *D* for 'Dorrie'.

Two

Dear Diary,
Oh, I can still taste it! And it's a whole day since the
willy-race. What makes it worse – what made me feel
sick at the time and still makes me feel sick – is that I
know P. arranged it all. She did nobble that soldier and
all of us round the table knew it. E., when we discussed
it later, is convinced that she 'wanked' him 'off' and then
gave him a 'blow-job', to make sure his 'lovely big balls'
(her words) were thoroughly drained before the willy-
race. I'm not so sure that she's right. Oh, it's quite likely
that the boy was 'wanked' and 'blown', but I'm not so
sure that P. did it herself. It would be just like her to
force some other poor girl to do it. One of my allies . . .

Yes, the thought has just struck me that it was
Edwina herself. That would explain her certainty about
the 'wanking' and 'blow-job', and the dreaminess in her
voice when she spoke of his 'lovely big balls'. But then
again, E. has developed a genuine passion for balls
since the beginning of the voyage. She loves their
variety, she's told me – I can hear her voice now,
discussing it so seriously that in the end it made me
giggle, and then her giggle too.

Theodora put her pen down and smiled sourly. If her
life were a film, this was just where there would be, what

14

was it called, oh yes, a *flashback*, a narrated flashback, like the one in *Working Girl's Progress* when Bella Tranter was remembering her schooldays. She closed her eyes, recalling the whispered conversation she and Edwina had had on deck, leaning over the rail and watching the creamy wake of the ship, glancing round frequently to make sure they weren't overheard. Miss Callaghan was prowling, but that made the forbidden conversation all the more exciting, as they pressed themselves against the railing and slowly and slyly rubbed their cunnies there.

'It's as though they're *fruit*, Dorrie,' Edwina had said, 'hanging from all sorts of different trees in a big orchard of *men*.'

Then her voice had gone into a dreamy chant, as she half-closed her eyes: 'Big ones and little ones and firm ones and squishy ones and hairy ones and bald ones and oblong ones and spherical ones and warm ones and coo—'

That's when I started giggling, making her giggle too.

'You've never seen as many balls as that *yet*,' I said.

'No,' she admitted. 'But . . .' chin tilting with resolution, blue eyes widening 'I'm *going* to. When we get to England, I'm going to see hundreds and *hundreds* of balls.'

'How?'

'I'm going to become a *whore*, Dorrie.'

I started to giggle again, though she sounded at least half-serious.

'No, I *am*, Dorrie. A high-class whore, a *fille de luxe*, that's what I'm going to become. Offering specialist services. Specialist service.'

'What kind of specialist service?'

'*Ball*-torture, Dorrie.'

Then both of us were helpless with giggles for at least a minute.

'What will you do?'

'I'll torture balls. No, stop it, Dorrie. Let me plan my future. I shall have a flat in Mayfair with silk curtains and French wallpaper and I'll advertise by word of mouth – stop it, Dorrie – advertise by word of mouth in all the best circles. They'll flock to me like moths to a flame, because I'll be something new and I'll be very young and very, very beautiful.'

'What will you wear?'

'Something in royal blue, to set off my hair, which I'll wear long and flowing over my bare shoulders. And I'll wear long, long blue gloves too, up over my elbows, with two rings on my left hand and three rings on my right.'

'Will you have a new name?'

'Yes. I'll call myself Bella Douloureuse.'

'And what services will you offer?'

'Only one. Ball-torture.'

'Will that be enough?'

'Yes. I was talking with one of the officers last week, remember, and he told me that the specialist whores can charge almost *anything* they like.'

'Are there lots of men who want their balls to be tortured then, Winnie?'

'Don't tease, Dorrie. Yes, there *are* lots of men who want their balls to be tortured. I know there are. I shall have a little altar made for them, with lots of different tops that I can choose from once I've seen what size and shape my clients are.'

'Tops?'

'Yes. Altar-tops. With two depressions in them, so that the client's balls can fit snugly when I begin the torture proper.'

'What about . . .' glancing behind me 'their *cocks*? Won't they flop over their balls and get in the way of the torture?'

'No. I shall have their cocks strapped up against their tummies by then. With surgical tape, going right around

16

their bodies, three times. I'll go through yards of the stuff every week. Yards and yards and yards. So I won't be able to see their cocks at all. Just their lovely, lovely balls, dangling beneath the surgical tape.'

'Not all balls are lovely.'

'Yes, they are.'

'Not old men's balls, surely? I bet they're really shrivelled and shrunken and – yuck.'

'No, old men's balls are lovely too.'

'How do you know?'

'Because they're *balls*, Dorrie. And all balls are lovely. Ripe for torture.'

I sniggered.

'*Chacune à son gout.*'

'*Oui,*' said Edwina, '*et mon gout, ma passion, c'est pour les boules.*'

'*Vraiment?*'

'*Vraiment. Devant Dieu.*'

'So how will you torture balls as a specialist whore in your flat in Mayfair with silk curtains and French wallpaper?'

'You won't make fun of me when you see how much money I make, Dorrie. But to answer your question: I will have a fixed routine and clients will have to pay through the nose for me to alter it in the slightest. But I shall always insist on the surgical tape and the cock being strapped out of sight. I quite like cocks, you know that, Dorrie, but nothing must get in the way of my true love.'

'*Les couilles.*'

'*Oui.*'

'So what will your fixed routine be?'

Edwina sighed and closed her eyes, saying dreamily: 'The client must strip and bathe under my supervision. I think I will, yes, I *will* have two maids to follow my orders, ball-maids, Dorrie, and they'll be, yes, they'll be twin midgets, beautiful young twin midgets, one called

17

Dextra and the other called Sinistra, both dressed in red silk and with long, long pigtails.'

'And will Dextra wear higher heels than Sinistra?'

Her eyes flew open and she looked at me with a frown.

'What? I don't . . . ah, I see what you mean. Yes. Yes, she will, at first. That's a very good idea. Thank you.'

'Glad to help. And what will your twin midgets do, exactly?'

She looked away and closed her eyes again.

'They'll help the client undress, and his cock will already be *very* stiff by the time they get his trousers down. But not just because of the beauty of Dextra and Sinistra.'

'What else will make it stiff?'

'I shall. Because all the while I shall be giving Dextra and Sinistra orders in a French accent. The officer said French whores, or English whores who can pretend to be French convincingly, earn *much* more in England, so I imagine a French specialist whore can charge the *earth*.'

'For giving orders in a French accent to two dwarfs undressing fat, lecherous, middle-aged men?'

'That will just be the *beginning* of the session, Dorrie, and not all of them will be fat or middle-aged. But I won't care if they are, so long as they have balls. Which they will. And not *dwarfs*, Dorrie, *midgets*. Midgets have limbs and bodies in the same proportion as we do, dwarfs' limbs are *squashed*. And that isn't aesthetically appealing.'

'Do you want aesthetic appeal?'

'Of course I do, Dorrie,' she said, opening her eyes and transfixing me with their clear blue innocence. 'I will be a *fille de luxe*, and all *filles de luxe* are great *artistes*, great *artistes* performing on a private stage.'

'Your officer told you that?'

'Yes.'

'Did you torture his balls?'

Edwina sniffed and shook her head with a pout.

'Ask me another.'

'Then you did torture his balls.'

'Ask me another.'

'Very well. What will you do when you're a *fille de luxe* in London and your twin midgets have undressed your clients?'

She looked away from me and down came her ivory-smooth lids over her eyes again. She sighed happily, re-entering her fantasy.

'They will put handcuffs on him.'

'Handcuffs?'

'Yes. Handcuffs. They'll handcuff his arms behind his back, then they'll *gag* him.'

'A silk gag?'

'No. Velvet. Black velvet, with just a drop of eucalyptus in it, to tickle his taste-buds and keep him *alert*.'

'Velvet blindfold too?'

'No. Not yet. That will come later. No, first he'll be handcuffed and gagged and . . .'

'And . . .?'

'He'll be led into my big bathroom. With no bath in it, as yet.'

'Why not?'

'Be patient, please. Yes, he'll be led into my big bathroom, my big *tiled* bathroom and *won't* his eyes go big and round as he sees what is *depicted* on some of the tiles?'

'And what is depicted there?'

'Some of what *will* await him and some of what he *fears* will await him. My, how the *contrôleuse* and her midgets will feast their eyes on the conflicting emotions in his face. After all, he is completely helpless and at our mercy, and how can he be sure quite how far we will go? Bella Douloureuse will maintain an air of mystery, y'know, and *rumours* will circulate about her, which he will surely have heard.'

'What rumours?'

19

'Rumours that will seem excitingly absurd in his silly men's club or regimental mess or wherever he has first heard them ... but will begin to seem much less absurd now. I will start the rumours myself, of course.'

'But what will the rumours be?'

'They will be about what Bella Douloureuse *sometimes*, with the connivance of the police and the government, gets away with. Because it will be said – no doubt truly, after she has been at work for a little – that she has clients in high office and even in ...'

She sighed happily.

'Even in what?' I whispered impatiently.

'Even in the royal family, Dorrie. The royal families of all Europe. Imagine that, Dorrie, torturing the balls of a *king*. Yes, and her royal connections will allow her to get away with a very great deal. Sometimes, you see, she will be bribed by wronged wives or mistresses to punish their erring menfolk. That's how one of the rumours will run. And a guilty conscience will be a fine spur to the imagination, particularly when he is prepared for the true beginning of the session.'

'Won't he try to flee, sometimes?'

'Yes, I'm sure he will. But he won't get very far. He will be handcuffed and naked, remember, and I shall coolly remind him that the flat is quite secure and that even if he does get out, he will be a laughing-stock on the street. If that doesn't keep him in line, Dextra and Sinistra will be more than a match for him.'

'Midgets will be a match for him?'

Edwina nodded, eyes opening for a moment to fix on mine.

'Oh, they'll be *trained* midgets, Dorrie.'

Her eyes closed again and she nodded as if to herself.

'Yes, they'll be trained midgets. Trained in *ju-jitsu* or something like that. I don't know the details yet. And they'll put him, willy-nilly, into a contraption that will be waiting in the as-yet-bathless bathroom for him. A kind of invalid thingy on it, you know, for lowering invalids or old people into a bath and then lifting them out. Yes, they'll get him into the invalid thingy, they'll *strap* him into it, and he'll be quite, quite helpless, and his *balls* will be dangling beneath him, waiting helpless for whatever comes next.'

'And what will come next?'

'Dextra and Sinistra will wheel the first bath in.'

'Wheel?'

'Yes. It will have wheels. And Dextra and Sinistra will wheel it *right* underneath his dangling balls.'

I suddenly snorted with laughter. Edwina suppressed her own snort of laughter and sniffed.

'*He* won't be laughing, Dorrie. Because the water in the bath, waiting for his helplessly dangling balls, will be very, very *cold*. Icy. In fact, it will have a layer of ice on it.'

'How will you do that?'

'The bath will have been in some sort of big fridge. To make the water cold. I don't know the details. My agent will arrange all that.'

'Your pimp, you mean?'

'Don't be crude, Dorrie. *Filles de luxe* don't have pimps. They have agents.'

'Like actresses?'

'Yes. Exactly like actresses, because . . .'

'They are great *artistes*, it's just that they perform on a private stage.'

'Exactly, Dorrie. But stop interrupting me or I'll stop talking and imagine it all in silence.'

'No. Please don't. I don't want to leave your client dangling helplessly over the ice-covered water. Please carry on.'

'It's not *him* dangling helplessly, Dorrie, it's his *balls*. The most vulnerable part of his entire body and now they're *entirely* at my mercy.'

'And will you be merciful?'

21

'No. Of course not.'

'What will you do?'

'I shall order one of my midgets to collar him.'

'Collar him?'

'Yes, collar him. Or rather, collar the most important part of him. That is, put a collar around the root of his balls, so they can't climb up out of harm's way.'

'You want them in harm's way?'

'Of course I do, Dorrie.'

'What will the collar be like?'

Eyes still closed, Edwina was silent a moment, frowning slightly.

'A bit like a handcuff, I suppose. But for his balls. A ball-cuff. Something that locks firmly into place around the root of his balls, with a solid click, and keeps his balls down and tautly stretched to meet their fate.'

'And what is their fate?'

'To be lowered, Dorrie. Lowered into the freezing water.'

'But what about the ice?'

'Oh, we'll have to break that. With his balls.'

'How thick will the ice be?'

'Pretty thick.'

'Half-an-inch?'

'Maybe.'

'An inch?'

Another moment of silent pondering.

'An inch sounds good. An inch of ice on the surface of the water. Which we'll have to *break* with his *balls* before his balls can be lowered *into* the water.'

'How will you break it?'

'We'll lower him slowly the first time, in that invalid contraption. So that his balls don't damage the ice at all. Just land on it and slowly and firmly flatten against it. That might, that usually will, that almost always will, make him swear and struggle. To absolutely no avail, of course. I might get a little sharp with him then. Tell him that *much* worse is to come for him or, I mean, for the most sensitive part of him, namely, his *balls*. But first we must *bathe* them. And if there is a layer of ice in the way, well then, the ice must be broken. That's when I'll order Dextra and Sinistra to raise him three inches, but very slowly.'

'Why very slowly?'

'Because some of the hairs on his balls will have frozen to the ice while I'm admonishing him and raising him very slowly will drag them out by their roots in the most painful way.'

'Why only three inches?'

'Because he's going to be dropped back onto the ice. Or rather his balls are. There will be a handle on the invalid mechanism and when you pull it, the whole thing will jerk violently downward by a specified amount.'

'And you'll pull it?'

'Not I, Dorrie. This is menial, and relatively unskilled work, so Dextra will pull it. On my hand-signal. *Whoosh!* Down he will jerk! And *bang!* His balls will hit the ice. But they won't break it, I think. Not the first time. It's too thick for that. No, all that will happen is that his balls receive a painful knock and doubtless he will *groan* with pain. It will echo between the tiled walls of the bathroom, Dorrie, but the beautiful young blonde *contrôleuse* – that's me – and her two midget assistants will be breathing lightly, calmly, unconcernedly, waiting for more of his ball-hairs to freeze to the ice. Then, in the silence, the diamond rings on the left hand of the *contrôleuse* will flash as she signals to her midgets to raise him off the ice again. Slowly, slowly, slowly ... so that more ball-hairs are torn out by their roots. Four inches this time. Four inches above the ice.'

'And then he'll be dropped again.'

'Precisely. On my signal. *Whoosh!* Down he will jerk! And *bang!* His balls will hit the ice again.'

'And he *groans* again.'

23

'Yes. A lovely male groan of ball-pain that echoes in my big tiled bathroom.'

'And will his balls break the ice?'

'Yes. A little. It's still too thick, you see, and he isn't being dropped from high enough. But they may crack it. A little of the freezing water beneath may begin to seep through. As before, we'll leave him in place to let more ball-hairs freeze to the ice . . .'

'If he has any left,' I murmured, surprised at my own relish in Edwina's beloved ball-torture. My eyes were closed too now and I was gloating, with moistening cunny, over the scene she was conjuring for me.

'Oh, I'm sure he'll have some left,' murmured Edwina. '*Notre Dame de Supplices* will see to that.'

'Who?'

'*Notre Dame de Supplices.* Our Lady of Tortures, Dorrie. I think, yes, I *will* have a big statue of Her in a niche at one end of the bathroom, overlooking the scene. So that he finds Her gazing serenely at him whenever he raises his eyes. I'll light a candle in front of Her before the first bath is wheeled in. So that She watches over the ice-torture and ensures that there are sufficient hairs on his balls each time they are left flattened on the ice and then slowly, slowly, raised again.'

'Isn't that rather blasphemous, Winnie?'

'Hmmm?'

'To have the Virgin Mary preside over a man having his balls tortured?'

'Oh, no, this isn't the *Virgin* Mary, it's the *Virago* Mary. But they will think it's the Virgin Mary, of course. It will add to the *ambiance française.*'

'Very well. And she, your Virago Mary, will make sure that he has enough ball-hairs left when he is raised for the third time?'

'Yes. But she's your Virago Mary too, you know, Dorrie. She's the Virago Mary of *all* beautiful young girls, if they only knew it.'

'Only of beautiful young girls?'

'Yes. Our Lady of Tortures has very exacting tastes and though She might attend – momentarily – a session of ball-torture being conducted by a spotty, fat, plain girl with an ugly accent or a persistent sniff or both, it will only be momentarily. Unless the girl is exceptionally good at her job. And that's not very likely, is it?'

'No. But does she only attend girls torturing boys?'

'Not quite. Only girls or women torturing boys or *men*, Dorrie. Men, for preference. With lovely big hairy balls.'

'And lovely long thick *cocks*,' I was unable to resist murmuring, feeling a trickle of pussy-juice escape my knickers and begin sliding down my inner thigh. Edwina sniffed, as though she had caught its scent.

'She is indifferent to the size of cocks, Dorrie. That is a low-bred taste. Balls and their welfare, their *mal*-fare, are Her central concern.'

'But in her aspect as . . .'

'No, Dorrie. You had never even *heard* of Her before, so don't go pretending you know better than I, who have been a faithful votary for *ever* so long.'

I murmured reluctant acquiescence, but I tucked away the thought that I would return to *Notre Dame de Supplices* in one of my own fantasies. And it would be in her cock-loving aspect too.

'Very well,' I said. 'Go on, then. She is presiding over the third raising of the balls.'

'Yes. The third slow, slow raising, and for the third time a lot of ball-hairs will have frozen to the ice and will come out by their roots, *twing*, *twing*, *twing*. How he will grunt and snort! The budding ache *inside* his balls, started by those bangs on the ice, will be encouraged to begin opening its sharp petals by the little jags of pain *outside* his balls but very near to them.'

She sighed happily and I asked:

'But what will his cock be d—'

Still with my own eyes closed, I sensed her eyes fly open and her head turn to me.

'I don't *care* about his cock, Dorrie. Nor does *Notre Dame de Supplices*. So stop mentioning it.'

'Sorry.'

I had opened my own eyes and given her a timid smile.

'Please go on,' I said. 'He's being raised for the third time, more ball-hairs being torn out by their roots. How high will you raise him?'

Edwina shook her head slightly.

'I won't go on if you keep making these constant . . .' she hissed the next word with venom '*cock*-interruptions. No more of them, d'you hear? *Pas de verges, absolument!*'

I looked around me, fearful that her voice had carried. What would Miss Callaghan think to hear her? But the deck near us was safely deserted.

'*Très bien,*' I said. '*Pas de verges. Absolument.*'

Now Edwina nodded.

'I'm sorry, Dorrie. I know how much you like them, but this is *my* future career I'm planning and I can't bring you and your tastes into it.'

'Can't I be your agent?'

Edwina laughed against her will.

'No. My agent will be a woman, but she must be as obsessed with balls as I am. None of this cock-nonsense. On my rest-days, we shall sit and discuss sessions of ball-torture together. And plan future ones.'

'How will she be able to discuss sessions with you, if she's not there when you conduct them? Unless she's one of your midgets.'

'Oh, she will be there all right, after a fashion. Peep-holes, Dorrie. There will be a peep-hole in each torture-room: bathroom, games-room and chapel.'

'Chapel?'

'Hold your horses, Dorrie. We have a long way to go before we reach that. He is still enjoying the bathroom. Being raised *slooooowly* for the third time, ball-hairs

26

teeeeearing from his *aaaaaching* ball-sack. Poor man. Poor, poor man!'

She sighed happily and I wondered if her knickers were as thoroughly soaked as mine.

'Yes,' Edwina said and I jumped slightly. Had she read my thoughts? No, it was not that, for she went on: 'Yes, my heart will be aching for him rather like his balls, but I am afraid my cunny will be smiling broadly with pleasure. Much like it is now. Oh, Dorrie, *what* a wank I am going to have later! I shall come *seven* times, at least!'

Again I jumped slightly, but this time with renewed fear that we would overheard. No, it was safe: the deck near us was still deserted.

'Be careful, Winnie,' I said. 'Keep your voice low. If you could only have heard yourself a year ago!'

'Something was missing in my life then, Dorrie. I should have responded to myself speaking of lovely balls. I shouldn't have been shocked, you know. Lovely balls. Big ones, small ones, firm ones, squi—.'

'Ascending ones,' I said. 'Get on with your plans for the future, Winnie. Delightful as this is, we don't want to be here all day.'

'Very well. His lovely, big, firm, hairy balls are being lifted for the third time from the ice.'

'How high?'

'Six inches this time. Don't say it, Dorrie. It's what you always say when someone mentions six inches.'

'Sorry. Go on. He's being raised six inches.'

'No, his *balls* are, Dorrie. The rest of him exists merely for the sake of his balls, which are now *swelling* to fill his universe.'

'Poor thing,' I said, feeling my own cunny throb with delight at the image of those big bruised balls positively *swelling* in response to the relatively mild abuse they had received so far. But Winnie admonished me.

'Swelling to fill his universe *metaphorically* speaking, Dorrie. They won't be *literally* swelling. Not much, anyhow, though they might later. No, I mean that he is just very *aware* of them. Of their *aching*, of the way hairs twing and ping oh-so-painfully from their lovely, wrinkled, leathery sack. As he's raised those six inches. And now he *has* been. His collared balls are dangling again, ready to fall on the ice. And he will be *trembling* in anticipation of it. Positively trembling, this great *big* man.'

'With his great big *cock*,' I was unable, again, to resist murmuring.

' "You dirrty-minded young slip," ' Edwina said in her by-now-nearly-perfected Miss Callaghan voice. I choked slightly and Edwina, as though encouraged, continued: 'Indeed. You very dirrty-minded young slip.'

I grunted with surprise. Edwina's second attempt at Miss Callaghan's voice had not only been even better, she had somehow seemed to project it from a yard or two *behind* us. Then I felt a swirl of air on the nape of my neck, and a moment before Edwina gasped at my side a slim but firm – oh, so very firm – hand closed where the air had brushed me. I smelt Miss Callaghan's perfume, discreet and well-mannered as the woman who wore it, as she leaned between the two of us and hissed, strengthening her own accent to mock us: 'And now you can come to my cabin to have this . . . *filth* slipperred out of you, my fine pair of whispering young *fanta-sistes*.'

The hand tightened and I heard Edwina cry out, barely aware that I cried out with her. Then we were plucked from the rail, all free-will and power to resist leaving us in the storm of Miss Callaghan's fury, and marched to her cabin.

Three

'Such *filth* I have never heard in my life.'

A deeper pink had entered the cheeks of the petite Scottish schoolmistress standing in front of the two girls, dark Theodora and blonde Edwina. Theodora bit her lip and glanced sideways at her companion, but Edwina was unresponsive, head bent and shaking slightly for a moment, as though to deny the tears that had begun to trickle down her velvet cheeks. Miss Callaghan gave a genteel grunt – something else Edwina could imitate almost to perfection – but the spark of defiance that lightened Theodora's misery and apprehension was quenched in an instant as Miss Callaghan demonstrated once again her uncanny ability to read the minds of her charges.

'Keep your eyes on *me*, Miss Theodora. If you're wondering how *long* I stood there listening to it, then wonder on. But it was *quite* long enough.'

Theodora swallowed despite herself. *Oh, dear God, no, no, dear Our Lady of Tortures, let her not have heard* anything *about our soldiers.*

'Yes, quite long enough,' Miss Callaghan repeated. 'Or should I say "Aye", Miss Edwina? Your insolence compounds your offence, and you shall be sure I will lay on with a will.'

Theodora swallowed again, and heard Edwina trying to sniff back her tears. As she spoke Miss Callaghan had begun unbuttoning the sleeve of her slim right arm, somehow contriving to make each pearl button open with a distinct and ominous click (there were various theories as to how she did this, and some of her girls even insisted that it was black magic). Now, flexing the fingers of her slippering hand and gazing with satisfaction at the faces of her two errant pupils, she neatly rolled up the sleeve and gave another genteel grunt (it's her *church* grunt, Edwina had always said, hypothesising and re-creating a whole series of further grunts for other settings: milliner's, grocer's, hatter's. But no spark of defiance lit Theodora's misery now. The memory merely emphasised her captivity).

Now Miss Callaghan turned away, crossing the floor of her cabin to one of her trunks. She paused, but did not look behind her as she spoke.

'Eyes to the front, Miss Theodora. You have just earned yourself three further strokes.'

Perhaps it was black magic after all. Theodora glared at the slim back bending over the trunk, trying to skewer it with the force of her hatred. *Get cramp, you old cow* (though Miss Callaghan was barely thirty-six). *Get prickly heat, appendicitis, beri-beri!* But the slim back bent and turned with serene indifference and now the catches of the trunk were clicking up (she *choreographs* it, Jacky had once said. Every sound, every movement is calculated for its deleterious – one of Philippa's polysyllables – effect on our nerves). Now mysterious creaks and rustles were coming from the trunk. *Yes, yes, she does. Every sound, every movement. If this is her slipper-trunk and she uses it almost every other day, why is the slipper buried so deep inside it? Because then she has to* delve. *Has to make this noise.*

She swallowed again. With a faint, almost inaudible sigh of satisfaction, Miss Callaghan had found what she sought. Now she straightened and turned, holding it in her right hand. That dread device of chastisement with

30

which all her girls were so often and so unwillingly familiar: The Slipper! At the sight of it Theodora felt the muscles in her bottom tighten and quiver with involuntary memory. Edwina gave a sniff of extra misery and Theodora knew without glancing sideways that tears were now running freely down her cheeks. Miss Callaghan nodded almost imperceptibly and advanced.

'Filthiness in the mind, girruls, must be attacked at the fundament. You apprehend my meaning, of course. Turn round, the two of you.'

The girls obeyed. Edwina was already trembling with fright and Theodora felt tears begin to prick at her own eyes. Poor Winnie. Poor, poor Winnie. Her velvet-cheeked bottom was widely acknowledged to be the tenderest among the girls of Miss Callaghan's class, and she had handed it to Miss Callaghan, so to speak, on a platter. Poor Winnie. But Theodora knew, without the slightest doubt, that when the slippering started she would have no more sympathy to spare for her companion: it would be devoted entirely to her own poor bottom.

'Lift up your skirruts,' came the voice from behind them. And there it was: a faint tremor had entered the velvet-sheathed iron of Miss Callaghan's voice, just for a moment. Yes, just for a moment. Theodora reached behind herself and took hold of the hem of her skirt, her fingertips suddenly sensitive to every detail of the cloth she held, and lifted it up, exposing her knickered bottom to Miss Callaghan's searching gaze. And now her ears, straining into the space behind her, caught a faint sigh of indrawn breath. Miss Callaghan was gazing on her twin *champs de bataille*. Yes, she could almost feel the scorching track of the older woman's eyes tracing the curves and clefts of the two bottoms.

'Now, bend forward.'

An extra-loud sniff from Edwina this time, and Theodora, feverishly anxious for distraction, risked rolling her eyes to her right, trying to catch a glimpse of her friend's face.

'And three more to add to the extra three you have already earnt, Miss Theodora,' came the calm voice from behind her; and Theodora bit her lip in fury at herself. How could she have risked it, knowing that her adversary could read the slightest movement, or even the slightest *lack* of movement, as a disobedient girl tried to conceal her guilt at some forbidden thought or action?

'And now, girls, with your permission, I am going to slide your knickers down to expose the cheeks of your bottoms.'

Theodora heard Miss Callaghan's feet move on the floor of the cabin and then that discreet, well-mannered perfume was in her nostrils again as Miss Callaghan stood directly behind her.

'Miss Theodora, with your permission?'

This ridiculous ritual! Only two girls had ever refused permission for their knickers to be taken down, and Miss Callaghan had soon bullied it out of them. Theodora swallowed.

'I . . . I grant it freely, Miss Callaghan.'

'Thank you.'

She felt her teacher's thumbs slip under the hem of her knickers and in one smooth movement sweep them off her bottom and half-way down her thighs. She tried to suppress a wince: some knicker-cloth had been glued to her flesh with cunny-juice and come painfully free. What a state her cunny was in! It was lucky her legs were well together, imprisoned by the knickers around her thighs. Yes, how ridiculous she must look from behind. And how humiliated she felt knowing that Miss Callaghan knew that she must know how ridiculous she looked from behind! Then came those two faint, those two ever-so-faint touches on her bare buttocks, left and right. All the other girls had reported them too, but no one had ever been able to decide what they were. Was

Miss Callaghan brushing the buttock-skin with a finger-nail? Or was she – only the most daring voiced the thought – stepping silently backwards and bending forward to *kiss*, just barely, the buttocks she was about to beat? Theodora strained to read the fading memory in her buttocks, but it was no good. The twin brushes had been too delicate and she was doing precisely what some girls said Miss Callaghan wanted the twin brushes to do: namely, make her victims throw all their attention into their buttock-skin, sensitising it before the violence of the storm about to break over it. She heard Miss Callaghan step sideways to Edwina.

'Miss Edwina, with your permission?'

Poor Winnie! Poor, poor Winnie! She was not only to be beaten but had to grant permission for the beating to be prepared. Theodora heard her sniff again and the click of another fat tear hitting the floor of Miss Callaghan's cabin. Now that delicate mouth would be opening, reluctantly shaping itself to speak.

'I ... I g-grant it freely, Miss –' Theodora heard Edwina gulp back her rising emotion 'M-Miss Callaghan.'

'Thank you.'

A fraction's pause, and then the whisper of Edwina's knickers sliding down to mid-thigh, pinioning her in place like Theodora before her. Now was the chance to see what Miss Callaghan did. If Theodora turned her head she would see whether the older woman fingered Edwina's bottom or *kissed* it. But she did not dare, she could not draw anything from the well of her free-will: the bucket hit dry bottom and came up empty. Her mind flashed suddenly to a mason-wasp she had seen at home, carrying a dead spider to the mud-cells it had constructed. But the spider was not dead, it was only paralysed with a deft sting. She was the juicy spider, Miss Callaghan the efficient wasp, paralysing her with the sting by which she had slid her prey's knickers down over her thighs.

Edwina had stopped sniffing. Was she too straining to read the memory of those twin touches in her buttocks? *Don't, Winnie, don't!* Theodora tried to thought-transmit to her. *You're doing exactly what the old bitch wants: sensitising your bottom for the slipper!* But it was Miss Callaghan who sniffed next – deeply, suspiciously.

'Girruls,' she said, and Theodora knew she was still exaggerating her accent for Edwina's benefit. 'What is that . . . that *smell*?'

Theodora was mystified for a moment, then realised what it was. Their cunnies! She had been directing almost all her attention to her buttocks: now her mind flashed between her thighs, reading the after-seethe, the after-ooze, of the arousal that had growled there during Edwina's ball-torture fantasy. Edwina would be even worse. But Miss Callaghan must have smelt it well before now: Edwina's juice, though initially hard to tap, was peculiarly pungent and spicy. A favourite game among Theodora's and Edwina's friends at the beginning of the voyage had been 'Winnie Welling': a group of girls was blindfolded by a Mistress of Ceremonies selected by lot, before each was helped into a chair. The Mistress then told an erotic story till the blushes on her audience's faces told her that all of them had begun to seep. Each girl then had to slip her hand into her knickers, rub her forefinger between her cunny-lips, and hold it to the noses of her neighbours on left and right for identification.

Edwina's cunny-juice was almost always identified first, and Theodora believed that at least two girls in their party liked it so much that they . . .

'Well, girruls?'

Miss Callaghan's voice interrupted her thoughts. 'Well? What is that . . . smell? You, Theodora. Tell me: what is it? Answer me, girrul. At once.'

She swallowed. What on earth could she say?

'It's . . . it's . . . it's stickiness, Miss Callaghan.'

'Stickiness? What on earth do you mean, girrul?'
She swallowed again.

'My front ... my ... my front bottom, Miss Callaghan, it's ...'

(*E. later told me that she almost fell over with shock at the thud of Miss C's slipper meeting my bottom and my wail of pain. Then she stood, heart thumping with fear, as Miss C thundered in outrage in a voice that must have been audible at least two cabins in either direction.*)

'What? Are you telling me that you are ...' and here her voice was lowered to a hiss of disgust '*leaking*, my girrul? Between your legs?'

(*I tried to speak but tears threatened to overwhelm me and I could only nod my head in reply, Miss C's expertly encouraged shame burning inside me only a little less than the stroke of her slipper burnt on my BTM.*)

'Answer me, girrul. Are you leaking?'

(*Oh, the OB knew exactly why I nodded and did not speak: I heard her grunt of pleasure as I tried to stammer out 'Yes' but got no further than the 'Y-' before bursting into tears. Then the OB set to work on E.*)

'I shall take that as a confession of guilt. And you, Miss Edwina, what about you?'

(*It was all a big act she was putting on. E's CJ must have been the first she smelt, but there she was beginning the whole routine again. Not that she needed to bother: barely had the question left her mouth than E burst into tears too. Then it was my turn nearly to fall over with surprise, because the slipper landed on E's BTM at once and she wailed with pain.*)

Miss Callaghan stood breathing heavily a moment after administering the stroke to Edwina's bottom.

'I shall take your tears too as a confession of guilt, my girrul. Oh, what a degraded pair of wee beasts we have here. Not content with whispering filth to each other, you must do so with your wee ...' here Theodora heard Miss Callaghan swallow 'with your wee pussies unwashed. Filthy stories, with filthy pussies.'

(*Yes, Dear Diary, she was pretending not to know of the connection between our 'filthy stories' and our 'filthy pussies'; that one had led inevitably to the other. But I am sure that the connection was at work in her own shrivelled-up old cunny, as she stood behind us and watched the two of us snivelling side by side, bent forward with our bare bottoms not merely on display, as she loves to see them, but glowing with the mark of her slipper.*)

'Well, girruls, I have a solution for both of your wickednesses. I shall use your filthy pussies to teach you not to tell filthy stories. Like *this*.'

(*Another wail from E, but there had been no sound of slipper meeting bottom and though I could hear Miss C pulling her towards me I was not sure what Miss C was doing to her till I felt E's face, wet and hot with tears, pressed against my BTM. Miss C had her by the back of the neck, forcing her to kneel behind me. Yes, that was it: next I felt Miss C shaking E, so that her face rubbed left and right on my bottom. Then I felt Miss C's other hand hook into my knickers and slide them, with a grunt, right down my legs to my feet.*)

'You shall go first, Miss Edwina. Miss Theodora, your legs farther apart, if you please. Thank you.'

(*I lifted one foot out of my knickers and opened my legs more, wondering what on earth Miss C planned for poor E. Was she going to rub her face on my cunny, smearing her eyebrows and nose and cheeks with my CJ? No, it was worse than that – far worse! I felt a quiver in E's face, tight-pressed to my bottom, Miss C's strong hand tightened again, then dragged her head back a little and forced it down against my cunny.*)

'Now, you young limb of Satan, you are ready. Lick. Lick, d'ye hear me? Lick it all up. That will teach you to tell Miss Theodora filthy stories, and when you have finished, Miss Theodora will perform the same service for you, to teach *her* not to listen.'

(*Oh, I nearly fell forward in horror as I understood why Miss C had forced E's mouth against my cunny. I was to be licked clean the way P, if the rumours are true, has herself licked clean sometimes. Poor E! But I am afraid that I was thinking mostly of myself in that moment: of what I would have to do to E, and – oh dear, do I dare to write it? Yes – of the pleasure E's tongue began to give me.*)

'Lick. Lick, you young limb. Lick all that pussy-filth away and learn not to indulge yourself in fictional filth. Lick!'

(*I had to restrain a gasp of pleasure as Miss C's strong hand shook E's neck, making her mouth rub against my cunny. Then I felt that mouth, oh-so-reluctantly, open and E's tongue emerge oh-so-shyly! But Miss C had to whisper furiously to her yet again before she did as she was told and began to clean up my 'filthiness'.*)

'Lick, you young slut! Lick up every last drip and trickle!'

(*What a sight it would have been for one of our soldier-boys! Myself, skirt lifted, knickers around my ankles, bending forward as our stern schoolmistress held the beautiful face of one of my schoolfriends to my 'leaking pussy'. Oh, the thought of it, as E's soft tongue began to slide and wiggle over the folds and lips of my cunny, multiplied my pleasure and I released an involuntary moan of joy. But Miss C wasn't having any of that.*)

'Silence, you filthy young beast. Oh, what can be done with you? Ah, I have it. Miss Edwina, *bite* her. Bite the beast. Gnaw and nibble on her. That will teach her to moan as her filthiness is cleaned away.'

(*But poor E wasn't able to obey for a minute or two, for at that moment she was sick over my knickers: I felt drops of it strike my feet, stinging with stomach acid. It was the heat, she told me later, the heat, the upset and excitement of Miss C's seizure and punishment of the pair of us, and the muskiness of my CJ. Miss C muttered to her furiously, and barely gave her time to recover before hauling her up again and forcing her mouth against my cunny, shaking her like a puppy presented to a damp patch on the carpet, so that I had to restrain another moan.)*

'There, bite her. We'll teach her to take pleasure in having her filthiness licked away. Bite her, Miss Edwina. Gnaw and nibble on her. Bend further forward, Miss Theodora, you filthy young beast, and open your legs wider. Allow your schoolfellow access to every inch of your pussy. Yes. That's it. But take hold of your bottom-cheeks too. Pull them apart. Not a sliver of your pussy must escape Miss Edwina's attentions.'

(I obeyed, bending further, opening my legs wider, taking hold of my bum-cheeks and pulling them apart, and barely noticing the tremor of excitement in Miss C's words in my own emotion: my humiliation, arousal and fear. The humiliation of being on open display for my schoolmistress, of knowing that her eyes had gloated on my slipper-marked bottom and the wet pink lips of my cunny before she forced E's blonde head against them; the arousal that had already been awakened by E's attentions and that perversely fed on my humiliation; and the fear of E's white and perfect teeth: biting, nibbling, gnawing. I gasped as she set to work.)

Miss Callaghan hissed with excitement.

'Yes. That is the way, Miss Edwina. Be cruel to her. Punish her pussy-lips for the pleasure she, she *purloins* from your purifying mouth. Punish them. Punish her.'

(E apologised later: she said that she had gone too far, and that she hoped my cunny recovered quickly. In truth, it was not so bad, or not so bad when the storm had blown over and I was surveying the blasted field. At the time, well, we were both over-sensitised by the circumstances in which E set to work on my cunny with her teeth, and she believed she was biting harder than in reality she was – and I believed she was too. The thought that it was gentle blonde E and her soft-lipped mouth at work increased the

sensations by contrast. Oh, I gasped and groaned and wriggled, and was unable to hold back the rage that flashed up in me at Miss C's soft laughter; but the rage galloped straight at poor E, who was doing no more than obey orders. When my turn came – and I knew, knowing Miss C, that it soon would – I would take great delight in punishing her cunny-lips even more ferociously than I believed she was punishing mine.)

'Good girl, Miss Edwina. Good girl. That's the way. Punish the filthy little beast. Bite her. Those are, I believe, the most sensitive parts of her entire young body, and the sensation of your teeth will linger in her nerves for hours to come. What a delicious thought. Yes. The sensation will linger for hours. So bite her, Miss Edwina. Nibble her, gnaw her, *consume* her.'

('. . . consume her,' were the old b—'s exact words; but on the word 'consume' E bit hardest of all and I released an especially loud groan, quivering where I stood. Miss C finally took pity on me and ordered E to resume her tonguing away of my cunny-juice. I sighed with relief, but now heightened-sensation-by-contrast was back again, surging in the nerves of my cunny and re-exciting me to oozing. My cunny had just been punished – severely punished, I believed – and was bruised and aching with teeth-marks, but now E's soft tongue and gently sucking lips were back, probing, tickling, pleasuring. Even the sharp odour of E's vomit, rising in the heat, served merely to spur my pleasure on and I knew that E would soon feel my juice gushing hotly against her face. Indeed, there it was: she inhaled incautiously and had to gasp and splutter. And that, of course, did not escape Miss C's sharply focused attention: she still had her hand on E's neck, reading every tremor therein even as her eyes and ears held the two of us secure in their net.)

'What is wrong, Miss Edwina? Tell me, girl.'

(When E did not answer, Miss C hauled her face off my cunny, and I moaned again – with frustration and disappointment that E's mouth had left me.)

'Tell me, girl. Why did you choke and splutter? Oh, Heavens, I can see, or rather *smell,* for myself.'

(*She sniffed lingeringly, and such was her dominance and the fear she had induced in me that I trembled even at this.*)

'Oh, the filthy young beast. She is leaking again. That is *fresh* pussy-juice. Here, out of the way, you useless lump. Let me examine the miscreant for myself.'

(*E was pushed unceremoniously to one side and Miss C, as she had no doubt been eager to do ever since she began listening to E's ball-torture fantasy, bent to examine my cunny. My face, already hot and sweating, flamed with further blood as I felt the tickle of her breath on my sticky thighs and cunny-lips, then heard her disgusted sniffs.*)

'Oh, she appears to be worse than ever. Well, we shall soon see if our eyes and noses report truly. Miss Edwina, stand up and slide your knickers off. Yes, good girl. Hand them to me. Now, open that cupboard over there and bring me what you find inside. That cupboard there, girl. Use your eyes. Yes, that's it ... Thank you, Miss Edwina. Now, just to be sure ...'

(*I had listened to E standing up, sliding her knickers off, handing them to Miss C, creeping knickerless across the cabin – and as soon as her back was turned, did there not come a faint sniffing as Miss C unfolded her knickers and inspected them? – opening the cupboard, sneezing delicately, as though she had released some dust or pungent odour, then the sound of her scampering back across the cabin and, panting a little, handing Miss C what she had asked for. But what was it? Oh, it didn't take me long to get a clue, for Miss C set to work with 'it' on my cunny: two pointed ends of wood began poking, pulling, probing, and I winced and shivered with the sensation of it, and barely suppressed a moan of reluctant pleasure as they reached and began to tug and tweak at my swollen cunny-button.*)

'Keep still, you filthy young baggage. You have brought this entirely on yourself: if your pussy were not so slippery, you would not be nipped and tweaked so. Ah, but let us probe to the heart of the matter . . .'

(After a moment of puzzlement I had realised what she was doing: she was using chopsticks on me, as though my cunny were a plate of Chinese food! Now she was pushing them deeper inside me, down the oozing throat of my cunny, using them to lever me apart as she peered and sniffed. E told me later that when she opened the cupboard she found the chopsticks sitting in a lovely little pure white porcelain bowl, their ends soaking in some chemical solution that made her sneeze, like a pair of medical instruments. Yes, Miss C had used them in this way before! But that would have been obvious, E said, simply from the way she set to work on my cunny: she knew exactly what she was doing, and I can imagine how E's blue eyes widened in her CJ-smeared face as she watched the tips of the chopsticks glinting as they flew hither and thither over my cunny, expertly tugging the lips apart, plucking at or stretching out individual cunny-hairs, working on my cunny-button as though it were a little mushroom stuck to my cunny-plate, then levering my entire cunny open so that Miss C could peer down the glistening pink throat of my inner cunny. E hasn't told me so, but I know that she tried to peer too, and inadvertently hit Miss C's head with her own. The faint clunk of collision and Miss C's hiss of annoyance were quite enough to inform me what faithful E had been up to. The chopsticks slid out of me then and I heard Miss C move away.)

'Mind yourself, Miss Edwina. Yes, it is as I thought, this filthy young specimen is quite as wet with her filthiness as she looks and smells. Well, it is evidently no use for you to continue licking her, Miss Edwina, so you will kindly return these to their bowl while I pursue an alternative route . . . Now, Miss Theodora, *this* is for looking wet! . . . and *this* is for smelling wet! . . . and *this* is for being wet!'

41

(*The faint sounds of movement behind me had given me no clue, and E, she told me later, had not dared to hiss in warning as, scampering back from the chopstick-cupboard, she saw Miss C take her slipper from the shelf on which she had dropped it and lift it ready to bring it down again on my unsuspecting bottom. With each 'this' she landed a blow, carefully pacing them to allow the second and third to inflict maximum pain. Yes, I was being punished for looking wet . . . for smelling wet . . . for being wet. On the final blow, Miss C had not pulled the slipper back but artlessly allowed it to slide off my bottom, brushing my cunny as it left me, with just the faintest, most delicately judged, contact on my cunny-button. The sensation of its rough leather sole on my blazing bottom-flesh, then on my sopping cunny-lips, then, just faintly, on my cunny-button, was enough to trigger my 'orgasm': it was a physical spark for the emotional gunpowder Miss C's humiliation and paining of me had heaped in my brain. And I blew apart, gasping and groaning as my thigh-muscles, bottom and cunny spasmed with pleasure – which was so intense that for a moment or two I did not realise what Miss C had done as she set me off. But there was no doubt about it: though I had not felt her insert it with a swift, expert jab, I could feel her middle finger inside my cunny, savouring its heat, its juiciness and its tremors and spasms. As my orgasm subsided, she slid her finger slowly out, twisting it from side to side as though to soak it in my CJ more thoroughly. Then, as she tickled very delicately at my cunny-button, I felt her kiss first the left, then the right cheek of my bottom, before she straightened and leant forward to whisper in my ear.*)

'Thank you, Miss Theodora. That was most delicious to observe and feel. But what I did with my finger must remain our little secret, eh?, or I shall be very, very angry.'

(*Then, with another little kiss for my ear, she turned her attention to poor E. I heard E gasp softly with surprise but could have guessed what Miss C had done to her – indeed, when E later told me I had difficulty crediting it, till I thought back and realised how well what I had heard matched the image E's gasps and murmurs had created in my head. Yes: that first gasp of surprise had been Miss C's middle finger, still wet with my cunny-juice, jabbing between E's soft-skinned, firm-fleshed buttocks, to land unerringly atop her pink and delicate bottom-hole, like the unopened bud of a flower. And E's further murmurs of protest and disbelief had been our 'perverrted' schoolmistress's attempts to 'get in': to overcome the resistance of E's tight-sealed bottom-hole and slide that middle finger into the dark and mysterious depths of her bottom. Oh, I shiver now at the realisation of what was going on beside me: that unspeakable assault on E's back-passage, while Miss C discussed what next to do with her victim. But I hear the thread of excitement in her voice now, woven through her feigned unconcern; yes, and can pinpoint the exact moment at which she triumphed and her finger slid inside that delicious citadel.)*

'Now, Miss Edwina, *what* are we to do with you, eh? Your companion here, foul little beast that she is, has merely leaked harder when I set you to licking her filthiness away. I wonder: can you be as corrupt as she? Perhaps so. After all, for all your demureness, your softness, you took the lead in that disgusting story. What were you talking about? Yes. Men's private parts. *Part* of men's private parts.

'So perhaps your – yes – perhaps your head is as stuffed with filthiness as Miss Theodora's plainly is. Unfortunately we cannot open it to see. You have locked your secrets tight away. Sealed them in, one might say, and for all my efforts, I can't, simply can't . . . Ah. Thank you, Miss Edwina. That is most satisfactory. Yes, I think I will give you the benefit of the doubt. Eh? I cannot probe to the bottom of your secrets, as it were, and it is fairer to assume that you conceal no

further filthiness in your bosom. Eh? So, let us set Miss
Theodora to work on you.'

(*Her words were accompanied throughout by suppressed murmurs and gasps from E, as first Miss C strove
to penetrate her pupil's delicate bottom, then, having
succeeded, forced her finger into its depths and rotated it
first one way, then t'other. Something in E's voice, as she
described her 'ordeal', made me wonder whether she had
taken any pleasure in the insertion, and some day soon I
mean to ask her so. If she blushes and denies it, I will
know my suspicions are correct. As for Miss C: there can
be no doubt that she took pleasure in the deed, though of
a kind I am at a loss to fathom. It must be the sense of
possession, of power, that one – that is to say, that she –
derives from overcoming the will of her victim. Poor E did
not, at least at first, want that cunny-juiced middle finger
up her bottom. She resisted, she sighed, she murmured –
no doubt her bottom quivered and flinched and her
bottom-hole clenched tighter and tighter – but Miss C's
stronger will prevailed and she triumphed, possessing that
bottom in a way no slippering could match. Filthy old b—
that she is. Well, after tormenting E, she turned her
attention to me: my neck was seized as E's had been – and
as soon as I knew where one of those fingers had been,
you may be sure I scrubbed that neck till it tingled – and
I was dragged sideways and forced to my knees behind
bent E's thighs.*)

'Open your legs, Miss Edwina, and your little school-
companion will commence work. Good girl. Now, you
filthy little beast, lick. Lick. Yes, that's right. Further
forward, Miss Edwina, and if you could just . . . ah, you
anticipate me. Good girl. Yes, very good girl.'

(*E had 'anticipated' her by taking hold of her bottom-
cheeks and tugging them apart, granting my mouth and
tongue fuller access to her oozing cunny and its musky
sweetness, in which trickles of sweat from her bottom-
cheeks had woven salty harmonics. I strove manfully –*

*girlfully? – to follow Miss C's orders and lick away her
juice, but it was obviously no use. She was gushing like a
crushed peach and I had difficulty merely breathing, let
alone licking and lapping, as Miss C's slender but
oh-so-strong hand held me sternly to my task. Perversely,
it was E I felt more resentment towards, at that moment:
she was flowing too freely, responding too copiously to the
pleasure of my moving tongue and lips; and my heart
bounded with malicious joy as Miss C deigned finally to
notice what was taking place. Now I would be ordered to
do to E what E had been ordered to do to me: that is, bite
her.)*

'Excellent, Miss Theodora. You are working extreme-
ly well. You will have her licked clean in no time, I
fancy. But let me just ... Oh, I cannot believe it. I
simply *cannot* believe it. You filthy, filthy young baggage, Miss Edwina. You are *worse*, scarce though I can
credit it, than your filthy little companion. And though
my first remedy for her was a failure, I recall, perhaps
it will work with you. Miss Theodora, *bite* her. Gnaw
on her, nibble her. She must be taught not to respond
so, ah, *fluently* when she undergoes a simple hygienic
procedure.'

*(I needed no urging to set my teeth to work on E's
tender cunny, like a plate of exquisitely prepared fish,
stewed in a salty-sweet sauce, but cunningly (ha!) held
myself back a moment, so as to convey the impression
that I was reluctant to begin.)*

'Come, Miss Theodora. Begin. Bite her. Have no
mercy on the beast. She must be pained, she must be
punished for the filthiness of her pussy. No, stay where
you are, Miss Edwina, you wee beast. Do not seek to
escape. Miss Theodora, I trust you to remain where you
are and deliver the punishment I have ordered for her.'

*(At the mere threat of my teeth, E had wriggled
uncomfortably and tried to inch forward; but Miss C was
having none of that. She released my neck – I sighed with*

45

*relief, feeling droplets of trapped sweat trickle finally free
– and seized E to position her for her punishment. I
believed I had delayed long enough to establish my
reluctance firmly in E's shapely blonde head: she would
not suspect that I was as delighted to bite her as to obey
Miss C's order. Yes: I sucked a juicy fold of cunny-lip
into my mouth and, as though misjudging my first
attempt, munched hard at it, producing a squeak of pain
and a jerk of protest from E and a murmur of satisfaction
from Miss C. Ah, how I smiled, my face safely hidden
against the cunny I was about to torment, for I left off my
vigorous munching, as though horrified by what I had
done, and when I set to work again I flew to the opposite
extreme, barely using my teeth at all. I pictured how Miss
C's face, beaming with pleasure at my apparent cruelty,
would begin to fall as no further squeaks and jerks of
protest were forthcoming from E. Yes, it would not be
long before she ordered me to increase the strength of my
bites and I, oh-so-reluctantly, my darling E, would be
forced to obey. But cunning E, grasping my apparent
intent, began to pretend that I was at work as vigorously
as ever: wriggling, squeaking, jerking. But Miss C's ear,
bless its perspicacity (as P would no doubt say), was
sharply tuned for deceit, and after half-a-minute or so, my
heart thudded with relief as she intervened.)*

'Miss Theodora, I do not believe you are biting the
beast as hard as she would have me believe. In fact, I do
not believe that you are biting her hard at all. But please
carry on as I monitor you.'

*(I heard Miss C bend and felt a slim hand, released
from its cruel hold somewhere on E's luscious young body,
slip carefully up over E's cunny to wait just beneath my
mouth, ready to read how hard it was at work. I paused,
then began to bite E's cunny again, a little harder than
before, but nowhere near hard enough, I knew, to satisfy
our cruel schoolmistress. Miss C's fingertips fluttered
against my chin, darting up and back, reading the*

movements in my and E's flesh. Then it withdrew, and I smiled again against E's cunny, wanting to kiss it with delight at what I knew Miss C was about to say. But I refrained, lest E realise what I was up to.)

'Miss Theodora, my suspicions are confirmed. You are being far too gentle with the beast. Bite her harder or I shall set to work with my chopsticks. Well? Bite her, girl. Bite her.'

(That free hand seized my neck again and thrust me forward hard against E's cunny. I was tingling with lust and anticipation – and, I must admit, glee at my own cleverness. One thing only was lacking in the charade I had played, in the web I had spun around both E and Miss C: I should now be weeping against E's cunny for sorrow at the pain I was about to inflict, so that even through her own heat and stickiness she felt my hot, sticky tears. But I could not conjure tears, for sorrow was the very last emotion I was feeling. Ah, I had paused long enough: time to set to work. I sucked in another juicy fold of cunny-lip and bit into it with slowly increasing force. E stiffened, sensing somehow from the first trickle of sensation in her nerves what I intended; and now she squeaked and wriggled, trying to jerk forward, trying to pull her cunny-fold from my lips and nipping teeth. Miss C hissed with pleasure and her hand flew from my neck, back to E's luscious body. I felt the force with which she seized my torturee and smiled again, knowing that E would be unable to move now as I continued my work.)

Four

All the preparations had been made: the bribery, the blackmail; the spying, the secret messages; and now the juicy fly was wandering complacently into the web that had been spun for it. But the fly wasn't wandering: Theodora had to push her hand over her mouth to restrain a spurt of laughter as she heard Philippa's feet trot eagerly past the cabin in which she was hiding. Philippa had been told that Theodora's Diary was available for viewing at last, stolen for an hour from its owner and held in an unoccupied cabin in a distant part of the ship. But just about now – yes, there it came: the cry of guillotined outrage as Philippa made that coded knock on the door of the cabin and was pounced upon by two girls, tall Zoë and Rhoda, who had crept from the door of the cabin directly behind her.

Theodora smiled in the gloom of her own cabin. Now they would be dragging Philippa backwards into the cabin, her cries cut off by a large palm over her mouth, her eyes rolling wildly with outrage and apprehension. Yes. But the play couldn't start without its director. She picked up her Diary, strolled to the door of the cabin, and opened it, smiling again as she heard the faint sound of struggling from further down the corridor cut off as a door closed firmly against it. That would be door-girl Winnie. Now Zoë and Rhoda would be gagging Philippa, tying her hands behind her back and turning her to face the door. Perhaps she would have seen the row of holes drilled in the left wall of the cabin and be trying to twist her head to look at them. But a strong hand on the back of her neck would soon stop that.

Theodora strolled down the corridor, hugging her Diary happily to her breasts. *At last, at last, I have her exactly where I want her!* She reached the door of the cabin in which Philippa was being held and knocked on it using the code Philippa had used a minute before on the door opposite. *Tit-tit-tat tit-tat.* Mockery of their fly, now that it was safely swathed in silk and awaiting the fangs of the spider. The door opened and there was Winnie's face, flushed and smiling with the same pleasure that lit her own. She entered the cabin, reaching for and squeezing Winnie's hand, heart thudding at the sight that greeted her in the centre of the cabin: Philippa helpless and wrathful in the grip of Zoë and Rhoda, eyes widening with understanding and fear above her gag now that she saw her enemy.

'Philippa!' Theodora cried gleefully, running across the room to plant a kiss on the soft, trembling, sweaty cheek that Rhoda held in place for her. She stepped back, shaking her head in mock surprise.

'Such an unexpected delight to find you here, Philly! But of course, it's not really unexpected, is it? You've come here with a definite purpose, haven't you, my darling? Connected with this, *n'est ce-pas?*'

She held up her Diary, waving it in front of her enemy's face.

'*Mon journal.* You have been *so* eager to read it, haven't you? To learn my most intimate little secrets and gain even more of an ascendancy over me. Well, my darling, and so you *shall* read it, or at least you shall be read to *from* it, by the author herself, your obedient servant Theodora.'

She bowed, hearing Edwina snigger behind her, and

49

straightened to see the grins on Zoë's and Rhoda's faces widening even further.

'Let me see,' she said, beginning to leaf through the Diary. 'What shall I read to you first? Oh, this might be good . . . But no.'

After a few moments of silent reading, she looked up, pursing her lips and shaking her head.

'That is rather *too* intimate. But perhaps . . . this?'

Another few moments of silent reading, another pursing of lips and shaking of head. Then Winnie, as they had planned – scripted – spoke up from behind her.

'Make it something recent, Dorrie.'

'Something the two of you have shared,' chimed in Zoë, and Theodora shivered slightly at the increased *deepness* of her voice. It must be the pleasure of seizing and subduing Philippa. She looked up from her reading.

'Recent?' she said. 'Shared?'

'Yes,' Rhoda said, or rather – Theodora shivered again – rumbled. 'Some recent experience the two of you have shared. So that Philly can see it from a different angle. *Your* angle, Dorrie. That will be an unusual experience for her.'

Theodora nodded.

'An excellent idea, the three of you. I shall read to her about something recent, something shared, to allow her to see it from *my* angle. Such an unusual experience for her. Hmmm. But what?'

She leafed back and forward through the Diary, pausing to read briefly, then shaking her head and leafing on. Then she grunted.

'Have you found something, Dorrie?' Winnie said from behind her.

'Hm?'

She glanced behind her, shaking her head fractionally to warn Winnie to take the smile off her face. She turned back to the Diary.

'Perhaps, Winnie. Perhaps. Let's see . . .'

She read on, nodding and grunting again.

'Yes, I think I *have* found something. It certainly meets all your criteria: it's recent, it was shared, and it will certainly allow Philly to see things from that new and unusual angle, namely *my* angle. Yes, I think this will do. Winnie, could you bring me the chair?'

She heard Winnie trotting to the corner of the cabin where the chair sat waiting, draped with a rug, and watched Philippa's face carefully for her reaction. Ah, there it came as the rug was tugged away.

'Is there something wrong, Philly?' she asked innocently as Winnie lifted the chair and carried it to her. 'Oh, sorry, I forgot. You're having a little trouble with your voice at the moment, aren't you? Thank you, Winnie.'

The chair had been set on the floor behind her. She half-turned to flick at its seat with the hem of her skirt, then sat down. Philippa had recognised the chair all right and Theodora felt a warm glow at the base of her belly at the apprehension in her enemy's face. She wriggled fractionally, pleasuring her buttocks against the cane-work of the seat, trying to encourage the glow to sink faster, to enter her cunny and excite her for the spectacle she would be witnessing in ten minutes or so.

'Now, where shall I begin? Here? Or here? No, perhaps *here* would be best. At the moment Philly threw the toast onto the table.'

She looked up, ostensibly to check that everyone was ready for her to begin, in reality to see if Philippa recognised the allusion to the toast. But of course she had, and now she was speculating furiously and fearfully about what revenge was planned for her. Would the holes in the cabin-wall be part of her speculation yet?

'Everyone ready? Win? Zo? Rho? You, Philly? Are you ready? I'll take that as a "Yes", dear. Right, you're all ready, and I'm all ready, so let's begin.'

She cleared her throat and began reading.

Yes, cher Journal, *imagine how I felt when I saw that the toast had a letter on it! Philippa or one of her minions, rather, must have painted it on with water before the bread was toasted. On both sides: a big 'D' for 'Dorrie'.*

'There you go, young lady,' Philippa said with a 'cat-that's-got-the-cream' smile, 'a piece of toast specially for you. Now you can soak up all that lovely come and eat it with . . .'

I interrupted her, shaking with anger as I appealed to the rest of the table and to our soldier boys.

'Look at that! She must have arranged all this, or she wouldn't have . . .'

But Philippa, her smile growing even smugger, anticipated what I was going to say and started to throw other pieces of toast onto the table. They had letters on them too: one for each of us around the table, it seemed, but as I goggled at them in chagrin, I realised with a sudden upsurge of hope that one was missing. And that was when Philippa threw a final piece of toast onto the table: 'P' for 'Philippa'.

'Get on with it, Dorrie,' she said. 'You've got all the toast you'll need. But cake first.'

She nodded to Frances, who stretched across the table, took hold of the plate of cake, and slid it across the table towards me. Everyone still had her tits on display and I noticed that three or four cocks were re-stiffening as their owners looked happily from pair to pair.

'Get on with it, Dorrie,' Philippa said again. 'And girls, please, cover yourselves. We aren't having to compensate for Dorrie's lack of expertise any more.'

Giggles around the table as my school-'friends' began to put their breasts away, though Edwina had the decency to look ashamed of herself as she did so. I reached out miserably and tugged the plate the last few inches towards me. Now the smell hit me: the sweetness of cream and sugar almost overpowered by the briny reek of 'come' pumped hot and fresh from five pairs of balls. No, four pairs of balls: my soldier hadn't made it as far as the cake. My stomach rolled with nausea, but I knew that Philippa was watching me eagerly, eyes shining with the hope that I would be sick, so I forced my nausea down, pushed a smile into my face, and scooped up a big handful from the plate.

A soldier-boy groaned as he watched me lift it to my mouth, and a glance at his cock showed me that it was fully erect again, straining ceilingward. Why is it so exciting for them to watch a girl eat their come? Is it the sexual perversity of it? The humiliation and disgust the come-eater feels, however hard she tries to hide it? Or is it the combination of cake and come? Poor dears: some of them would never have seen a cake so magnificent in their lives, and yet here was a 'posh bint' eating it while it was soaked with the product of their lower-class testicles. I tried desperately to keep these questions in my head as I took the first bite, but it was hopeless: the flavour and texture of the cake were impossible to ignore and for one horrid moment I thought my throat was going to lock and refuse to let me swallow it.

How Philippa would have enjoyed that! Chance for a game of 'Suffragette and Semen' – I had already seen her force-feeding poor Annette with come-soaked cake and knew how much she enjoyed it. But no: my throat was responding now and I could gulp down that first mouthful and even emit an 'Mmmmm' of pleasure. I decided to eat fast, cramming down the cake before I started on the pools of come on the table, soaking them up with the toast, and was confirmed in my plan by a secret glance at Philippa and the disappointment in her face.

Theodora stopped reading and looked up at her gagged enemy.

'You were disappointed, weren't you, Philly? Seeing me able to cram so much in and swallow it with such apparent ease? But remember, darling, that what goes around, well, comes around.'

She stared at Philippa's face, waiting to see if the meaning of her words had sunk in, then nodded and smiled with satisfaction, wriggling fractionally as she felt the glow in her belly settling at last into her cunny. Philippa had known something more was planned for her than simply a reading from Theodora's Diary; now she knew it would involve 'come' in some way. Was that row of holes in the wall in her consciousness again? But Theodora kept her eyes firmly on her Diary, not glancing up to see if Philippa was trying to look at the wall.

'Where was I?' she said. 'Ah, yes, I'd just seen the disappointment in your face, Philly.'

She cleared her throat and continued reading.

Knowing that made it easier to go on. I scooped up another handful of come-soaked cake and crammed it into my mouth, having to restrain the urge to laugh now. The soldier-boys were staring at me wide-eyed and open-mouthed, groaning occasionally with lust as they watched me eat. Yes, I was being 'tarty', 'sluttish' even, but the feeling of power it gave me helped compensate for the humiliation of falling into the trap Philippa had set for me. When I finished the mouthful and ran my tongue around my lips, licking off the cream and come that had accumulated there, eyes closed in apparent ecstasy, I heard more groans; and when I opened my eyes I saw that all five cocks were standing rigidly to attention, even that of my own 'nobbled' soldier-boy.

'Privates on parade,' I said, nodding around the table at one cock after another as I scooped up a third and final

*handful of cake. The soldiers and the other girls laughed,
except for Philippa. No, she frowned momentarily then, I
saw, as I kept a close eye on her with my peripheral vision.
This wasn't going at all the way she'd planned! Up with
the third handful to my mouth, cram it noisily in with
murmurs of appreciation, gulp it down, then lick my lips
and fingers noisily clean before reaching nonchalantly for
'my' slice of toast and popping it neatly atop the largest
pool of come on the table. As I pushed the toast to and
fro, soaking up the come on one side before I turned it
over and soaked up the come on the other, I said chattily
to Philippa: 'This hasn't been at all bad, you know,
Philly.'*

*Ah, nonchalance cometh before a fall! My anger and
excitement were still bubbling beneath my pleasure at
turning the tables on Philippa, and I was really not so
much in control of the situation as I thought. This was
brought home to me all too strongly as I lifted my slice of
toast and took a large bite out of it. I do not know
whether the come I had soaked up was especially pungent
or the toast, unlike the cake, did not offset its pungency
with sweetness, but the result was the same in either case.
The flavour of come flared in my mouth and my stomach
revolted.* Une jacquerie gastrique, cher Journal! *Yes, I
threw up all the cake I had so successfully swallowed, and
guess whose was the one face around the table not to
watch with mingled disgust and pity?*

Theodora snapped her Diary shut and looked up at her
enemy.

'It was yours, wasn't it, Philly? Your face. How happy
you suddenly looked, knowing what you could now
force me to do. But I won't read my description of it.
It's still too painful, but it won't be so for much longer.
Not once I've forced *you* to do something even worse.
Yes, darling,' she repeated with satisfaction, watching
her enemy's face, 'even *worse*.'

She smiled, then glanced at Philippa's two guards and nodded.

'Time to introduce her to the chorus-line, girls,' she said. Philippa grunted with pain as Zoë and Rhoda seized her by the upper arms and turned her to face the row of holes in the cabin-wall. Theodora finished re-tying the ribbon around her Diary and stood up.

'Can you guess what awaits you, darling?' she said. She strolled over to the wall, still carrying her Diary, and stood at the left end of the row, looking towards Philippa.

'Ten holes, darling,' she said. 'Can you guess? About three inches across and about two-and-half feet off the ground. Cat got your tongue, darling? Let's hope not, because you'll need your tongue shortly. And your lips. Here, perhaps this will help you think.'

It was Winnie's cue to throw the cushion; Theodora caught it in one hand and dropped it neatly on the floor beneath the first of the holes.

'Mustn't have you hurt your knees, darling,' she said. 'No, mustn't have that happen when you suck your way through this little lot.'

She hit the wall softly three times with her Diary, watching Philippa's face as the holes were filled in sequence, one to ten, by the stiff cocks that had been waiting for her signal. Oh, she felt her sticky cunny throb against her knickers at the horror and disbelief that sprang into Philippa's face with the first cock, then deepened with the second, third and fourth – Philippa's whole body twitched to mark the emergence of each – and seemed to sink into a kind of shock with the fifth, sixth, and seventh. On what must have been the eighth, Philippa fainted, relaxing in Zoë's and Rhoda's grip with a sigh.

Theodora looked sideways just in time to catch the emergence of cocks nine and ten. The biggest and longest of the lot: she had been to great pains to ensure that the row of cocks emerged in strict sequence of size, working the greatest possible havoc on Philippa's nerves. Yet she had been almost *too* successful, as the limp body of Philippa testified. Their script had to be torn up now, but she thought she could improvise something new to fill the gap between this moment and the moment at which Philippa, fully conscious again, took the first cock into her mouth. She jerked her chin at Zoë and Rhoda.

'Strip her, darlings.'

She watched as Rhoda held Philippa up by her armpits, flopping head safe over the tall girl's broad left shoulder, while Zoë expertly and swiftly stripped her skirt and knickers off. Then it was Rhoda's turn: Zoë clasped Philippa from behind as Rhoda, working from the front, undid all the buttons of Philippa's blouse, large hands moving nimbly as a pink tongue wiggled in the corner of her mouth, then peeled the blouse open and reached behind Philippa's body to undo her bra. The smaller girl murmured uneasily, sensing somehow in her faint what was being done to her as Rhoda plucked off her bra in one smooth movement, exposing her firm eighteen-year-old's breasts, glistening with sweat and set with stiffened pink nipples that wiggled like little tongues as Rhoda drew her blouse off too.

Now Philippa was quite naked but for her socks and shoes. That was the way Theodora preferred her, however: girls seemed *more* naked that way, rather as they did when stripped of everything but a hat.

'Display her for me, darlings,' she said. 'Let me admire that lovely body of hers.'

She was speaking for the benefit of the ten soldier-boys waiting eagerly behind the holes, cocks thrust into the unknown, but she would have been quite happy to issue the order if she had known that none of them could hear her. Philippa did have a lovely body, as though the share of beauty that might have gone to

57

sweeten her personality had been poured instead into her breasts and buttocks, her legs and arms, and that smooth, innocent face of hers, presently lolling on her slender neck. But quite enough of Philippa was visible as Zoë and Rhoda held her up and turned her like a large doll, glistening faintly with sweat as though fresh from a bath. Theodora felt her cunny throb and ache with desire.

'*Ah, la belle gonzesse!*' she cried, longing to rush across the room and drag the unconscious girl from the large hands of her captors, then wake her with trickling kisses over her breasts and buttocks before riding those buttocks *à la tribade*, sliding and grinding her hot, oozing cunny on their smooth curves. She dragged herself out of the fantasy almost with a physical effort, and, realising that the French would be a little above the heads of her listeners on the other side of the wall, called out: 'What an arse! And what *tits*! Mmmmm, she looks good enough to *eat*!'

She glanced sideways at the row of cocks now, and saw that all were twitching eagerly and that five or six of them had risen even further, so that their shafts must have been rubbing uncomfortably against the upper edge of the holes through which they were pushed.

'Hold your horses, boys,' she said; then, to Zoë and Rhoda: 'And she certainly is good enough to eat – to eat this lovely row of cocks. Carry her here, darlings, and set her in place, ready to begin.'

Out of the corner of her eye she saw the first cock twitch even more violently. Ah, the owner thought he would soon be being sucked. And he was quite right: he would be. She walked to the cock, dropped her hand over it and squeezed it, feeling the floor shake faintly beneath her feet as Zoë and Rhoda carried Philippa to her. But she didn't squeeze too hard. He was a most excitable boy, this one, and she didn't want him going off prematurely. She stooped to put her mouth nearer to the hole through which the cock was inserted.

'Hold on, sweetie,' she whispered through it. 'The star of the show fainted when she saw your cocks and we'll have to bring her round first.'

On 'fainted' she felt the cock throb in her hand, and when she straightened from the hole and delicately thumbed back the hot foreskin, tilting the cock upward a little, she saw that the mouth of the cockhead was glistening with pre-ejaculate. Ah, what excellent timing! Zoë and Rhoda had reached the wall and were lowering the limp Philippa onto her knees in front of the cock she was holding. She tightened her grip on it, holding it in place as she said, 'Untie her gag, Rho, and rub her face on it, Zo. That will wake her up so she can begin sucking.'

Zoë grunted with sadistic anticipation as Rhoda quickly untied and drew Philippa's gag away. Now Zoë took hold of Philippa's hair, lifting her face up and presenting it to the swollen cock Theodora held ready. Zoë rubbed it left-right, up-down against the head of the cock, then leaned forward a little to watch as she rubbed Philippa's nostrils on the cock, ensuring that its hot smell entered her nostrils, then tugged her head back a little to rub the cock along the unconscious girl's lips. That was the end both for the cock-rubbing and for Philippa's faint: Theodora felt the too-sensitive cock, already stimulated to excess, throb heavily in her hand, and watched, a little surprised in the first moment, but soon beginning to smile broadly, as it spurted thickly over Philippa's face.

The effect of powerful shafts of hot semen at point-blank range was apparent almost at once. Philippa murmured loudly in her faint, but as her eyes flickered and seemed about to open, Theodora swung the cock slightly upward and landed the fourth shaft of semen directly atop the bridge of her nose, so that it sprayed over her eyes, then swung the cock downward to land the fifth shaft neatly through Philippa's mouth as it opened in protest. *That* woke her up fully: she spluttered and coughed, trying to shake her head and move away from the still-firing cock. But Zoë's hand was locked as firmly as ever in her hair and the further three shafts spurted against her face as the previous five had done. Theodora murmured with pleasure at the humiliation of her enemy, longing to masturbate as she felt her cunny ooze even more thickly.

But she must remain as much in control of herself as she was in control of Philippa: this was the price that the 'dominant' paid for the pleasure of domination. The cock had ceased firing; she shook it briskly, splattering Philippa's thickly coated face with a few last droplets of semen.

'If you could only see yourself, darling,' she said. 'You're barely recognisable through all that lovely come.'

Philippa was blinking, trying to open her eyes, and blowing air through her lips, trying to clean them so she could speak – 'fubbering', Jacky called it.

'I fubber, thou fubberest, she fubbereth,' Theodora said, then letting go of the cock and lifting her hand as she called 'Spoon, Winnie!'

Still watching Philipa's semen-soaked face and the firm, pink-nippled breasts onto which the semen was rapidly dripping, she heard Winnie trotting eagerly to the shelf where the spoon sat ready, then back across to the cock-wall.

'Thank you, darling,' Theodora said as the spoon was placed in her hand. 'What a mess you've made of your first suck, Philly! Time to clean you up with our come-spoon, I think.'

She squatted on her heels to begin gliding the spoon briskly over Philippa's left breast, filling it with semen and making Philippa jerk as the cold metal circled her stiff nipple.

'Ow,' Philippa said, and muttered something under her breath.

'Sorry, darling,' Theodora said. 'But I'll do it again and worse if you don't keep your mouth shut and open it only for purposes of sucking and swallowing. Right? For the next hour or however long it takes, you are merely a warm, wet, animated orifice for the pleasuring of our soldier-boys. So just shut up and do as you're told because there are a *lot* of cocks to get through and a lot of lovely come for you to swallow and you've barely started yet. There, your first mouthful. *Ooopen* wide and let Mummy pop it in.'

She lifted the spoon to Philippa's mouth, but it remained stubbornly closed and even with Rhoda's large hand locked in her hair Philippa tried to shake her head.

'Naughty girl!' Theodora scolded. 'But Mummy knows the remedy for such stubbornness. Zo, nose, please.'

Another large hand moved over Philippa's face and two strong fingers pinched Philippa's nose firmly shut.

'If you don't start doing exactly as you're told, Philly,' Theodora said conversationally, 'we can always find somewhere else for those lovely big cocks to go, you know. Rather than the warm, wet, animated orifice in your face, we can always use one of the warm, wet, animated orifices lower down.'

She heard Winnie gasp with shock at the threat, and looked up at her, winking and shaking her head slightly. But she was quite convinced that Zoë and Rhoda would do it if she ordered them: seize Philippa and thrust her against the wall in such a way as to allow the cocks to enter her cunny or – Philippa felt herself shiver deliciously at the thought of it – her bottom. Philippa's breasts were shuddering with the effort of holding her breath, and Theodora felt tiny droplets of semen striking her hand as she held the spoon ready.

'Trust me, darling,' she said to Philippa, 'we'll do it. Push the cocks up *both* of them, one after another.'

The threat of having ten fat cocks forced first up her cunny, then up her bottom, had its effect at last even on the stubborn Philippa and her mouth came open with a gasp. Theodora popped the semen-laded spoon neatly inside and turned it over.

'Don't spit, darling,' she said. 'Or Mummy doesn't know *what* she'll do. Just swallow like a good girl, and let Mummy feed you the rest.'

Philippa was spluttering with a look of intense disgust on her face, and Theodora knew she was considering whether to spit the mouthful of come out over her tormentrix, fouling her clothes or splattering her face. But Philippa had managed to open her eyes a little now and the look of cool assurance Theodora was wearing apparently convinced her that the threat was quite real, for she made a convulsive effort and swallowed the mouthful of come with a noisy gulp. Theodora looked up to see broad grins on the faces of her three helpers, and chuckled happily as she looked down again to guide the spoon over Philippa's right breast.

'What a *good* girl she is! Doing *exactly* what Mummy tells her . . . and here's her reward: another spoonful of delicious creamy come to swallow.'

Philippa's mouth came open almost at once this time, as though she had decided to get her ordeal over as quickly as possible. Theodora popped the spoon in and turned it over, depositing the come on her tongue.

'Swallow, darling,' she said, sliding the spoon out and beginning to guide it over Philippa's face. Chin first, to catch the come before it dripped onto her breasts again. She murmured distractedly '*Good* girl' as Philippa swallowed again, then lifted the third spoonful to her enemy's lips.

' 'Nother one, darling.'

Philippa's mouth *did* come open at once this time. Was she starting to like the taste? Theodora popped the spoon in, turned it over, slid it out.

'Dorrie?'

It was Winnie's quiet voice and she glanced up for a moment.

'Hmmm?'

'Look.'

'What is it?'

She glanced up again and followed Winnie's pointing finger.

'Oh. I see. Could you just . . .?'

And Winnie trotted off happily down the line of cocks to sort the problem out. Two of them, numbers six and eight, had started to droop a little and Theodora watched out of the corner of her eye as Winnie knelt in front of number six. Theodora stopped guiding the spoon over Philippa's face to watch what Winnie was going to do. Ah, she was unbuttoning her blouse, reaching inside to unclip her bra, sighing with relief as she peeled the sweat-moistened cups from her breasts and dropped the bra on the floor beside her. Now what would she do? She was leaning forward a fraction, lodging the bulbous head of number six gently between her bared breasts. What next? Oh, with a delicate grunt she raised and lowered herself on her knees, rubbing the cock with her breast-skin. Theodora smiled as the cock sprang fully erect again with an almost audible click, then smiled harder as Winnie looked at her, beaming with pride and satisfaction.

'Well done, darling,' she said. Then she returned her attention to spooning Philippa's face clean of come, watching out of the corner of her eye as Winnie shuffled sideways to cock number eight and performed the same trick with her breasts. She was doing it just right, recognising . . .

'Oh!'

It was Winnie. Theodora was lifting a fourth spoonful of come to Philippa's lips, and frowned a little. What had happened? She couldn't look just yet.

63

'Fourth spoonful, darling,' she said to Philippa, and clucked with satisfaction as Philippa's mouth opened at once again and she could pop the spoon straight in. Now, what was Winnie up to? She looked sideways and clucked again, but this time with annoyance. Cock number eight, to Winnie's evident surprise and chagrin, was spurting thickly over her breasts.

'Winnie!' Rhoda shouted. 'You clumsy idiot!'

Rhoda had noticed too and was glaring with anger at the younger girl.

'No, Rho,' said Theodora, sliding the spoon out of Philippa's mouth and setting it gliding over her face again. 'I saw how carefully Winnie was working,' she continued. 'Number eight is obviously too excitable as well.'

Another spoonful would do it: it was well past time for Philippa to start sucking cock, not merely swallowing come. But what about Winnie? She lifted the fifth spoonful to Philippa's lips, thinking hard. Out of the corner of her eye, she saw that the cock had stopped spurting. Winnie was leaning her torso backwards, keeping the come on her breasts as she peered down at it. Ah, she knew what to do.

'Fifth spoonful, darling,' she said. 'Then you can start sucking cock number two.'

Did Philippa's mouth stay shut a moment longer this time, and open reluctantly to accept the fifth spoonful of come? Perhaps the poor dear had forgotten that she was here to suck and swallow, not to be spoon-fed.

'Good girl,' Theodora said, sliding the spoon out. 'Now, move her along, Zo, Rho. Number two has been waiting long enough.' Then, raising her voice, knowing that the prick-owners' ears would be pricking behind the wall: 'Winnie, darling, it will all drip off your firm little titties in the end, even if you sit like that. Go and lie on your back in the middle of the floor. Then Rho or Zo will bring you a couple of fans and you can waft your titties. Help the come dry and then in fifteen or twenty minutes or so, when Philly's sucked her way down this row of lovely stiff cocks and swallowed lots and lots of hot, fresh come, she can lick it off your titties.'

Winnie obeyed at once, lowering her back to the floor as she knelt on it in front of the cock that had soaked her breasts, then straightening her legs and pushing herself in little jerks to the middle of the room, where she began to fan her breasts with her hands as she waited for Zoë or Rhoda to bring her the real fans Theodora had promised. Philippa was in front of cock number two now, staring at it with narrowed eyes between come-splattered eyelashes.

'Zo, could you get the fans for Winnie?' Theodora said. 'Let Rho hold her by the hair, then you can change back for number three.'

' 'Kay,' Zoë said. She let go of Philippa's hair, picked two or three strands of it from between her fingers, dropped them to the floor, and went to fetch the fans for Winnie. With a smile, Rhoda inserted her large hand into the rumpled mess Zoë had made of Philippa's hair. Philippa had sighed with relief as Zoë let go; now she grunted with pain as Rhoda took hold and tightened her grip.

'Hold her firmly, Rho,' Theodora said, feeling fresh juice beginning to leak from her crusted cunny. How delightful it was to dominate and control Philippa like this! 'I don't want her to be shy as I introduce her to *Monsieur le Deux*.'

She slipped her fingers around the second cock, holding it firmly but carefully, not wanting to provoke another premature ejaculation. She looked up as Zoë handed Winnie a pair of fans and the smaller girl, lying on her back in the middle of the floor, began to fan her breasts.

'*Monsieur le Deux*, may I introduce you to young Philippa?' she said, dragging her eyes away from the delicious sight. 'Well, *mademoiselle*, don't you have a kiss for your new acquaintance? She's a little shy, I think, Rhoda, so perhaps you can help her.'

She glanced up at Rhoda, who grinned and provoked a squeak of pain from Philippa as her hand tightened even further in the older girl's hair. She pushed Philippa's head forward so that her mouth pressed against the head of the cock Theodora was holding ready for her. Theodora smiled happily, then jerked her chin at Rhoda, indicating that she should pull Philippa's head back.

'What a sight you are, Philly,' she said, dropping out of character for a moment. 'Isn't she, you two?'

She looked up at Rhoda and at Zoë, who had returned to stand beside her tall friend. The two of them nodded, rumbling 'Yes' with a grin as they waited for Theodora to continue her verbal tormenting of her rival.

'Yes, you really are a sight,' Theodora said, looking back down at Philippa's face. 'Not a sight for sore eyes, but a sight to make eyes sore. Face smeared in come, eyebrows and eyelashes all matted and stuck together with come, and you've even got come in your hair. And you know, it takes a mother's eye to see your beauty through all that, darling, but fortunately that's exactly what I've got. So come on, open your mouth for Mummy and forget your troubles in sucking on this lovely treat she's prepared for you. Something hot, meaty and filling for you, because we all know that's what you like best . . . And there's a good girl!'

And Philippa *had* been a good girl: Theodora jerked her chin at Rhoda again, indicating that she should push Philippa's head forward again onto the cock, and their captive opened her mouth meekly as anything, allowing the cock to slide inside.

'*Good* girl,' Theodora said, wondering whether Philippa was up to something. 'Deep enough for now, Rho, thanks. Now, darling, isn't that nice? Close your mouth on it . . . yes, good girl . . . and now suuuck . . .'

About a third of the cock's length was inside Phi-lippa's mouth and Theodora thought she had rarely seen her enemy look so attractive – partly by contrast with the vein-crawled *alienness* and masculinity of what had, well, *invaded* her fresh-skinned young face. Ah, and Philippa was obeying orders again: sealing her mouth on the cock and sucking. Theodora tried to put a look of maternal pride on her face as she watched Philippa's cheeks hollow and eyes close with apparent pleasure; then she snorted with laughter at the transformation that took place. Philippa's eyes sprung open with shock and her fresh young breasts shook and bounced with a sudden access of coughing.

'No!' Theodora said. 'Don't let her, Rho! Push her
. . . Yes, that's it. *Exactly* right.'

The cock had evidently begun to discharge heavily and prematurely inside Philippa's mouth, catching both forced fellatrix and fellatrix-forcers by surprise. But Rhoda had reacted quickly as Philippa tried to pull her mouth off the cock, holding her head firmly in place, then pushing it forward further over the cock as it continued to discharge. Poor Philly must have taken the first spurt directly down her unprepared throat, Theodora thought. No wonder the poor thing had choked and spluttered. But now she seemed to be pooling the spurts inside her mouth. Yes, from the way her cheeks were bulging that was exactly what she was doing. She tutted loudly.

'Oh dear, you *are* having a time today, aren't you, Philly? Two cocks, two premature emissions. And copious emissions, I might add. But perhaps you'll have better luck with *Monsieur le Trois*. First, though, you'll have to swallow everything you've got in your mouth. Not that lovely big cock, I mean, but what it's very kindly *discharged* into your mouth. Yes, darling, you can't fool Mummy. She can see you're holding come there. Swallow it, darling, then we can go on to number three and see if that, finally, will allow you to get some decent cock-sucking practice in.'

But whether cock number three was another premature ejaculator or not neither Theodora nor Philippa would ever learn, for even as Philippa began to swallow the come pooled in her mouth, they heard an explosion in the distance and the floor of the cabin shook beneath them. Now a klaxon began to sound and the row of cocks, save for cocks four and ten, began to slide back through the holes in the wall. The girls in the cabin stared at each other in surprise, but Theodora was pleased to see that Rhoda did not relax her grip on Philippa's hair. A faint sound of upraised voices came from the cabin where the cock-owners had been standing, and cock four quivered and shook before withdrawing through its hole. How much longer cock ten stayed where it was, waiting for a mouth that would never come, Theodora did not learn, for she did not watch: Miss Callaghan's distorted voice, evidently speaking through a megaphone, was now audible in the distance through the wail of the klaxon.

'Torpedo!'

It was Winnie, sitting up on the floor, still automatically working the fans over her bare, semen-soaked breasts. Yes, they had all caught the word. The door of the cabin next to them crashed open and they heard the sound of many feet running down the corridor. A heavy fist pounded on their door and a male voice – Theodora caught the note of disappointment and realised it was one of the would-be suckees – shouted through it: 'We bin 'it, girls! On deck, quick!'

Then his feet too were pounding down the corridor.

'Release her,' Theodora said to Rhoda. 'Philly, Winnie, get dressed, quick as you can! Forget bra and knickers!'

Theodora ran to the door of the cabin, threw it open and looked out. Two soldiers, one of whom appeared to

68

be still doing up his trousers, were just disappearing around a turn in the corridor. She looked back into the room.

'No, come on, all of you, now! Do it up *later*, Winnie!'

And she motioned fellatrix-forcers and forced fellatrix out of the cabin. Winnie was holding her blouse modestly closed over her bare breasts, and Theodora reached out and did up her top button.

'Silly girl,' she did. 'Now, come on, run!'

They ran, but had barely gone two yards before another explosion shook the ship beneath them. Philippa, still unsteady on her feet, stumbled and fell, and Theodora turned back to seize her by the elbow and haul her to her feet.

'Thanks,' Philippa gasped. 'But it makes no difference, you know. I'm *still* going to pay you back for this.'

Theodora slapped her resoundingly on her bottom, storing the memory of the firm, bare buttock her hand had met beneath the thin skirt.

'We've got to get safe out first, Philly. So shut up and run!'

She seized Philippa's hand and hauled, pulling her rival after her. Zoë and Rhoda had already turned the corner, but Winnie had stopped and was staring back at them.

'Run!' Theodora shouted at her. 'Forget about us!'

Philippa was running by herself now and Theodora released her hand. Trust Philippa to be making threats in the middle of an emergency, *and* to the girl who was trying to help her. Her ego really was too big: she needed plenty more resounding slaps on her bottom, without even a thin skirt in the way, and Theodora smiled even as she pounded down the corridor. *And I'm the one to do it*, she thought to herself. Suddenly she heard Winnie coughing ahead of her, and now she smelt it too – and saw it. They were nearing the door that opened on deck and wisps of acrid smoke were drifting down the corridor. Miss Callaghan's voice began speaking through the megaphone again and Theodora was near enough to catch all the words this time:

'Girruls! Remain calm and orderly! There are plenty of lifeboats for everyone and sailors are on hand to assist you!'

Then Theodora, with Philippa on her heels, was running through the door. What a scene of confusion met her eyes on deck! Billows of thick black smoke were pouring between milling groups of frightened schoolgirls, while Miss Callaghan, half-obscured through a billow of smoke still passing over her, was standing slim and erect at the rail, megaphone lifted to her lips. As Theodora watched, she lowered it and spoke to a sailor standing next to her. Other sailors were hard at work readying lifeboats at the rail. Another explosion shook the ship and Theodora moved forward, trying to see where Winnie, Zoë and Rhoda had gone. Philippa had run off somewhere too. Now Miss Callaghan was lifting the megaphone to her lips again.

'Girruls! Please move to the rail now and wait to be helped into the lifeboats!'

Theodora had just taken the first step to obey when she heard a deep male voice speak behind her.

'This 'er, Miss?'

She was spinning on her heel even as Philippa's voice, rich with spite and satisfaction, said 'Yes.' She dropped to her knees, realising by instinct what was happening, but the owner of the male voice moved too quickly for her: an arm swept around her waist, plucking her off her feet, and a large and sweaty palm closed over her mouth. Something large and hard was pressing into her lower back as she was crushed to the sailor's body and she realised breathlessly, indignant at her own lack of indignation, that it was his stiff cock. What a size it must be!

'Over here,' she heard Philippa say as a billow of smoke poured over them, and she was carried, kicking helplessly, to the rail where one of the lifeboats was waiting. She tried to turn her head, looking for Miss Callaghan or one of her own friends, but the hand was too strong and Philippa was issuing another order.

'Shield them. Don't want Cally or anyone else to see.'

Damn that smoke! Theodora thought as she sensed Philippa's gang crowding around her and the sailor, shielding them from discovery. Miss Callaghan was speaking through the megaphone again.

'Into the lifeboats now, girruls!'

She felt the sailor's deep voice vibrating in his body as he spoke.

'Ah'm gonna need an 'and here, Miss, 'cause Ah've got to keep mine on 'er mouth.'

Theodora blushed despite the heat as her cunny throbbed with pleasure, releasing another gush of juice against her soaked knickers. His cock was hard as ever, pressed against her body, but now other hands were fastening to her too, helping the sailor lift her over the rail and lower her into the lifeboat. His hard cock left her body, but suddenly she was kicking and struggling again, squeaking through the large hand still firmly planted over her mouth. Someone was lifting her dress and tugging at her knickers. What on earth was Philippa planning to do with her? Have her raped by the sailor? No, it wasn't that, and Theodora felt an unmistakable pang of disappointment through her relief. Her knickers had been deftly pulled down her legs and over her kicking feet.

'Gag her,' she heard Philippa say. She drew in breath to scream in the moment between the sailor releasing her mouth and her own knickers being forced on her as a gag, but Philippa had thought of everything. As the sailor let go, Theodora felt her nipples being seized and cruelly twisted and, as she cried out in pain and surprise the knickers, soaked with cunny-juice, were pushed hard into her mouth. The sailor's hands finally left her body and she was being lifted and laid in the lifeboat, held down firmly so that she couldn't struggle free and remove her gag.

'Now, Miss?' she heard the sailor say, and she blinked furiously, trying to clear her eyes of the tears caused by a combination of smoke and nipple-tweaking.

'Certainly,' Philippa was replying. 'Jacky and Frances, position her. You other girls, make way.'

Theodora felt two pairs of large, strong hands fasten to her body as the other hands released her. She was dragged none-too-gently from the floor of the lifeboat and forced to kneel. A firm pair of buttocks descended on her feet, locking them in place, and all she could do was watch, half-choked, half-blinded with smoke, anger and fear, as the sailor climbed into the lifeboat too. How tall and muscular he was! Was he coming with them, to steer? Maybe, but there was something more immediate on his mind: the girl he had just helped kidnap. He was stepping along the lifeboat to lower himself with a grunt onto a seat in front of her. She tried to breathe shallowly so that she wouldn't catch the odour of horrid sweat, but her lungs perversely inhaled extra-hard and she almost fainted with the animal-like stink of him. So masculine, so dominant!

'Grab her by the hair, Jacky,' she heard Philippa order and she felt a hand seize her hair. Her stomach rolled with fright and excitement, but her conscious mind was still groping for an explanation. What were they going to do to her?

'You can start now, dear,' said Philippa, and Theodora heard a zip coming down. Her stomach rolled again and even as Jacky forced her head forward and down to the base of the sailor's stomach the truth exploded in her brain. She was going to be forced to suck him! Oh, she could smell the hot reek of his cock rising against her face! This must be what Philippa had promised him for helping in her kidnap, she realised. The lifeboat shook as it began to descend towards the sea and simultaneously Theodora felt the head of the sailor's cock strike her face. It was hot, almost burning her skin, and seemed as big as a child's fist. The sailor had gripped his cock and was holding it steady against her face. Jacky chuckled behind her and began to rub her face against it, and she shivered with disgust as she felt the fleshy bulb of the glans leave a smear of semen on her skin.

But now Theodora started with surprise. Jacky had dragged her head back up a little, cool breath had tickled her right ear and Philippa had begun to whisper to her. She had been concentrating so hard on the cock and Jacky's hand in her hair that she hadn't noticed as Philippa wriggled down the crowded lifeboat to her side and leaned down to put her mouth against her prisoner's ear.

'Tables,' Philippa had said. 'How quickly they can turn, darling, can't they? Ten minutes ago, you were forced me to suck. Now, darling, *I'm* forcing *you*. But you won't have time to make a leisurely job of it. Speed is of the essence, darling, and I want you swallowing *his* essence chop-chop. Is that clear? Just in case it isn't, darling, here's a little reminder.'

Philippa's mouth left her ear and after a moment she felt her kidnapper's fingers seize hold of her right nipple, still aching from its tweaking of a minute before, and twist it sharply. She moaned with pain, feeling the renewed ache worsen with the cruel laughter that sounded around her.

'Do her left, Jenny,' she heard Philippa say, and the slim fingers of the redhead Jenny darted to her left nipple and tweaked sharply. Cool breath puffed against her ear again and Philippa whispered.

'Now accept him, darling. Accept him hard, accept him deep, and swallow everything he gives you. Or else.'

She stiffened as Philippa's mouth left her ear and her kidnapper's fingers took hold of her right nipple again, but this time they merely caressed it before lifting away.

'Jacky,' she heard Philippa say. 'She's ready to begin.'

The sailor grunted with anticipation as Jacky pulled Theodora's knicker-gag free of the prisoner's mouth and forced her head back down between his thighs. Theodora's head was spinning with emotion like a chip of wood on a mill-race and her will seemed paralysed, nailed helpless into her body by the bitter ache in her tweaked nipples, unable to raise her head and prevent her mouth opening meekly to accept the cockhead that awaited it.

'*Festina lente*, Jacky,' she heard Philippa say through the thunder of blood in her ears. 'We don't want to *asphyxiate* the poor darling.'

And yes, for a moment, as the cock entered her mouth, she had panicked at the prospect of choking. It was so big she had to strain her jaw to accept it, and if Jacky had continued to force her head down at the same rate it would have surged to the back of her mouth and maybe even blocked her throat. But Philippa's order had been obeyed: Jacky was forcing her head over the cock more slowly now, giving her time to adapt as the giant cockhead slid further into her mouth, followed by the seemingly wrist-thick shaft. Her lips were smeared with cock-sweat and she felt a trickle of pre-ejaculate on her tongue as her nostrils filled with a rich, feral cock-smell. Then cool breath puffed against her ear again.

'Now, darling,' Philippa whispered. '*Pleasure* him.'

She felt her ear kissed and Philippa withdrew, whispering something to Jacky. Theodora's jaw-muscles were aching, so large was the cock that had invaded her mouth, and she wondered how on earth she could cram it in. But now, as though catching the thought, Jacky stopped forcing her head further over the cock. The trickle of pre-ejaculate had increased and she felt it running over her tongue. Now Jacky's hands tightened on her head and she felt herself dragged off the cock, then pushed back onto it, dragged off, pushed on, dragged off, pushed on. Another puff of breath on her ear.

'*Collaborate*, darling. Suck him. And hum something. "I'm Called Little Buttercup" from *H.M.S. Pinafore* would be nice.'

Philippa's fingers brushed softly at her right nipple, warning her of what would follow if she disobeyed, and the ache re-awoke there fiercely simply at the prospect. Head spinning, jaw and nipples aching, Theodora struggled to remember the tune as she tried to suck the cock being forced in and out of her mouth, sliding a little further, she somehow managed to notice, each time. Oh God, she couldn't remember it and Philippa would tweak her nipples again. But suddenly she was flooded with relief: Philippa, sweet Philippa, kind, sweet Philippa, had recognised that she was not being insubordinate, simply forgetful and was humming the first bar of the song in her ear.

'For I'm called Little Buttercup, dear Little Buttercup, though I could never tell why . . .'

She caught up the tune and began to hum it as loudly as she could as the cock cycled in her mouth. Giggles sounded from the crowded lifeboat through the pulse of blood in her ears, then faint shrieks as the lifeboat rocked as it began to descend and then splashed solidly into the ocean that awaited it, shuddering through all its timbers. *How appropriate!* flashed through her brain, for at the same instant the timber-solid cock in her mouth, excited beyond endurance by her warmth, moisture and humming, shuddered heavily and began to squirt what seemed like an ocean of semen into her. She almost choked trying to gulp down the first shafts, but there was another whisper from Philippa, whose expertise in fellatio she was noting even in the midst of her confusion and lust, and Jacky tugged her head into a new position, relaxing her neck somehow and allowing her to swallow the briny flood. The cock was still firing and the sailor had forced it right to the back of her mouth, so that she half expected to feel his huge, hairy balls rubbing against her chin.

But no: if the length of his shaft was in proportion to its thickness, her lips were barely half-way down it and his balls were nowhere near her chin as they tightened to the root of his cock, emptying themselves of semen in tribute to the pleasure she had given him. And now, at last, the shafts of semen were faltering and weakening, and the ache in her jaw, lost in the sensations of receiving and swallowing, struck her again. There: he had slid his cock into her mouth and been pleasured and ejaculated thickly and copiously in perfect silence, but now, as the last shaft of semen left his cock and splattered chokingly, burningly, deliciously, against her upper throat, he released a deep groan of satisfied lust.

The lifeboat shuddered again and Theodora, dazed by the speed and strength with which she had been kidnapped and forced to perform a blow-job, heard Philippa issuing sharp orders. Jacky gripped her head hard and tugged it backward, and the sailor's cock, already beginning to soften and shrink, slid fast out of her mouth – too fast for her to get her teeth out of the way. She heard the sailor yelp with pain as her teeth raked him. Then, with a pop, the cock was out of her mouth and Jacky released her. She swayed where she sat, blinking as she tried to focus her eyes and feeling the load of semen she had swallowed sliding warm and thick into her belly. Where was the sailor she had fellated? She wanted to see him, to see his face. Oh, he was climbing out of the lifeboat, back up to the ship, Jenny accompanying him part of the way, pushing his cock back into his trousers and buttoning him up.

76

A male voice shouted out an order from the deck above and the lifeboat rocked. They were being released. Jenny dropped lightly back and Theodora heard her whispering in an awed voice: 'He was *huge*, darlings. Poor Dorrie's jaw will . . .'

But she lost the rest in giggles and a sudden rattle and creak of oars. The lifeboat was free and being pushed off from the ship's side. It rose and fell on the first wave and Theodora felt a first twinge of seasickness in her semen-filled belly. Someone was pushing her way along the lifeboat, finding a seat directly ahead of her, sitting down facing her, humming as she unbuttoned her own blouse and tugged down her bra-cups one by one to expose her firm, stiff-nippled breasts, then leaning forward to seize her, Theodora, by both hands. Oars began to splash clumsily in the water and Philippa, still holding Theodora's hands, grunted with annoyance.

'Clumsy sluts,' she said. 'You can have a turn at the oars later, Dorrie. But I've got a treat for you first, darling, as a reward for your recent endeavours. You can lick my titties and suck my nipples, which are rather *tumescent* after what I've just witnessed. I was *so* proud of you, darling, seeing you accept that *gargantuan* cock and swallow every last drop of what it pumped into you. Was it like a fire-hose, darl—'

But Theodora had an effective response: her anger at her rival's gloating and proposed 'treat' made her incipient seasickness strengthen and the mention of what she had swallowed was enough to trigger a gripe of nausea. As she felt the contents of her stomach shooting up her throat she leaned forward, ignoring the renewed ache in her jaw as she opened her mouth as wide as she could to cover Philippa's bare throat and breasts in a mixture of vomit and fresh semen.

Five

Theodora groaned and woke. She was lying face down on what felt like soft sand, blindfolded, ankles tied loosely but effectively together, wrists tied behind her back, and she was dressed only in her knickers. She could see nothing, but a patch of warmth lay on her bare back that she realised was sunshine.

'Oh, our princess has woken,' said a nearby voice. 'Would you like a pee, princess?'

Someone else giggled and Theodora swore.

'Untie me, Jenny, you slut,' she said. She heard movement and felt Jenny's soft hands on her body, helping her sit up. Her nipples felt puffy and hot, retaining the memory of the fingers that had pinched and twisted. Other memories were returning in a rush and what she saw as Jenny tugged her blindfold down suddenly wasn't a surprise any more. She was sitting in the shade of a group of three palm-trees overlooking a beach of sun-blasted, almost glaringly white sand and a lagoon blue as Winnie's eyes, shielded from the wider ocean by a surf-creamed reef whose roar was reaching her ears as a gentle, soothing whisper.

'Thanks, Jen,' she said. The redhead, who was dressed only in knickers and bra, sat back on her heels and tutted.

'Philippa does go a bit far sometimes,' she said. 'I'd untie your hands too, darling, but I daren't risk it.

You'll have to go back on your face when we see her coming back.'

'Where is she?'

'Off exploring,' said the other voice. Theodora turned her head and saw that it was Caroline, a slim, black-haired girl who had tugged her bra-cups down and was fanning her sweat-gleamed breasts with a green leaf. 'The bitch,' Caroline added softly, then looked over her shoulder down the beach with a shiver of fright at her own daring.

'I thought you were one of her biggest allies, Carrie,' Theodora said.

Caroline looked back.

'She went far too far in the boat. Didn't she, Jen? After you threw up on her titties.'

Theodora moaned softly: the pain in her nipples had suddenly flared as she was reminded of what Philippa had done to her in the boat.

'Yes,' Jenny said, shaking her head as she stared at Theodora's breasts. 'She was like a madwoman. Your poor nipples, Dorrie. Would you . . .' Theodora heard her swallow in the shade of the palm-trees 'would you like me and Carrie to soothe them for you?'

'Yes, please,' Theodora said. She wondered if she was being set up: were Jenny and Caroline trying to lull her into blaspheming against their mistress? Then she sighed with pleasure and relief: Jenny had shuffled forward and lowered her mouth to her aching left nipple, licking it gently, then closing her lips on it and sucking. Caroline was shuffling towards her too, the pink tip of her tongue passing over her lips in anticipation. Her mouth dropped too and Theodora sighed again.

'Thanks, sweeties,' she said. 'But I fainted pretty soon, you know.'

Jenny released Theodora's left nipple with a pop.

'We know,' she said. 'Then the bitch tweaked your nipples and cunny-lips till you came round again.'

She closed her mouth over Theodora's nipple again, licking, sucking. Theodora shivered with pleasure, feeling fresh cunny-juice beginning to flow again through the crusted mess in her knickers. The two mouths on her nipples were so deliciously soft and gentle, simultaneously heightening and soothing the pain there. Caroline released her right nipple with a pop, looking up at her and smiling as their eyes met and she saw the pleasure glowing in Theodora's.

'We'd have tried to make her stop, darling,' she said. 'But we were afraid she'd turn on *us*.'

Theodora shook her head.

'Don't worry. I saw that you didn't like doing it. But there were plenty who did.'

'Hmmm,' Jenny murmured in agreement, still sucking her left nipple.

'Don't get angry, darling,' Caroline said. 'It will make it harder for you to come.'

The black-haired girl lowered her mouth to Theodora's right nipple again and a moment later Theodora felt a small hand trying to work its way behind her thighs. She resisted a moment, then relaxed. If Philippa was setting her up she might as well make the most of it. Caroline's hand slid into her knickers, stroking, exploring, and she felt rather than heard the younger girl giggle as she sucked her nipple, excited and pleased by the fresh cunny-juice she found. Then the stroking fingers reached her clitoris and began, very gently but very expertly, to masturbate her. Theodora screwed her eyes shut, trying by force of will to hold down the wave of pleasure that rushed up in her. She didn't want to come too quickly: if Jenny and Caroline were working at Philippa's orders, they'd report it gleefully, knowing it was a sign of her agitation and upset. She opened her mouth, carefully examining the state of her lips and tongue and throat before she started speaking, in case she stammered or spoke too huskily, overwhelmed by the skill with which Caroline was 'diddling' her.

'Wh-where are Winnie and Zoë?' she asked. Damn. Her voice had been a bit unsteady for a moment there. Caroline pulled her mouth off its nipple with a pop.

'Somewhere on the other side of the island, darling,' she said. 'With Miss Callaghan. Is that nice?'

She was rhythmically squeezing Theodora's clitoris between her thumb and forefinger while her three other fingers tickled at the moist, swollen folds of her cunny-lips.

'Yes, lovely,' Theodora said, trying to suppress a gasp. 'But wh- – oh! – why are you – oh! – not all – oh! – with Miss Callagh—'.

She broke off, shuddering with pleasure as Jenny, very gently, began to nibble, then suck, then nibble, then suck her left nipple. Caroline, as though knowing by instinct what her fellow titty-sucker was up to, began to nibble, while squeezing and tugging harder at Theodora's clitoris. Theodora's mouth was still open to speak, but now it widened and she began to gasp uncontrollably, sliding faster and faster down the slope that led to the abyss of orgasm.

'Ah! ah! ah! ah! ah! *Aaaaah!*'

As she had quivered on the brink of orgasm Caroline had formed a fist with her cunny-diddling hand and deftly thrust it between her cunny-lips; now, as her orgasm began and she shuddered harder and harder in its grip, she pushed the fist deep, rotating it against the stickily spasming walls of Theodora's cunny, so that Theodora felt its knuckles tenderly raking her most intimate flesh. She thought of the sailor's cock she had sucked, imagining how that would have felt instead, spearing into her, *shouldering* into her, brutally forcing her open for the cockhead to slide into her depths and ram itself against her cervix before withdrawing to ram itself against her cervix again. But no: the thought of it was almost certainly more pleasurable than the reality, and certainly less bruising: she was glad to have Caroline's delicate fist inside her instead. It now stopped

81

rotating, locked in place by her tightening cunny-walls as Jenny and its owner sucked frantically on her nipples, trying to prolong and deepen her orgasm.

It was already the deepest and longest Theodora had ever experienced, in part, she thought, because of the helplessness she felt with her ankles and wrists tied together. But finally it was over. Still groaning from a slack, dribbling mouth, still shuddering with aftershocks, she heard the moist pops as Jenny and Caroline pulled their mouths off her nipples, and managed to gasp out:

'Thanks, girls.'

'Our pleasure, Dorrie,' said Jenny, planting a kiss on the nipple she had just pleasured so expertly. 'After what Philly did to you, you deserved a treat.'

'*Cave!*' Caroline suddenly hissed. Theodora blinked and tried to focus her eyes. Caroline was looking down the beach, and now Theodora could make out a group of figures approaching through the heat-shimmer.

'Sugar,' Jenny said. 'Speak of the devil and she appears.'

She planted another quick kiss on Theodora's nipple, turned where she knelt and began to crawl away.

'Come on, Carrie,' she said over her shoulder.

'Can't,' Caroline said. 'I'm stuck.'

'What?'

'Sorry,' said Theodora. 'It's me. Ow. Pull more gently, please, Carrie.'

'Sorry. But I can't be caught like this, can I? Try and relax, Dorrie.'

She could feel Caroline trying to withdraw her fist from the fleshy tunnel into which she had inserted it.

'Ow!' she said more loudly. Caroline stopped watching Philippa's approach for a second and looked at her, raising her eyebrows in apology, then looking away again for Philippa.

'Sorry, darling,' she said. 'But I'll end up like you if I don't get my hand out quick. Please relax.'

'Suck her nip again, Carrie!'

It was Jenny, crawling back to them, planting her mouth over Theodora's left nipple again. Caroline gasped with fright and obeyed, closing her mouth over Theodora's right nipple and sucking hard. Theodora moaned with pleasure and all at once, with a squelch, Caroline's fist slid free from her cunny, accompanied by a gush of juice.

'It's free! It's free!' Caroline whispered frantically to Jenny, almost falling over as she turned and began to crawl away from the prisoner, trying to keep her recently cunny-trapped hand clear of the sand. Jenny's head came off Theodora's nipple and she began to crawl for safety too. Theodora suddenly realised what they had forgotten.

'But what about my blindfold?' she hissed. 'Quick!'

She suppressed a spurt of hysterical laughter as Caroline swerved and came crawling back towards her, sucking and licking at her cunny-juice-plastered hand, trying to destroy the evidence before Philippa reached them. She reached Theodora, tugged the blindfold back into place with a gasp of panic, and was off again, crawling frantically. Theodora turned over and laid herself on the sand, closing her eyes, trying to control her breathing, trying to pretend she was sleeping. After about thirty seconds she heard five or six pairs of feet approaching through soft sand, then her heart was hammering in her chest as she heard Philippa's arrogant drawl.

'Look what we've found for our little prisoner.'

She heard Jenny and Caroline murmur with interest.

'But what are you going to do with it?' Jenny asked.

'I'm sure we'll think of something.'

The lascivious menace in her voice was unmistakable and Caroline gasped with horror.

'But you can't!'

'Just watch me,' Philippa said. 'As we give her another in the series of little treats I have planned for her. Gwen, Jacky, prepare her.'

83

Six

'So what did they do to you?' Winnie asked sleepily, cheek pressed to Theodora's breast.

'I won't tell you unless you give me another of your lovely long sucks.'

'All right. Titty or cunny?'

'Cunny, please.'

'I'm on my way.'

She felt her cunny stir with anticipation, releasing more juice, as Winnie began to kiss and nibble her way down her body to it. Oh, but it was good to be safe again, back with her gang and out of Philippa's clutches. The rescue had come right on the heels of the 'little treat' Philippa had given her. Still weeping with humiliation, she had heard running feet on the sand, sudden cries of surprise and anger from Philippa, Gwen, Jacky and Frances, sounds of a struggle, then felt the hands that had held her down for the 'treat' releasing her, heard the struggle continuing, felt other hands, friendly hands seizing her, lifting her, carrying her into warm sunshine, then into shade again, a thicker, moister shade.

She gasped with pleasure. Winnie's mouth had kissed and nibbled its way to her cunny and begun one of its lovely long sucks.

'Th-that's lovely, darling,' she said, voice uneven with pleasure. 'But can you hear me properly? I don't want anyone else to overhear.'

She gasped again. Winnie had hummed 'Yes' against her cunny and she could begin telling the story of the 'little treat'.

'Well, I was still pretending to be asleep when Gwen and Jacky grabbed me, darling, and I had no idea what Philippa had brought for me. But Philippa pulled down my blindfold and showed me what it was before she began . . . A little *tortoise*, darling.'

Winnie's mouth came off her cunny and in the warm darkness she sensed her friend's blue eyes open and staring up at her.

'She showed you a *what*?'

'Carry on, darling. Please. It's lovely.'

The mouth returned to its work and Theodora, suppressing a shudder of pleasure, went on with her story.

'A little tortoise, darling. That's what she showed me. And she told me she was going to put it *up* me.'

Winnie grunted with disbelief.

'I know: that's how *I* felt – oh, yes, lovely, but more slowly, please, darling, or I'll come before I start the story properly. Yes, that's right. Lovely. Lovely. Now, where was I? Oh, yes, *I* couldn't believe she was going to do it either, darling, but she was. Gwen and Jacky held me down, then Philippa pulled the blindfold back up – to heighten the sensations, she said, and it *worked*, you know, we'll have to remember that trick – and two others – Frances was one, I think, but I couldn't tell who the other was – got my ankles untied and dragged them apart before Jenny was ordered to drag my knickers off.

'Then there was a lot of *most* humiliating discussion about the state of my knickers before they began to discuss the state of my cunny. While Frances and the other girl held my ankles well apart and Carrie and Jenny sat on my back so I couldn't struggle, Philly and Gwen and Jacky *poked* and *probed* my cunny while they

85

were discussing it, darling, and you can imagine what happened next.'

There was a sticky pop as Winnie raised her face from the cunny she was licking and sucking.

'Your cunny *oozed*.'

'More than that, darling.'

'It *gushed*.'

'Yes, that's more like it. But carry on, please. Yes, lovely. Yes, they *poked* and *probed* it while they were discussing it and inevitably I got rather excited. You know how strong *emotion*, any kind of emotion, when you're excited, excited sexually I mean, always *heightens* the excitement, and I was in a *very* humiliating position, darling. Cunny on full display, being poked, being probed, being *insulted*, well, I'd say I was rather more than gushing, I was flooding. Of course, I protested, but that only made it worse, because Philly ordered Jacky, I think, to gag me too. With my own knickers. I could hardly breathe for the smell of my own cunny-juice, darling, and now Philly was claiming that the fresh juice I was "*exuding*" – one of her big words again, darling – at the other end was attracting flies. "Can't you hear them?" she said, and everyone else said they could and had me half-convinced I could hear them too.

'But I *think* the sensation of them landing on my cunny and running up and down it, licking my cunny-juice, was just Philly or someone with a palm-leaf. Because I don't think a fly could have landed on my cunny without getting well and truly stuck or even *drowning* in my cunny-juice. Then Philly said, "Oh, come on, we'll have to push it up her quick, before we can't see what we're doing for flies", and . . .'

But the whispered story was interrupted: from somewhere outside Winnie's hut, in which Theodora was lodging before her own hut was built the following day, came the sound of running feet and a cry of 'Miss Callaghan!' Theodora, on the verge of her first orgasm, clutched a second too late at Winnie's head, but it had lifted from her cunny and Winnie was shushing her plea for it to be returned.

'No, hush, Dorrie, darling, let me listen. What's going on?'

The cry of 'Miss Callaghan!' went up again, and now they heard the occupants of other huts talking excitedly as they spilled out into the night.

'Come on!' said Winnie, grabbing Theodora by one hand as she wiped at her face with the other. 'Let's see what's happening.'

Theodora groaned with frustration and let Winnie pull her from the bed of palm-leaves. They quickly pulled on their bras and knickers, then ran out of the hut to find the rest of the girls a dozen yards off near the stream, excitedly clustering around Miss Callaghan and a sobbing girl from Philippa's side of the island. Pale girl-flesh gleamed in the starlight, for the moon had set and they hadn't yet discovered how to make lamps or candles, and almost everyone else was dressed only in bra and knickers too, with the exception of Miss Callaghan, of course, and even she had discarded her shoes and stockings. Hand in hand, the two of them hurried over to find out what was going on – Theodora glad that the heavy scent of night-blooming flowers was hanging in the air, masking the fresh musk of her cunny-juice. And no one would notice its gleam on her thighs, if she stood well back.

'Oh, it's Jacky,' she heard Winnie say. And it was, but a Jacky quite different to the stern, cruel lieutenant she had seen during the day. *This* Jacky was sobbing and near-hysterical, even with Miss Callaghan's hands firmly locked on her shoulders and shaking hard.

'Control yourself, my girrul,' they heard Miss Callaghan saying as they joined the group. Theodora heard Winnie whisper to Ruth, a slim, dark-haired girl whose firm, heart-shaped bottom Philippa delighted to spank.

87

'What's going on?'

'Shush,' Ruth whispered back. 'Listen. Something bad's happened with Philippa's lot.'

Her voice was rich with satisfaction and excitement. Theodora had learned the arrangements Miss Callaghan had made after the two lifeboats reached the island, leaving the burning ship behind them. One group of girls, under Philippa's command, had been allowed to camp on the other side of the island, so that more of the sea could be scanned for possible rescue by both day and night. Theodora, still sleeping off the effects of the tortures Philippa had subjected her to in the lifeboat, was carried with the second group despite the attempted protests of Theodora's friends.

'No,' Theodora heard Miss Callaghan say. 'Calm yourself, my girrul, and start at the beginning. Who do you say has disappeared?'

'F-f-f-' Jacky gasped. Who was it? Frances? Fiona? Then Jacky got the name out: '*Philippa*'s dis-disappeared, Miss Callaghan.'

The answer struck Theodora like an electric shock, and she heard murmurs of excitement and dismay from the other girls.

'Are you sure?' Miss Callaghan asked.

'Y-y-yes, Miss Callaghan. S-s-she went into the jungle with F-Frances and J-J-Jenny to watch the moon rise from the t-t-top of that hill, Miss C-Callaghan, and . . .'

Theodora had grunted as Jenny's name was mentioned, and felt Winnie's hand momentarily tighten on hers in sympathy. Philippa hadn't taken Jenny into the jungle to watch the moon rise *at all:* there had been some more *sinister* motive. Had she discovered or guessed that Jenny was a traitor? Jacky was continuing her story: an hour after the three girls had left for 'the hill', Frances and Jenny had burst back into the camp, crying out that Philippa had disappeared suddenly while the three of them had been climbing the final slope to

88

the top of the hill. At first they had thought it was a game, but Philippa hadn't re-appeared and they had grown worried.

'Th-they said Philly c-c-*couldn't* have disappeared there unless she *meant* to, Miss Callaghan, or unless something *else* m-m-meant her to. Or s-s-*someone* else.'

'What on *earth* do you mean, you foolish girl?' Miss Callaghan demanded. 'The island is deserted.'

Jacky explained that Frances and Jenny had seen what they thought was a footprint just near where Philippa disappeared.

'B-b-but it was a l-l-*large* footprint, Miss Callaghan. A m-m-*man's* footprint.'

A murmur of excitement and fear went up among the listening girls. They hadn't explored the island fully yet, but Miss Callaghan had insisted that it was deserted and certainly they had seen no sign of other inhabitants.

'Have you seen this footprint for yourself?' Miss Callaghan asked.

'N-n-no, Miss Callaghan.'

'And were Frances and Jenny *certain* it was a footprint?'

'N-n-no, Miss Callaghan. But what else c-c-could it have been?'

'Oh, a hundred things, you foolish girl. In the morning I shall examine it for myself and I am sure it will prove something quite innocent. Philippa is playing some silly game with you, and will turn up safe and sound before very much longer.'

But Jacky was shaking her head vigorously. Two or three girls standing near her moved back with murmurs of distaste as they were splattered by mingled drops of tears and snot from her glistening, anguished face.

'N-n-no, Miss Call–' Jacky was stammering, but Miss Callaghan interrupted her.

'No. Say nothing further till you have given your nose a thorough blow. You, Theodora, fetch her a leaf.'

Theodora suppressed a grunt of indignation. Miss Callaghan had been trying to provoke her ever since the rescue, seeking an excuse to punish her. She was determined not to supply one and released Winnie's hand, trotting briskly to a nearby 'Snot-rag bush', as the girls had informally christened a certain shrub whose large, soft leaves substituted quite adequately for handkerchiefs. She tore a leaf off and trotted back, pushing her way through the soft flesh of near-naked girls to Miss Callaghan and the still snivelling Jacky.

'Here you go, Miss Callaghan,' she said.

'Thank you, Theodora.'

Miss Callaghan took the leaf from her and Theodora turned to go back to Winnie, but a moment later an icy tremor ran down her spine. Miss Callaghan had *sniffed* behind her and her instant fears at the meaningful *tone* of the sniff were stomach-churningly confirmed when the older woman spoke.

'Stop, Theodora! *What* is that smell?'

Oh, Christmas! She had forgotten the fresh cunny-juice still oozing from her cunny and trickling down her thighs. She took an extra stride before she turned to face Miss Callaghan, swallowing away a lump of anxiety in her throat and answering as lightly as she could.

'What smell, Miss Callaghan? I was a little sweaty earlier on, after my rescue, but I had a lovely bathe in the sea and . . .'

'Shut up,' Miss Callaghan rapped. 'Here, you, Jacky, take this. Come here, Theodora.'

Theodora, her heart hammering, walked reluctantly back to her form-mistress.

'Come *here*, I said.'

Miss Callaghan's slim but oh-so-strong right hand flashed out and seized her by the wrist, dragging her closer. The stern form-mistress sniffed theatrically, putting distaste into the sound now.

'*What* is that smell? Answer me, girl.'

'N-n—' Theodora began. She broke off, swallowing hard as treacherous giggles sounded around her. Her anxiety had made her sound just like Jacky for a moment. But she had herself under control now.

'Nothing, Miss Callaghan,' she said with a confidence she was far – oh, so very far – from feeling.

'Don't lie to me, girl. I *distinctly* detected an *aroma* on the air when you handed me the leaf, which faded as you departed but has now returned in full strength.'

Theodora swallowed again.

'It's nothing, Miss Call—'.

She broke off with a cry of pain: Miss Callaghan's fingers had tightened on her wrist and now her form-mistress forced her hand downward, sliding its fingers over her belly, pushing it into her knickers, rubbing it hard over her oozing cunny, then dragging it up again, holding it in the air. Theodora could see cunny-juice glistening on it and felt her chest suddenly swell and relax with a sob of fear. No way out now: Miss Callaghan would sniff the hand disdainfully and announce to the assembled girls what it was and then spank her or, worse, send someone for her slipper. But no, Miss Callaghan wasn't leaning her head towards the seized and glistening hand at all. Instead:

'You, Winnie, come here.'

Theodora's eyes had blurred with tears and even if she had turned her head she didn't think she could have seen Winnie pushing her way through the girls as she obeyed Miss Callaghan. But Theodora could hear the reluctance in her friend's steps and her heart pounded again as she realised that it was not there simply because Winnie didn't want to betray her friend. Miss Callaghan was preparing to punish them *both*.

'Sniff this,' Miss Callaghan ordered as Winnie reached them, and thrust Theodora's hand at her face. Theodora suppressed a moan of pain: Miss Callaghan was holding her wrist so tightly that her hand was starting to feel numb. She heard Winnie sniff cautiously.

'Sniff *harder*, girl,' Miss Callaghan ordered. 'And tell me – tell *all* of us – what you smell.'

Winnie sniffed again.

'Harder, girl. Harder. And tell us all what you smell.'

Reluctantly, Winnie sniffed harder.

'Well?' Miss Callaghan demanded.

'I . . . I don't know, Miss Callaghan.'

'Don't lie to me, young lady! You know exactly what it is. Tell me.'

'It's . . . it's . . .' Winnie began, then said something inaudible.

'What was that? Louder, girl.'

Theodora heard Winnie swallow. Miss Callaghan snorted with impatience.

'Answer me, girl!' she snapped. 'What is it?'

'C-cunny-juice, Miss Callaghan,' Winnie said almost in a whisper.

'Repeat it. Loud enough for everyone to hear.'

'Cunny-juice, Miss Callaghan.'

'Louder!' said Miss Callaghan over the giggles that greeted the announcement.

Theodora heard Winnie, as though lost to shame, draw in a deep breath.

'Cunny-juice, Miss Callaghan!' she shouted, and Miss Callaghan impatiently hushed the further giggles.

'Cunny-juice?' she said wonderingly. 'But what on earth is that? Theodora, can you tell me?'

'It's . . . cunny-juice, Miss Callaghan. Juice from a . . . from a cunny.'

'I could perhaps have worked that out for myself, Theodora. Expand on your explanation. What provokes it to flow?'

Theodora swallowed.

'Excitement, Miss Callaghan.'

'What kind of excitement? An exciting book? A thunderstorm? A hard-fought game of chess?'

More giggles. Theodora blinked back the hot tears that were stinging her eyes and shook her head.

'No, Miss Callaghan. Not that kind of excitement.'

'Then what? You, Edwina. Tell me, what kind of excitement provokes this ... this cunny-juice ... to flow?'

'S—' Winnie began, then broke off with a gulp.

'Yes? Carry on, girl. Tell me what kind of excitement provokes this cunny-juice to flow.'

Theodora heard Winnie swallow again.

'Sexual excitement, Miss Callaghan,' Winnie said, almost whispering again.

'Repeat it. Loud enough for everyone to hear.'

'Sexual excitement, Miss Callaghan.'

'Louder!'

Theodora heard Winnie draw in a second deep breath.

'Sexual excitement, Miss Callaghan!' she shouted. No giggles this time; instead, Theodora felt a thickening air of silent expectation. Miss Callaghan was setting the two of them up for something, that was plain, and it was going to be public. Their form-mistress seemed to have lost her inhibitions since the shipwreck, as though something told her that none of them would see civilisation again. Suddenly she sighed with relief. Miss Callaghan had released her hand and was speaking almost conversationally:

'Ah. So there we have it. Cunny-juice, the juice of a cunny, is provoked to flow by sexual excitement. But the solution to one mystery merely supplies us with another. That is to say, we now know that Theodora's cunny-juice was provoked to flow by sexual excitement, but what provoked the sexual excitement? Or should I say, *who* provoked it?'

The dart of her hand and Winnie's cry of surprise and pain were almost simultaneous: Miss Callaghan had grasped Winnie by the back of her neck and was tilting her face up to the starlight.

'But I believe that we have the solution of the second mystery to, ah, hand, as it were.'

Theodora swallowed again. The smears of her cunny-juice on Winnie's pain-tightened face were clearly visible.

'Miss Theodora, can you enlighten us?'

She started to shake her head, but Miss Callaghan released a warning hiss.

'Be careful, my girl. Be very, very careful. Consider the possible consequences of your refusal to answer.'

Theodora tried to swallow but her throat was too dry and tight. She closed her eyes, feeling fresh tears start to trickle through her eyelashes and down her cheeks. She shook her head, whispering, 'No, Miss Callaghan.'

'No? But what is this, on Miss Edwina's face?'

Theodora blinked hard at her tears, swallowed, sniffed, and said, 'Smears.'

'Hmmm? What was that?'

'Smears, Miss Callaghan.'

'Smears? But smears of what?'

Theodora closed her eyes again and shook her head.

'So you are refusing to answer. Very well. You, Miss Edwina, tell me. *What* are the *smears* on your face?'

With her eyes closed Theodora's hearing was even sharper: she could hear the hushed breathing of the other girls as they waited to see what punishment Miss Callaghan had in store for them. Now she heard Winnie swallow hard and the dry pop of her lips as they opened and Winnie stammered, 'C-c-cunny-juice, Miss Callaghan.'

'Repeat it, girl. Loud enough for everyone to hear.'

'Cunny-juice, Miss Callaghan,' Winnie repeated.

'Louder!'

Theodora heard Winnie draw in a third deep breath.

'Cunny-juice, Miss Callaghan!'

Miss Callaghan paused a moment before replying, and when she spoke her voice was dripping expertly with disgust and disbelief.

'The smears on your face are cunny-juice, Miss Edwina?'

No sound from Winnie. Theodora opened her eyes just in time to see her friend nod reluctantly.

'Answer me, girl. A nod is insufficient. Are the smears on your face cunny-juice?'

Winnie's mouth worked with anguish.

'Yes, Miss Callaghan,' she said in a whisper. But Miss Callaghan did not pause to play the repetition game again.

'Yes? And are these smears of cunny-juice *extensive*, my girl? Answer me.'

A pause, then Winnie shook her head.

'No, Miss Callaghan.'

'No? But to my inexpert eye they appear so. What about yours, Miss Theodora? Do the smears of cunny-juice on Miss Edwina's face look extensive to you?'

Theodora sniffed. What could she say? Miss Callaghan shook Winnie's neck impatiently.

'P-perhaps, Miss Callaghan,' Theodora said.

'Perhaps? What nonsense. You, Jacky, kindly dispose of that noisome leaf and inform the class: are the smears of cunny-juice on Miss Edwina's face extensive or no?'

Jacky had stopped snivelling as she gloatingly watched Miss Callaghan's interrogation of her two victims; now she jerked a little with surprise as she was drawn into it herself.

'Er,' she began.

'Leaf,' Miss Callaghan snapped. 'Drop it. Good girl. Now, tell the class: are the smears of cunny-juice on Miss Edwina's face extensive or no?'

Theodora Jacky's teeth glint in the starlight as her enemy smiled. Ah, she was recovered from her surprise and upset now.

'I can't quite see from here, Miss Callaghan. Just a moment.'

The dark-haired girl pushed her way through the

crowd of girls surrounding Miss Callaghan and her prey, then peered carefully at Winnie's helpless face.

'Well?' said Miss Callaghan impatiently.

Jacky paused a moment longer, then nodded hard.

'Yes, Miss Callaghan. I do.'

'Do what, you foolish girl? Do think they are extensive or do think they are not?'

'Do think they are extensive, Miss Callaghan.'

'But then it follows quite clearly that if Edwina has extensive smears of cunny-juice on her face, then her face must have been in intimate and prolonged contact with a cunny. Do you agree, Jacky?'

'Oh yes, Miss Callaghan. Very intimate and prolonged contact.'

Theodora heard air whistle faintly through Miss Callaghan's nostrils as she drew in a breath of satisfaction.

'Ah. So now we have both mysteries solved. The origins of cunny-juice in general, and the origins of *this* cunny-juice in particular. Has Edwina been *licking* Theodora's cunny, do you think?'

'Oh yes, Miss Callaghan. Definitely.'

'And *sucking* Theodora's cunny?'

'Yes, Miss Callaghan. Definitely.'

Miss Callaghan sniffed loudly.

'Then that is disgusting. Truly disgusting.'

'Oh yes, Miss Callaghan. It makes me sick just to think of it.'

'Then both of them must be punished. Take off your bra, Jacky.'

'Miss Callaghan?'

'Take it off, girl. Take it off, at once.'

'But Miss Call—'

'All will become clear, Jacky. You will not be subject to the punishment, but you *may* be an essential part of it. So bra off, girl.'

Theodora heard Jacky swallow hard, then the snap of

her bra-strap coming undone. She watched Jacky's bra come off, exposing her firm and still growing breasts.

'Thank you, Jacky,' Miss Callaghan said, almost cooingly. 'Hand your bra to someone and then place your hands on your back, so.'

She demonstrated, placing her own hands flat to her back directly behind her breasts, fingers pointing downward.

'Good girl,' she said, as Jacky imitated her. 'Now, you two, Ruth, Naomi, get me some of those fruit. You know, the ones by the little stream. The rather *bitter* ones.'

'Yes, Miss Callaghan,' the two girls murmured, and they plunged off through the dimly lit undergrowth. What did Miss Callaghan want the fruit for? Theodora wondered, her mouth tingling as she remembered the specimen she had sampled earlier in the day ('It's *very* rich in vitamin C, girrul!'), but something inside her already knew as her teacher beckoned to her.

'And now, *you* two, Misses Theodora and Edwina,' Miss Callaghan said, the temperature of her voice plunging to freezing. 'Zoë, Rhoda, please bring our miscreants to me.'

Theodora, who had guessed what Miss Callaghan was planning now, barely felt Zoë, no, it was Rhoda, take her by the upper arms.

'Breasts forward, Jacky, please,' Miss Callaghan said. 'Push with your hands.'

Jacky obeyed and Miss Callaghan walked to stand in front of her.

'I am now ready to smear your breasts with the soft, pulpy flesh of a certain rather bitter fruit, Jacky. No, stay where you are! But whether or not I do so will depend on our two young miscreants here. They now have a simple choice. Either I will smear your breasts in that fruit and they will lick and suck them clean or . . .'

She broke off, tutting with annoyance. Theodora had gasped and nearly fainted as a wave of nausea swept over her – and Edwina *had* fainted. Zoë grunted as she took the slender blonde's sudden dead weight, keeping her prisoner on her feet. But suddenly Theodora's head cleared. She could see Jacky smiling broadly, her teeth gleaming white in the semi-darkness.

'Wake her,' Miss Callaghan said impatiently and eager hands reached for Edwina's nipples.

'No, girls!' Miss Callaghan said. 'Not there. We must leave those unmolested in case the two of them choose not to take the first fork of the road that now lies before them. Ruth, dear, please squeeze young Edwina's earlobes till she wakes and can listen to all I intended to say. But gently, dear. Gently.'

Theodora, heart still hammering in her chest, watched and listened as Ruth pushed through the the crowd of disappointed would-be nipple-squeezers around Edwina and reached up with both hands for her victim's ears. Theodora shivered and felt her cunny pulse involuntarily with excitement. Ruth was an expert at squeezing sensitive body-parts, somehow knowing the exact rhythm and pressure to awaken the maximum of sensation with the minimum of effort, and if she had been a crueller girl she would have been a formidable weapon in Philippa's armoury.

But Miss Callaghan's admonitions had been unnecessary: Ruth was always gentle, always glad to give pleasure and reluctant to inflict pain. She brought Edwina out of her faint swiftly and efficiently, first tickling the entirety of the younger girl's ears with her fingertips, tracing their whorls and edges, as though learning the geography of what she was about to work on, then taking the delicate lobes between forefinger and thumb and beginning to squeeze, humming under her breath some tune Theodora did not recognise. After a moment Edwina sighed with pleasure, murmured something in response to the tune Ruth was humming, moaned with increased pleasure, and woke up, only to burst immediately into tears as her eyes opened on the scene in front of her: Jacky's bare breasts gleaming in the moonlight, ready to be smeared with fruit for her and Theodora to lick clean. She shook her head.

'Please, Miss Callaghan!' she began to sob. 'Don't make us do it! I'll be sick, I know I w—'

'Shut up, you foolish girrul,' Miss Callaghan snapped. 'You did not give me time to finish before you lapsed into that childish and unnecessary faint. Indeed, if you had listened to me with the requisite care and attention, you would have known not to faint before you heard all I had to say. Which is this. Either I will smear Jacky's breasts in fruit and the pair of you will lick and suck them clean, or you will accept *another* punishment whose nature will not be disclosed to you before it commences. Very well?'

Theodora, realising that Miss Callaghan was in no mood to be argued with, quickly nodded.

'Yes, Miss Callaghan,' she said, and stared hard at Edwina, trying to make her realise that she should answer quickly too and not provoke their teacher. But Edwina was still blinking and sniffing back tears. Theodora's stomach rolled uncomfortably, for Miss Callaghan had grunted with satisfaction.

'I said "Very well", Miss Edwina. A response would be much appreciated.'

Theodora shook her head in frustration as Edwina failed to reply yet again. At this rate Miss Callaghan would withdraw her offer and force them to lick Jacky's breasts clean. Or would she? Was the unknown punishment even worse than that?

'Answer me, Miss Edwina! Are you and your co-miscreant ready to choose between the alternatives I have offered? Well?'

Edwina gulped and choked back further sobs.

'I'm ... I'm sorry, Miss Callaghan. Please could you ...'

'Och, God give me strength,' Miss Callaghan interrupted her, provoking one or two faint and immediately suppressed giggles from the eagerly watching girls around her. 'It is perfectly simple, girrul. The road the two of you travel now forks. *Metaphorically* speaking, ye understand. To the left, it will take you to Jacky's fine young breasts, glistening with fresh fruit for your delectation; to the right, it will take you to a punishment whose nature will not be disclosed before it begins. *There*, girrul, is your choice, *there* your dilemma. Better the devil you know or the devil you *don't* know? Well?'

Seven

Theodora had lost count of how many times she had raised her head to see if dawn was coming. Fifty? A hundred? And each time the stars in the east had glittered coldly back at her, a strewn dust of crushed gems – diamond dust mostly, but she could see emerald dust, sapphire, ruby too – that was serenely indifferent to the punishment that awaited the two of them. But now she thought that dawn *was* coming: the black velvet on which the gem-dust was sprinkled was paling fractionally, blushing ever-so-faintly with the climbing sun. Soon it would be pink, red, and then the blazing rim of the sun would peer over the windowsill of the horizon, a vast golden eye greedy for the spectacle that awaited it: the two young and beautiful girls strapped naked and helpless to black rocks overlooking the sea.

They had chosen the devil they didn't know in the end: poor Winnie had nearly been sick simply at the thought of licking fruit off Jacky's breasts, and though Miss Callaghan had refused to tell them anything *positive* about the alternative punishment, she had revealed something *negative:* that it would not involve any licking, sucking or swallowing. For a moment Miss Callaghan had seemed on the verge of saying something more, but she caught herself – or *pretended* to catch herself – just in time. What had it been? What had she been going to say? Theodora had asked herself that even more often than she had raised her head to see the first sign of coming dawn. Miss Callaghan had said nothing, but her teeth had glinted in the darkness and Theodora had known she was smiling. But smiling about what? Something had struck her as humorous in the information she had given. The *negative* information. They were not to lick, suck or swallow – and that was amusing. But why? Why? Because someone would be licking, sucking or swallowing something from *them* instead? But how could that be a punishment?

Oh, the creation of mystery had been quite deliberate: Miss Callaghan had meant to torment her pupils' minds as well as their bodies, during the hours that followed their strapping to the rocks overlooking the sea.

'There, girruls,' she had said. 'You can rest here till sunrise, at which point your chosen punishment will begin.'

But Theodora had not rested at all, as far as she could tell, though Winnie, exhausted by the emotional strain of the choice Miss Callaghan had forced out of them, had gone to sleep almost at once. Perhaps her rock was smoother or perhaps its knobbly bits were positioned less uncomfortably or perhaps Winnie's body was softer in the right places – whatever it was, Theodora envied her. The strain of waiting, of speculating what Miss Callaghan was going to have done to them, might be even worse than the punishment itself.

She raised her head again and sighed as she saw that the east was definitely pink now. A moment later, as though to confirm what she saw, she heard Miss Callaghan's voice sound faintly in the distance, admonishing some unfortunate girl as she led her party back to the punishment site. Soon the crackle of disturbed undergrowth was unmistakable and Theodora began to hear the gasps and pants of the girls climbing the hill. It *was* difficult to reach this spot – she herself had grazes and cuts on her legs and arms from being marched there during the night – but she thought there was excitement as well as effort in the sounds, and her stomach rolled at what might be awaiting them.

Edwina moaned in her sleep and suddenly awoke with a gasp. Theodora looked sideways at her in the faint light and tried to smile as she sensed rather than saw the fear and apprehension in the wide blue eyes beneath the sweat-darkened blonde hair that straggled along Winnie's smooth pale forehead.

'They're coming for us, Win,' she whispered. 'But be brave – don't give that old bee the satisfac—'

She broke off, hearing someone burst through the bushes a few yards behind them and Miss Callaghan calling out again.

'Miss Jacky! I did *not* give you permission to charge on ahead in that undisciplined fashion. Stand right where you are, girrul, or you can join those two little beasts in the *ordeal* that lies ahead!'

Theodora shook her head frantically at Winnie, trying to make her realise that Miss Callaghan's words had been *intended* to reach their ears, but it was too late. With a gulp, Winnie began to cry, feebly trying to break free of the tropical vines that held her firmly to her rock. Theodora heard more girls bursting through the bushes behind them and had to resist the temptation to start struggling herself. Her ankles were tied apart, exposing her inner thighs and the tender orifice that nestled between them, with a tenderer (and tighter) sitting above it. Cunny and bottom-hole. Ah, they felt suddenly much more sensitive, squirming as though they were trying to burrow into her flesh for safety.

'Stay where you are, girruls!'

Miss Callaghan's voice rang out clearly, only a few yards away now, and Theodora heard Edwina squeak with fear. She sniffed. There was another smell in the warm, flower-scented tropical air – hotter, sharper, *wetter*. She realised that Edwina's bladder, never the strongest of organs, must have opened when she heard Miss Callaghan's voice so near. 'Winnie wee' must be trickling down the rock beneath Edwina's own splayed thighs, released from the pink-lipped throat of her cunny. Would it nourish some beautiful flower directly beneath that beautiful cunny? A rose? A *Gloire de Pis de Fille de Luxe?* Theodora choked back a gout of hysterical laughter, wondering whether her bladder would open too. More girls were crashing through the bushes behind them now and Miss Callaghan's voice rang out again, full of dominance and impatience, seemingly exasperated at its owner's being slightly out of breath from her climb.

'Right! Here we are, and here *they* are. Our two little beasts, awaiting their richly deserved punishment. Ruth, where are you? Ah, there you are. Don't hide away, girrul. You have a very important task ahead of you and I don't want to see any shirking. None at all, d'you hear me? Have you got them ready? Let me see. Good. And Jacky, do you have *yours* ready? Let me see. Good. Very good. Excellent, indeed. Then I think we can make our way to the waiting, ah, *orifices.*'

Theodora's bladder nearly *did* let go when she heard that. Everything Miss Callaghan had said had been calculated for its effect on *them*, of course, but now Theodora realised why the old bee had been so amused when she supplied that negative information. 'No swallowing', she had promised, and it was true – they wouldn't be swallowing anything. Not swallowing anything at all. 'Quite the reverse' – that's what Miss Callaghan had started to say before she stopped herself. Quite the reverse: nothing would enter their *mouths* to travel *down*, something would enter their *bottoms* to travel *up* instead. Theodora knew it now, knew it beyond a shadow of a doubt.

She raised her head for the final time and saw that the eastern horizon was on fire. In minutes, in seconds, maybe, the sun would peer over at them and their punishment would begin. Her heart was thudding so loudly in her ears that for a moment she could barely hear Miss Callaghan ordering her party forward to the rocks, but she swallowed hard and everything was suddenly clear again.

'Move forward now, girruls. Ruth and Jacky, take up your positions and wait for my order to in—, to do that which will commence the punishment. Zoë and Rhoda, check that their bonds will hold them if they struggle. As surely they will.'

'Insert', that had been the word Miss Callaghan had bitten off, still playing her little game with her two helpless pupils. The party of girls crowded eagerly forward to the rocks and the two schoolfellows whose naked bodies glimmered atop them. Theodora felt Rhoda-or-was-it-Zoë? checking the vines that held her firmly down, while Zoë-or-was-it-Rhoda? checked Edwina, sniffing a little as she smelt the 'Winnie wee'. Miss Callaghan was loudly issuing orders to the remainder of the girls, but her ear was as sharp as ever and she broke off abruptly.

'Why are you sniffing, girrul? Tell me.'

Good-natured Zoë-or-Rhoda, reluctant to get Theodora in worse trouble, grunted unhappily.

'I, ah, I think Theodora's had a little accident, Miss Callaghan.'

'What? Ah.'

Miss Callaghan sniffed herself.

'I see – or rather smell – what you mean, Miss Zoë. But we've no time to get to the bottom of that. Not when we've got *other* things to get to the bottom of, as it were.'

Giggles from the waiting girls and Theodora congratulated herself sadly on the way she had cracked the puzzle. They *were* going to have something pushed up their bottoms and everyone else knew it but thought *they* didn't. Miss Callaghan began speaking again, her voice suddenly crisp and urgent. Theodora closed her eyes and braced herself for what was about to come.

'Ruth, Jacky, are you ready? Then lubricate them, quickly. The sun is about to rise.'

Theodora's whole bottom was highly sensitised now and she felt the faint puff of breath as Ruth-or-was-it-Jacky bent forward and fast-moving fingers, moist with some slick plant-juice, invaded the hollow in which her bottom-hole lay. It was Ruth: the fingers were gentle but expert, lubricating her outer bottom-hole, then prising her open to rub the plant-juice inside her too. She did not try to resist – it was going to be bad enough without that, she was sure. Edwina cried out from beside her and Theodora ground her teeth in silent fury. Trust Miss Callaghan to set cruel Jacky to work lubricating Edwina's delicate bum-hole. That should have been Ruth's job, while Jacky worked on *her* bum-hole.

'Enough!' Miss Callaghan snapped. 'Get ready to insert. And you two, yes, you, *Miss* Theodora and *Miss* Edwina, if I see the slightest sign of resistance from either of you there will be hell to pay.'

Theodora closed her eyes more tightly still, as though by shutting out the light she could prevent what was about to happen. But she couldn't, of course: Ruth had pressed something to her bottom-hole, ready to insert it on Miss Callaghan's order. What was it? What was going to be pushed up both of them? Her universe now centred on her bottom, and her bottom centred on her bottom-hole as she wrung every sliver of sensation out of it, trying to decide what was going to be inserted into her, deep, deep into her most intimate and sensitive flesh.

'On the count of three, girruls,' Miss Callaghan's voice rasped, unsteady with barely disguised excitement, and Theodora had to fight to prevent her bottom-hole tightening against the coming intrusion. Was the sun about to slip above the horizon, fully lighting the hideous scene atop the hill? Was it? Was . . .

'One,' Miss Callaghan said and Theodora felt the expectation and excitement thicken in the air around her. Hearts were beating faster, lips were being licked, eyes were shining, she knew it.

'Two.'

Yes, she knew it, because their treacherous schoolfellows were readying all their senses to feast on the banquet of pain and humiliation that was about to be served to them.

'Three.'

The word was spoken quietly, almost casually, as though it were of no real significance and indeed the insertion into Theodora's bottom was anti-climactic: merely a lump of something sliding into her bowels under the firm but gentle pressure of Ruth's index finger. Edwina whimpered beside her and she knew Jacky was pushing something up her bottom too. The same thing, no doubt, but what was it? She thought that there was a string attached to it, so it could be pulled out later, but she couldn't tell what it was. Ruth pushed it as far as she could, then slid her finger out, rotating it slightly, as though to pleasure her victim, apologising for what she had done.

But what had she done? What had she pushed up inside Theodora's bottom? Animal, vegetable or mineral? Not mineral – it didn't feel hard or heavy enough. And somehow Theodora didn't think it was animal either. Which left vegetable. But vegetable what? She cried out with surprise and pain: a firm left palm had landed on her bottom, sounding simultaneously with what must have been a firm right palm landing on Edwina's bottom.

'Open your eyes, miscreants,' Miss Callaghan's voice said as she stood between them and Theodora obeyed after a moment, blinking in the strong sunlight now

107

blazing directly into her eyes as she lay strapped to the rock. Miss Callaghan had strolled between them, slapping at their bottoms as she passed, and now, having turned to face them, stood smiling down on them. Edwina cried out again and at almost the same moment Theodora felt an odd sensation beginning in her bottom. A sensation of . . .

But Miss Callaghan interrupted her thoughts, lifting up two lumps of some roughly carved yellow substance dangling on cords of braided plant-fibre.

'Are you beginning to feel it now, Miss Theodora? Miss Edwina there obviously is, but she was always a sensitive soul. Ah, I see that you are.'

Theodora had flinched, wriggling where she lay strapped to her rock. The sensation of *heat* in her bottom was definitely strengthening now.

'It's some kind of ginger, girruls,' Miss Callaghan said. 'Here, sniff.'

She held the lumps out on their cords, one to each of them, dangling them beneath their noses.

'Can you smell it?'

And Theodora could. Spicy, pungent, *hot*.

'These are what have been pushed up your sensitive young bottoms,' Miss Callaghan continued. 'The strings are there so that we can retrieve them when we're ready. Because, my dears, as you will short—' She broke off for a moment, shaking her head in mock sadness as Edwina released a moan of discomfort. 'Yes, shortly discover, it would be rather hard to retrieve them otherwise, even with your active and willing assistance.'

Theodora wriggled again on her rock, suppressing her own moan of discomfort. She wasn't going to give Miss Callaghan the satisfaction, not yet anyway, though she strongly suspected that the lump of ginger inserted into her bottom would soon have her moaning willy-nilly. Edwina, apparently oblivious to the satisfaction she was affording Miss Callaghan, moaned again, then grunted.

Miss Callaghan tutted and Theodora, who had lowered her eyes, trying to concentrate on holding back another moan of discomfort, saw the shadow of her head shake with mock sadness. She closed her eyes, biting her lip and feeling tears begin to prickle under her eyelids. The heat in her bottom was rapidly becoming painful. Edwina grunted again. Miss Callaghan tutted again.

'You won't be able to force it out, Miss Edwina, I promise you. It sets up some kind of reaction in the rectal *wall* that lodges it there very firmly. We haven't quite got to the, ah, *bottom* of the phenomenon yet . . .' this provoked sycophantic laughter from their watching classmates 'but Miss Catherine hypothesises that the wall swells around it, and Miss Zoë that it makes the wall sticky with *mucus.*'

Edwina moaned again even more loudly and Theodora ground her teeth to hear more laughter. What *cats* they were, to take pleasure in gentle Edwina's suffering. She bit back a further moan of her own. I'm not, I'm *not* going to give them the satisfaction. Miss Callaghan tutted again and continued.

'We shall discover the truth in the end, I am sure, with sufficient experimental material to work on. Girls' bottoms, that is. Myself, I am inclined to believe that it is, as it were, six of one, half-a-dozen of the other.'

Even through the growing pain in her bottom, Theodora caught the lascivious, gloating tone in Miss Callaghan's voice as she uttered that final phrase and her eyes flew open in apprehension. Oh, she had been right, for Miss Callaghan swallowed, as though her throat had constricted with lust, and continued:

'Yes, six of one, half-a-dozen of the other. Which would be *most* appropriate, my dears, given the bargain I am about to offer you.'

She paused here, but not to swallow again – and lust had been exactly what had constricted her throat, Theodora was now certain – rather to exchange glances with or nod at or otherwise signal two of her 'girruls', for Theodora heard two pairs of feet suddenly scamper away from the rocks on which she and Edwina lay bound, speeding on some errand for their mistress. But they weren't heading back down the hill, rather they were running down to the sea. Why? Theodora thought distractedly. What were they going to get from the sea? She bit back another moan, frowning a little at the apparent irrelevance of Miss Callaghan's next words.

'Who has my watch? You, Lily? Give it to me, quickly . . . Oh, you useless lump, you've forgotten to wind it.'

Through the latest and loudest of Edwina's moans of discomfort Theodora heard Miss Callaghan angrily begin to wind her watch up, grunting contemptuously at Lily's stammered attempt to apologise.

'Shut up. There will indeed be no lack of experimental material with fools like you on the island, Lily. I can just picture *you* where Miss Theodora now is, or Miss Edwina. But we will see about that later. For now, our two guinea-pigs – or should that be ginger-pigs? ginger-plugs?' (more sycophantic laughter from the spectators) 'are no doubt very eager to hear about the bargain I have to offer. It is this, my dears. Please be advised that the ginger in your bottoms has barely begun to work its magic on you. If you think you are in discomfort *now*, the passage of time will soon disabuse you. Half-an-hour, beginning now, is all I believe you will be able to stand and half-an-hour is what I intend to give you. Ah, most excellent timing.'

Theodora heard the two pairs of feet scampering on their return.

'Have you got plenty?' Miss Callaghan called, but another moan from Edwina drowned the replies. It was apparently positive, however, for Miss Callaghan continued:

'Very good. Ah, yes, I see that you have. Quick, girruls. Let's not keep our ginger-pigs waiting any longer.'

The feet sounded louder as they approached and Theodora could hear gasps of effort. What had they fetched for Miss Callaghan? She raised her head, waiting to see, and there they were: Hilary and Ophelia, grinning as they cresting the slope that must lead down to the beach, their firm young breasts bouncing beneath blouses made half-transparent with sweat, both girls holding up in their hands great, dripping bunches of *sea-weed*. Theodora's bewilderment was so great that she forgot the growing heat and pain in her bottom for a moment.

'Excellent, girruls,' Miss Callaghan cried out. 'But quick, show it to our ginger-pigs while I explain its significance to them.'

Hilary and Ophelia, grinning even more broadly, hurried to obey, Hilary taking up position in front of Theodora, Ophelia in front of Edwina, who sniffed in bewilderment, distracted from her own ginger as the smell of the seaweed – hot, salty, marine – struck her nostrils. Where beams of sunlight struck the weed held up proudly in Hilary's hands, shining beneath her armpits or around her flanks, it glowed and glistened green and gold. Miss Callaghan sniffed too, apparently savouring the strong odour of the weed, then continued:

'As I have told you, Miss Theodora, Miss Edwina, I intend you to spend half-an-hour with ginger up your bottoms, but you can cut short the ordeal – if ordeal it be, my dears – at any moment by simply asking for the ginger to be removed. But you will have to pay a forfeit, of course, and it will consist of being *whipped* on your bare bottoms with strands of this fine seaweed before the ginger is pulled out. Six of one, half-a-dozen of the other – which is to say, six strokes will be *your* forfeit, Miss Theodora, and half-a-dozen strokes *yours*, Miss Edwina. So the choice is yours, girruls. Half-an-hour of ginger-up-the-bum or six brief strokes of seaweed. And to help you make your minds up which you might prefer, Miss Hilary and Miss Ophelia will now spread the seaweed on your bottoms, so you can both become better acquainted with it. I hope you searched it thoroughly for crabs, you two, or our poor ginger-pigs might find that there's a nasty nip in the rear.'

More sycophantic laughter from the spectators as Hilary and Ophelia, still grinning, carried their bunches of seaweed along Theodora's and Edwina's helpless bodies and heaped them atop the ginger-plugged bottoms that awaited them.

'There is always the possibility,' Miss Callaghan continued, 'that the coolness of the seaweed will help you endure the heat of the ginger, but somehow, so far, it hasn't quite worked like that.'

Theodora could already understand why: far from helping her endure the heat of the ginger, the coolness of the seaweed sitting slimy and heavy on her smooth bottom was rapidly making it worse. The sun had cleared the horizon now, blazing fiercely in promise – or threat – of another gorgeous day, and Theodora, starting to feel slightly delirious, had a sudden vision of a second sun blazing in her own bottom, rising through her bowels till it burst above the horizon of her bottom-hole. Edwina was whimpering loudly, evidently feeling the contrast of cool weed *on* her bottom and hot ginger *up* it even more than Theodora was. She heard Miss Callaghan laugh with satisfaction, then ask:

'Any crabs in the weed, then, girruls? If so, let's hope they don't get loose and start roaming. For girruls of such refinement and education to have crabs on their cunnies would be a *dire* disgrace, would it not?'

And she laughed again, though no one else seemed to share her merriment and Theodora herself could not understand what she was going on about. Why would crabs on their cunnies be a disgrace? She couldn't understand. It wouldn't be pleasant, of course, but why would it be disgraceful too? Still, just the thought of it had made her bottom and splayed cunny, over which lower strands of the seaweed were draped, feel even more sensitive and vulnerable, which made the seaweed feel even cooler and slimier, which made the ginger feel even hotter. She was unable to prevent herself wriggling at the increased discomfort, provoking more giggles from her traitorous schoolfellows. Miss Callaghan's sharp eye detected the wriggle almost before it began, for Theodora heard her draw in a satisfied breath before purring with venomous, vindictive sweetness:

'So it's not helping, the cooling seaweed on your bottom, Miss Theodora?'

More and louder giggles. Edwina must have wriggled too.

'Nor you, Miss Edwina?' Miss Callaghan purred. 'Well, I do apologise. This is something we will have to remember for next time, isn't it, girruls? "Seaweed on bottom, ginger forgotten"' – mockingly adopting an accent like Edwina's for the mock proverb – 'is evidently quite, quite false. Quite the reverse, it seems. "Seaweed on bottom, ginger gets *rotten*". And . . .'

But with that she was interrupted, for Edwina, her will breaking under the strain of simultaneous pain and humiliation, cried out:

'Pax! Oh, pax, Miss Callaghan! Please take it out! It hurts too much!'

Another satisfied intake of breath from Miss Callaghan, and Theodora knew that their teacher's eyes, glowing with pleasure, were raking Edwina from head to foot, gathering every quiver of discomfort.

'What, girrul? So soon? You want the ginger out already?'

'Yes, Miss Callaghan! Please! Please! Quickly!'

'But you must accept the forfeit, girrul. Six slow strokes of slimy seaweed' – she lingered lasciviously and cruelly on each stressed syllable – 'will be directed against your poor, poor bott—'

113

'Yes, Miss Callaghan!' Edwina was apparently too agitated to care that interrupting Miss Callaghan might provoke their teacher to refuse her request. 'I understand! You can whip me with seaweed, but please, *please* take it out!'

Miss Callaghan snorted and Theodora trembled for a moment in sympathetic fear for her beautiful blonde friend. Was the cruel Scotswoman going to seize on Edwina's interruption as an excuse to refuse her request? No, thank the Virago Mary, she wasn't.

'Very well, Miss Edwina. We will whip you with seaweed and take it out. In that order, you understand? The ginger must remain *in situ* while you are whipped, for reasons that . . .'

'Yes, Miss Callaghan! I understand! Please whip me! Whip me! And take the ginger out! Quick! Quick!'

Another 'wilfully insolent' interruption – another opportunity for cruel Miss Callaghan to refuse Edwina's request. But Theodora had started to realise the truth: that Miss Callaghan had no intention of refusing it. Edwina was going to be whipped with weed however much she interrupted. Another snort from Miss Callaghan, but Theodora could tell that she was acting, and then their teacher began to issue crisp orders:

'Right, Ruth, Zoë, Jacky! Get the weed off Edwina's bottom and select some strands for whipping. Quickly! The poor wee girrul is evidently suffering greatly – aye, *greatly* – and we mustn't have another second – not a-no-ther *second* – of delay. Quick, girruls! Chop, chop!'

Theodora, closing her eyes to fight off her own surrender to Miss Callaghan's offer, heard brisk activity begin as the bunch of seaweed was pulled from Edwina's bottom and strands of it, with giggles and hurriedly whispered consultations and advice, were selected for the whipping. Edwina was moaning feebly, apparently wandering bewildered in a maze of bottom-pain.

114

'Right!' Miss Callaghan's voice cracked through the giggles and whispers. 'Who wants to whip her?'

Theodora felt the hot, sticky tears already leaking slowly under her eyelids quicken and increase in volume as she listened to the responses, imagining the arms that had shot skyward, exposing dark patches of sweat in hot young female armpits, tightening cloth over lust-swollen young breasts.

'Me, Miss Callaghan!'

'Me!'

'Me!'

'Oh, me, Miss Callaghan! Please!'

'Me!'

'Please, me!'

Miss Callaghan laughed, and Theodora imagined her shaking her head with malicious glee.

'So many? In fact, it's all of you! Well, we'll have to choose fairly. Keep your hands up, girruls, while I find a suitable coin.'

'*Keep your arms up?*' So Miss Callaghan too liked the patches of armpit sweat and the pink nipples on display through sweat-transparent cloth, Theodora thought. Dirty old woman!

'Now, you and Ruth first, Zoë,' Miss Callaghan began. 'Please choose heads or tails . . .'

But Edwina interrupted her for the third time, unable to stand the delay of the coin-tossing even at the risk of losing altogether the chance to have the ginger pulled free of her bottom.

'No! No! Please, Miss Callaghan, whip me now! Whip me!'

Even in her own pain, even full of sympathy and concern for her friend, Theodora felt the erotic force of Edwina's words: a beautiful young blonde, bound naked to a black rock, pleading – positively pleading – for her tender, ginger-plugged bottom to be whipped with slimy strands of freshly gathered seaweed. But she

115

had no fear now that Miss Callaghan would use the 'wilfully insolent' interruption to refuse Edwina's request. Her friend was going to be whipped whatever she said. Miss Callaghan grunted with mock surprise and began to purr in response to Edwina's plea:

'Oh, I *am* sorry, Miss Edwina. I was forgetting my own advice about delay. But if I can't choose one of your schoolfellows fairly I won't choose one at all. Therefore, *I* will have to wield the weed against your poor bottom. Here, Jacky, hand me those strands and you, Ruth, gag Miss Edwina with another strand.'

Theodora was unable to restrain a loud moan of self-pity (for herself) and sympathy (for Edwina) at this point, but no one seemed to notice: the prospect of Edwina's gagging and whipping with seaweed was far too attractive, far too heart-quickening – nipple-stiffening – cunny-moistening. Oh, yes, far too cunny-moistening: Theodora's tears began to flow in earnest now as she realised that the moisture and slime trickling between her thighs was not wholly from the seaweed that still sat fat and smug on her own bottom. She heard Edwina's cries of protest cut short as seaweed was stuffed into her mouth and shook her head with disgust and self-loathing. She too, Edwina's best friend, was aroused by the prospect of the beautiful young blonde being gagged with seaweed and *whipped* with seaweed, and a shock almost of electricity jolted through her body as Miss Callaghan grunted and swung the first stroke – *splat!* – against the round silken mounds of Edwina's delicious, eighteen-year-old bottom.

'One!' Miss Callaghan called, taking a deep, unsteady breath. 'And watch closely, girruls – or even more closely, I should say. The ginger in our young blonde miscreant's bottom prevents her clenching her buttock-cheeks to resist the strokes of my seaweed whip. They therefore remain relaxed, almost flaccid, and the strokes consequently set up the most *fascinating* patterns of oscillation in her toothsome buttock-flesh. Just watch, girruls!'

Another grunt, another *splat!* of seaweed landing on Edwina's bottom, and now the horror Theodora felt at enjoying merely the sound of the whipping was almost stronger than the pain of the ginger buried in her own bottom. But sharper even than those two sensations – she could no longer disguise it from herself – was her *envy* of Miss Callaghan. How she longed to be the one whipping the bound and helpless blonde Edwina as their schoolfellows watched with shining eyes, stiffening nipples and moistening cunnies. Another grunt from Miss Callaghan, another *splat!* of seaweed landing on Edwina's deliciously fleshy, ginger-sensitised buttock-cheeks, and Theodora groaned involuntarily with mingled lust, envy and self-loathing. A clear, self-righteous voice suddenly cut through the giggles and whispers of the audience.

'Ooh, Miss Callaghan! Look!'

It was the mouse-like Naomi, Theodora thought – long suspected of being one of Miss Callaghan's spies.

'What, girrul?'

Miss Callaghan broke off from the whipping, panting with excitement and her own lust.

'It's Theodora, Miss Callaghan! Look what she's doing!'

Startled, Theodora herself became aware of what was happening in her body: she was trying to rub – to *grind* – her inflamed loins against the rock to which she was bound, as though her cunny had independent life and had seized the opportunity of its owner's confusion to seek pleasure for itself.

'Stop her!' Miss Callaghan snapped; then Theodora heard her, with a despairing cry of lust, as though Edwina's reddening buttocks were twin suns sucking in her will like a doomed comet, swing back the strands of seaweed for the fourth time and lash them – *splat!* –

against their helplessly waiting, and now helplessly quivering, target. Eager hands were fastening on Theodora herself: tearing the seaweed from her bottom, seizing her hips, dragging them upward so that seaweed could be pushed between her thighs. For a moment Theodora, or rather her cunny, welcomed the assault, thinking that the seaweed would provide the friction and pressure she needed for orgasm, but in the next moment she realised that it was too slippery, too slimy, too insubstantial. She tried to thrust at it nonetheless, unable to control or even slow the instinctual mechanisms that seemed to be running in her lust-, guilt- and ginger-maddened brain and loins, but it slipped and slithered uselessly, meeting the juice-slippery, juice-slimy tissues of her cunny with its own slipperiness and slime.

With a groan, she gave up, hearing the seaweed whip land *splat!* on Edwina's buttocks for the fifth time. What did they look like now? Had they reddened under the strokes as she assumed, or was the seaweed as useless for whipping as it was for *frottage*? She tried to hope that it was, that Edwina had not suffered under the strokes, but her cunny, still leading its independent life, throbbed and gaped with the opposite hope: that the seaweed made an excellent whip, tough and springy for all its uselessness as a cunny-goad, and that Edwina had suffered *exceedingly*, biting into the seaweed stuffed in her mouth, so that its briny slime flowed thickly on her tongue, dominating and humiliating another of her senses.

The hands had left her now, leaving her cunny well-padded with seaweed against the rock, and Theodora knew their owners were eagerly watching for the sixth and final stroke, after which the ginger would be pulled from Edwina's bottom. Miss Callaghan seemed unable for the moment to deliver it, panting and gasping as though she had just run a race, and Theodora had to suppress an hysterical giggle at the thought that sprang

118

into her brain: that Miss Callaghan's knickers were full of seaweed too – strands of juice-slimed cunny-hair reeking hotly of brine and the sea. Theodora heard Miss Callaghan swear under her breath in some language her pupil did not recognise (Gaelic?), seeming to admonish herself, to whip at herself with words of self-reproach; then the sixth grunt came and – *splat!* – she had swung the sixth stroke. A sigh of released tension went up from the eagerly watching schoolgirls, then a peal of laughter. Theodora later learned that it was provoked by Edwina's frantically bouncing and squirming buttocks, as she protested at the delay in pulling the ginger from her bottom. Theodora ground her teeth in fury, vowing that she would be avenged on *all* of them but on Miss Callaghan most of all, with Jacky and Ruth and Naomi singled out for special attention too. Her ginger-lump seemed large as a cabbage now, burning juicily in the depths of her bottom, and she was suddenly gripped by the irrational fear that it couldn't be pulled out – nor out of Edwina's bottom. No, it would have to stay there until it burnt itself out and shrank again to ordinary size.

She shook her head, trying to work out what Miss Callaghan was saying through her subsiding gasps of delight-in-domination. Oh, it was:

'Pull it out. The poor wee girrul has suffered enough. Pull it out.'

Theodora shook her head again, squeezing her eyes shut even tighter as she willed herself to stay silent, to keep her mouth closed, *not* to plead for her own whipping with seaweed in exchange for her own ginger being pulled out of her bottom the way lucky, *lucky* Edwina's was about to be.

Eight

Trying to control her breathing, Theodora tiptoed across the cool marble floor of the dimly lit room, head swinging fast as she looked for somewhere to hide. Ah, there: she almost ran to the place and slipped into the niche between a bank of orchids and the wall, panelled with some dark tropical wood. Now she wished she could control the beating of her heart, which seemed loud enough to alert any passing guard. Oh, she knew she was being silly to think *that* was possible, but if a guard carried out a random check of the dormitory she had left and discovered that her bed did not contain what it should – well, Heaven knew what would follow. But she had to run the risk: she was under direct orders from Philippa herself. An hour-and-a-half before, during a dull mathematics lesson from one of the Doctor's underlings, they had heard the trumpets sound from the ramparts of the *château*, announcing another successful kidnap. A new girl would be arriving soon to be interviewed by their gaoler. Philippa had been briskly dominant when they were sent to the dormitory for their afternoon siesta.

'Intelligence, Theodora. It is our only weapon against this madman, and each of us must do our bit to gather it. It's *your* turn now, as the last girl kidnapped: you must conceal yourself in his interview room and over-hear what he says to the new arrival, whom we may not

120

see for a day or more. Very well? Then good: off with you.'

And with a firm pat on her bottom she had been despatched to sneak breathless and dry-mouthed down corridor after corridor till she reached the room where she herself and all the other girls of the dormitory had been interviewed after their kidnap. A large gilded chair sat at one end of it on a five-stepped dais, with a black velvet cushion waiting beneath the chair. Theodora had felt herself blush at the sight of the cushion, and the blush lingered in her cheeks as she crouched behind the orchids, praying that their creamily sweet odour wouldn't make her sneeze. The cushion meant that the new arrival was going to endure what she had endured: kneel atop it and – she shivered with anticipation: a pair of fast-moving feet had interrupted her thoughts, coming down the corridor outside. Was it a guard tracking her down with one of those horrid snakes? No: the doorway she had just passed flickered with light and the guard who strode through it dressed in eighteenth-century costume was not hunting her down but carrying a lit candelabrum.

He set it on a table near the dais on which sat the gilded chair and strode out, and Theodora suddenly smiled. She had at least *one* thing to tell Philippa: that the entire class was going to end up in the *château* sooner or later. There were eighteen candle-holders in the candelabrum and though only ten of them were filled, that was one more than she had counted when she herself was interviewed here two days before. Evidently a candle was being, and would be, added with every new kidnap, till all the shipwrecked girls were together again. She couldn't think how they would use this information, but it was *something*.

She had been peering over the top of the orchids as she examined the candelabrum; now she crouched again as two more pairs of feet sounded in the corridor. Was one of them *le Docteur?* Yes: she could hear the husky whisper in which he always spoke. He seemed to be dictating something. Yes: he was. Now she could hear the scratch of quill-pen on paper.

She raised her head cautiously, peering between the orchids, reminding herself to breathe shallowly in case their scent and pollen made her sneeze. There they were in the doorway: the Doctor and a secretary taking down notes at his dictation, both of them wearing eighteenth-century costume, buckled shoes clacking on the marble floor as they made their way to the dais. The Doctor climbed the steps and settled himself in the gilded chair. Here he paused in his dictation a few moments, lifting a lid in one of the arms of the chair to take up a pinch of something. He dropped the lid and delicately administered what he held between his thumb and forefinger – evidently snuff – to his nostrils, sat rigid for a moment, then sneezed so loudly that Theodora, although she had been expecting the sound, jerked a little with surprise. Then he continued with his dictation, Theodora straining with little success to decipher the scientific jargon in his whispered French, until a small bell tinkled somewhere in the room.

'*Merci*, Antoine,' the Doctor whispered to the secretary after a final remark Theodora did not understand. 'Please make fair copies and distribute them to the laboratories.'

Well, at least she had understood that. The secretary bowed his head and hurried from the room as three more pairs of feet sounded in the corridor. Theodora swallowed nervously: two pairs of feet were shod but one pair was bare and reluctant, just as *hers* had been a few days before. A freshly kidnapped girl was being hauled into the Presence and Theodora's mind whirled with memories of her own kidnap: the shock of it, the speed with which she had been plucked off her feet after she had lost sight of her companions for barely a moment, the sense of helplessness as she was gagged, bound and carried away into the jungle, then the disbelief as she arrived at the *château* at the other end of the island. But Miss Callaghan had organised a thorough search – how could they have missed this? This poor new girl must be in the same dazed condition, but who was it? Zoë? Frances? Little Jenny?

No! Theodora's heart thudded with mixed emotions, for guard and girl were in the doorway, the flickering candlelight gleaming off both tear-tracks on the girl's cheeks and blonde hair. It was Edwina! And somehow she was looking more luscious than ever, with her panting breasts almost bursting through fresh vents in her school-uniform. Poor darling! She must have been dragged through some rough vegetation during the kidnap. She heard the Doctor grunt with satisfaction and shift in his chair as Edwina was dragged to stand in front of him by two short but burly guards, also in eighteenth-century costume. The Doctor gazed greedily at his new captive for perhaps a minute, nodding three or four times as his eyes expertly measured her figure and read the emotions in her dazed, barely conscious face. Then he began to speak.

'Relax your grip, you oafs,' he whispered in English. 'You will bruise this exquisite morsel.'

The guards obeyed, but Edwina slumped between them and the Doctor grunted with exasperation and lifted another lid in an arm of the gilded chair.

'You have treated her too roughly, you barbarians,' he whispered, raising something small that glinted in the candlelight. 'Here, *ma petite*,' he continued, rising from his seat and walking down the steps of the dais to his captive. Theodora was shaking her head with anger and frustration. It was all an act, all a complete pretence. Look at how long he had gazed at Edwina in her distress before pretending concern for her! Using English, of course, so that the poor dear would understand him and be fooled. And the smelling-salts he was administering now, deftly presenting the bottle he had taken from the arm of the chair first to one nostril, then the other – he was bringing Edwina out of her half-faint only because he was eager to begin the interview.

It had worked too: Edwina moaned with surprise as the harsh scent of the smelling-salts penetrated her right nostril, shaking her head so that the Doctor had to gently take hold of her hair as he administered the smelling-salts to her left nostril. He stepped back, gazing at the renewed light of intelligence and awareness in his young captive's face, then nodded with satisfaction as she sneezed sharply, sniffed and sneezed again.

'Bring her nearer,' he whispered to the guards as he climbed the steps of the dais backward and sat down in the gilded chair. 'But gently, you oafs!'

The guards brought Edwina to the foot of the dais. Theodora could not see her face fully from where she half-crouched, half-stood behind the orchids, but it was apparent that she was gazing upward at the Doctor, whose own face, Theodora could see clearly, was full of concern and sympathy. She wanted to cry out: 'Don't trust him, Winnie!'; and shook her head softly in frustration. Now the Doctor smiled and from the minute movement of Edwina's head Theodora knew that her friend was smiling in response. Oh, it was heart-wrenching to see the poor fly winging its way so naïvely, so trustingly into the spider's parlour.

'*Bonjour, ma belle petite*,' whispered the Doctor, then continued in English: 'And I must, of course, apologise for the speed and roughness . . .' here he glanced left and right with a frown at the guards who were still keeping firm hold of poor Edwina 'with which you have been brought into my presence. But it was, alas, a necessary precaution.'

Ask him why it was a 'necessary precaution', Theodora wanted to shout. Don't let him fool you the way he fooled me.

But she had to keep silent, merely watching as the spider began to stalk its tender prey. It was the Doctor's *whisper*, Theodora had realised, that was his most effective tool of manipulation and deceit. It made him sound so gentle, so harmless, yet so fascinating withal, and his interlocutrix, having to strain her ears slightly to catch every syllable, was distracted from the sinister intent that lay beneath it.

'But tell me, my dear,' the Doctor was now saying, 'what is your name?'

Edwina shook her head slightly (*shaking off the spell of the bastard's voice!*, Theodora thought angrily) and stammered, 'Ed-Ed-Edwina, *monsieur*.'

'Ah. Edwina. What a beautiful name! Though your friends, no doubt, call you Winnie?'

'Y-yes, *monsieur*.'

'Then may I too call you Winnie, my dear?'

A brief pause from Edwina: she was swallowing, Theodora thought.

'Y-yes, *monsieur*. Please do.'

'Excellent. Then I certainly shall. But you will forgive me if, for now, I address you as Edwina. It is such a beautiful name and I am reluctant to abandon the sweetness it brings to the tongue. A beautiful name for a very beautiful young girl. But you are wondering, *peut-être*, how it is that you might address me?'

'Yes, *monsieur*.'

'I am Doctor Alphonse, my dear Edwina, a scion of a most noble family. Do you wish to know *which* family?'

Edwina nodded.

'Yes, *monsieur*.'

'Call me Doctor, *ma* Edwina. So again I ask: do you wish to know *which* family?'

'Yes, *mon*—, yes, Doctor.'

'Then let us play a little game, *ma* Edwina. Three clues for you. First clue. My family is descended from Petrarch's Laura. Can you guess who we are?'

'Pe-Petrarch?'

'Yes, my dear. But I see that the name is only vaguely familiar to you. And of Laura you know nothing? Ah, too bad. But here is your second clue: the most famous of my line was an author of, shall we say, somewhat *sulphurous* reputation. Can you guess?'

'S-sulphurous?'

'Yes, *ma* Edwina. Sulphurous. *Non?* No shaft of light, ah, penetrates your darkness? Then here is your third clue. Today is the one-hundred-and-ninety-ninth anniversary of the birth of that author of sulphurous reputation. Now can you guess?'

Edwina shook her head, blonde locks rippling.

'*Non? Mais c'est mon ancêtre le plus fameux.* Donatien Alphonse François, marquis de Sade.'

Again Edwina shook her head.

'You do not know him?'

'No. I'm ... I'm so sorry.'

'Then, my dear, it will be my delightful task to teach you more. Much more. Much, much more.'

With evident reluctance he looked away from the face of the girl who was gazing up at him in mesmerised fascination.

'You,' he said to one of the guards. 'Fetch our beautiful young guest *l'arbre généalogique.*'

The guard nodded, released Edwina, and hurried away.

'And you,' the Doctor said to the remaining guard, 'assist Edwina up the steps. Here, my dear, you shall kneel on this as I take you through my family history.'

He had reached under the chair and pulled out the black velvet cushion, dropping it on the dais in front of him as Edwina, tottering a little, was helped up the steps by the remaining guard.

'*Et voilà*,' said the Doctor, 'lower your very pretty knees atop that, my dear. *Très bien.* You, release her and stand back to await further orders.'

126

Theodora lifted her right hand to her mouth and bit on the knuckles as she watched the guard help Edwina kneel with a sigh of relief on the velvet cushion in front of the Doctor. The guard walked down the dais a little, then stood to await his further orders, two steps below the oblivious Edwina. Theodora shook her head. Oh, the fool, the poor fool, the poor sweet fool! Could she not see the bulge in the Doctor's trousers and realise what awaited her? Theodora closed her eyes, blinking away stinging tears as she answered her own question. No, poor Edwina could not see it any more than she herself had done in the same position, for the Doctor gave her no chance: a slender but powerful hand went under Edwina's chin, lifting her face to his and shielding the ominous trouser-bulge.

'There, my dear Edwina. Are you comfortable? Yes? Then here, as if on cue, comes *l'arbre généalogique* for your perusal under my guidance. But you wish to speak, my dear? Forgive me: I am pushing your chin too high. Now, what is it you wish to say?'

With her chin released a little, Edwina was able to speak.

'Are you – are you going to show me your family tree, Doctor?'

'Exactly so, my dear Edwina. My family tree.'

The first guard had now returned and was hurrying down the chamber holding up a length of parchment so long that it was nearly trailing on the floor. Theodora caught a glimpse of the gold, red and black calligraphy with which one side of it was covered, as the Doctor's ancestry was traced from Petrarch's Laura, whoever *she* was.

'Here,' whispered the Doctor as the guard reached the dais. 'Climb to us and pull it free under my direction, as I instruct our beautiful young guest. Yes. Now, my dear Edwina . . .'

His whisper grew even softer, even more conspiratorial, as he began to instruct Edwina in the family tree, holding the scroll over his lap and tracing his lineage through generation after generation as the first guard stood patiently, tugging the scroll slowly over one arm. Theodora felt a little sick at the knowledge of what would soon come. The Doctor was whispering and tapping the parchment, and though Theodora could not hear him properly she knew he was giving particulars of each ancestor, male and female, even sketching their appearance and character. Was Edwina already feeling bored, as she herself had done? Oh, it seemed so: she was stifling a yawn and her slender shoulders were shaking slightly. But the Doctor, watchful as a cat, was not at all discomfited. He suspended his instruction, looking down at Edwina with an understanding smile.

'But my darling girl!' he whispered. 'You grow weary, and no wonder, for I forget in my pride of ancestry that what is most fascinating to me is too often far from fascinating to others. Particularly the young, who are generally wrapped too fast in the present to pay concern to the recent, let alone the distant, past. I shall take pity on your *ennui*, my dear Edwina, and – how do you say? – *skip* centuries, bringing us almost to the present. But I must pause, *ma belle petite*, to indicate him who is the chief jewel of my family's crown.'

He nodded at the guard, who tugged the scroll upward until the Doctor nodded again. Now he tapped the parchment again as it lay draped over his lap.

'*Voilà*. Donatien Alphonse François, marquis de Sade. *Le divin marquis*, *ma chère* Edwina. Of whom, alas, you have never heard. But no matter: there will be ample time and opportunity for further instruction, so I leap two centuries to bring you to my own parents.'

Here his voice dropped again and Theodora closed her eyes and lowered her head, shaking it with frustration as she felt tears prickle again behind her closed eyelids. He was nearly at the end of the scroll, no doubt to poor Edwina's relief, for she could have no idea what awaited her. Against her will, Theodora opened her eyes and lifted her head, watching the final act in the drama. Here it came: the Doctor nodded at the guard, who tugged the scroll a final few inches, bringing it to the Doctor's own position. Theodora's stomach rolled as she heard Edwina grunt with surprise.

'But what is wrong, my dear Edwina?' the Doctor whispered – Theodora ground her teeth again at the clear note of mock-concern in his voice. But poor Edwina evidently heard nothing of it: she raised her face to his from the scroll.

'There – there's nothing but a hole, Doctor.'

'A hole?'

'Yes, Doctor. A hole where you should be.'

'Where I should be?'

'Yes, Doctor.'

'Then, my dearest, my sweetest, my most beautiful Edwina, the hole had better be *filled*, had it not?'

Theodora's stomach rolled again and she had to swallow her nausea. It was so obvious to her what was about to happen, but poor Edwina was utterly oblivious! The second guard, the one standing behind her, two steps down the dais, was tense with anticipation, and the scroll was rustling as the Doctor worked with one hand on something beneath it.

'Is this, *peut-être*,' he announced, his whisper huskier than ever with a barely controlled excitement, 'an acceptable substitute for my name? You might call it, my dear, my *second* family tree.'

Edwina looked down again at the hole, but her cry of surprise at what had emerged through it was cut short: with the slightest of nods the Doctor had issued his order to the guard who stood behind her, and he had pounced, seizing Edwina by the neck and plunging her head downward over the large and erect cock that awaited it. Theodora's head swam sickeningly for a moment, but she could not close her eyes or look away:

Edwina's cry of surprise, she knew from bitter personal experience, had opened her mouth exactly right for the cock to spear inside it. The Doctor sighed happily and nodded again slightly to the guard, who released Edwina's head as the Doctor himself took control of it, entwining his hands lovingly in her soft blonde locks and pulling her down more firmly over his cock. Edwina was struggling feebly to pull backward, issuing moans of disbelief and disgust, softened and muffled against the thick shaft of cock-flesh filling her mouth.

The Doctor nodded again to the guard, who straddled Edwina's back, locking her in place with his thighs as her struggles continued. Theodora heard the Doctor tut with disappointment.

'But is this not an acceptable substitute, my dearest Edwina? Ah, there is no pleasing young people today. Richarde, *les tétons, s'il vous plaît.*'

He had glanced up at the guard still holding the scroll, who now carefully lowered it to the steps of the dais and moved to Edwina. Another wave of sickness ran through the watching Theodora as she remembered her own sense of helplessness and horror at this moment: the large erect cock filling her mouth, another large erect cock rubbing against her back as the guard straddled her, and then the hands of the other guard working at her clothing, tugging and tearing at it to expose her breasts, taking hold of them, rubbing them, squeezing them, juggling them as the Doctor, beginning to mouth-fuck her, hoarsely whispered his questions about the size and firmness of her breasts. Now poor darling Edwina was enduring exactly the same.

'*Comment sont-ils?*'

The first question, 'How are they?', through poor Edwina's moans and murmurs and the liquid sounds of the mouth-fucking the Doctor was forcing on her. And the breast-molesting guard was replying, describing Edwina's breasts in a terse, strained voice, obviously almost overcome with his own lust. Theodora closed her eyes and placed her hands over her ears, not wanting to hear the Doctor's questions and the guard's responses, but unable to summon the will to press her hands down firmly enough and block out the dialogue entirely. But it was one-sided: she could only hear the guard's responses and Edwina's futile protests, not the Doctor's questions.

'... They are firm, *maître Docteur* ... *Non*, not excessive in size, but deliciously firm ... *Oui*, very tender, very sensitive. If I squeeze thus, *maître Docteur*, hear, oh, hear how she squeaks and wriggles ... *Oui* ... *Oui*, the nipples are soft and sensitive as the noses of mice, *maître Docteur* ... *Non*, they have not stiffened as yet ... I shall try, *maître Docteur* ...'

Here Theodora at last found the will to press her hands firmly over her ears and block out the sounds of Edwina's mouth-rape altogether. Poor, poor darling! But beneath the churning in her stomach and the sourness in her throat she could not disguise from herself that the lips of her cunny smiled on the scene – gaped on it, indeed, and oozed with the lustful juice seeping through the walls of her cunny-throat. And her nipples: unlike poor Edwina's, *they* were stiff, painfully so, indeed, for she could feel the slightest brush of cloth against them as she moved.

What a cat you are, Theodora!, she apostrophised herself. No, that was not the word. *What a slut!* You are taking pleasure in what is happening to poor Edwina and secretly – no, don't lie to me, you can't lie to me, because I *am* you – secretly you want it to happen again to *you*. Oh, her secret was out and her right hand dropped from her ear, flashing to and under the hem of her dress and working its way expertly upward to the oozing lips and folds of her cunny as the renewed sound of the mouth-fucking and breast-molestation filled her ear and inflamed her brain. Things had advanced greatly in the time she had blocked her ears and though she kept her eyes shut as she frotted furiously at her cunny, every detail of the scene was blazing in her imagination. The Doctor was gasping and groaning in his husky whisper as he drove his cock over and over to the limits of Edwina's mouth, and his orgasm could not be more than seconds away.

But another orgasm was evidently being brewed in another pair of fine hairy balls: even as the breast-molesting guard continued to repeat his description of Edwina's mammary charms in a mechanical, lust-dazed voice, the other guard was gasping and groaning as he frotted his erect cock against Edwina's slender back. Had he torn her clothing away and taken his cock out fully, so that he could rub the glowing head against her silken, sweat-moistened skin? Theodora was suddenly and shockingly aware that she too had begun to gasp and groan as she frotted herself behind the orchids: she was sliding too fast down the slope to the cliff of her own orgasm and the churning sea that awaited her at its foot. She closed her mouth and tried to hold her cries back, trying desperately to remember how the back-straddling guard had pleasured himself against *her* when she had been in Edwina's position.

Had he torn her clothing away and rubbed his naked cock on her naked back, skin to skin? Or had he contented himself with rubbing his naked cock on her clothed back? She could not remember but the question was suddenly of enormous importance – it was a way of clutching at grass and bushes as she slid down the slope to the orgasm-cliff, not arresting her descent but slowing it, so that she did not abandon herself entirely to it and unconsciously begin to vocalise again. Her frotting hand was soaked with cunny-juice to the wrist now and she longed to form it into a fist and thrust it deep into her cunny-throat. Two or three of her school-friends could do it, she knew from whispered rumours and one practical demonstration, but she couldn't: her maiden-head was still intact and she wanted to keep it that way.

Oh, she abandoned her attempts to remember how the guard had frotted himself on her back and let herself slide helpless down the final stretch of slope, for the guard was now gasping loudly in orgasm. It was skin-on-skin, she decided: his sperm must be squirting against Edwina's bare back and into her blonde, sweat-darkened hair. She reached the lip of the orgasm-cliff and plunged over, retaining only just enough will to lock her mouth shut and hold in her wail of joy. Her thighs had locked around her hand, almost paralysing it, so that she could work at her spasming cunny with only her fingertips. She completed her fall from the cliff-top and hit the water of full orgasm, feeling its hot bubbles drive through her body from her feet upward until they reached the dome of her skull and compressed there, making her feel as though her brain was going to explode with pleasure. She toppled slowly sideways, desperate not to make another sound that might alert the Doctor and his guards to her presence, and finished lying on her side, the knuckles of one hand crammed into her mouth as the fingertips of the other fluttered at her cunny.

She lay dazed with pleasure for she-knew-not-how-long, then came out of after-orgasm abruptly, suddenly aware of the silence in the room and of the ache in the hand trapped between her thighs. What was happening? There was a *watchfulness* in the silence and her ears, sharpening again after being deafened by orgasm, caught a faint tread of footsteps. She struggled to free her hand from between her thighs and sit up. There: it came free, releasing a gush of cunny-juice – the air was thick with the smell of it – and she was able to sit up and peer through the orchids to see what was going on. Oh! Her stomach lurched and her half-softened nipples stabbed with pain, as though the memory of what they had endured in the lifeboat was resurrected to symbolise her fear of what she might endure next. *For a tracker was in the Doctor's chambre d'entrevue, padding across the floor in his soft-soled shoes as he held the leash of one of the enormous tracking-snakes.*

Fascinated despite herself, Theodora watched its tongue flickering in and out as it tasted the air for her scent and followed the exact path she had taken as she came into the room and looked for a hiding-place all those hours before. But now she jerked, barely able to suppress a squeak of surprise and fright.

'I think,' came the Doctor's husky whisper, still weak with the cock-sucking he had forced out of Edwina (had he achieved orgasm too or had the entry of the tracker suspended the fellatio?), 'that she is most likely concealed behind *there*, my boy.'

The padding footsteps of the tracker altered direction on the floor and Theodora almost fainted as she realised that they were now coming straight for her. She closed her eyes, moaning deep in her throat, but her frantic prayer to Our Lady of Tortures was interrupted by the pleased chuckle of the tracker as he reached the wall and peered into the niche. A moment later his strong left hand closed in her hair and she was dragged forth, dazedly aware that the snake's head was swaying near her face, its tongue flickering in and out faster than ever as it sampled her full scent.

'Ah, *c'est toi, ma chère* Théodora,' came the Doctor's whisper. 'But what on earth shall we do with you? Ah, I know. You can collaborate with your little friend in the task I have set her.'

She heard the feet of one of the other two guards trotting across the floor and felt his hands seize her. The tracker released her hair and she was half-dragged, half-carried to the dais and up the steps to the Doctor's gilded chair. Through the rainbow blur of her tears she saw him wave his right hand to her – the left was locked in Edwina's hair, holding her head ready to be forced back over his cock, which throbbed and twitched just beneath her friend's mouth. So the fellatio had been suspended after all. But what did he mean that she could 'collaborate with' Edwina? Two girls couldn't suck one cock. But a moment later, provoking laughter from the three guards who watched, she cried out with surprise and horror. The Doctor's right hand had dived into his trousers, rummaged there, and lifted forth beside the cock that already jutted from them a *second* cock, seemingly identical in every respect to the first, save that it was not glistening with the spittle of Edwina's suspended fellatio.

Nine

'Did it give you a shock?' Edwina whispered.

'Of course it did, darling,' Theodora whispered back. She kissed her friend's ear, nibbled it, then pulled her mouth away with a cruel chuckle as Edwina wriggled with pleasure and tried to thigh-trap the hand that had been resting motionless on her cunny.

'Not just yet, darling,' Theodora said. 'I'll frot you to your heart's – or rather, cunny's content – when I've finished telling you the story.'

She began to whisper again, her mouth almost sealed to Edwina's ear. Yes, it certainly *had* been a shock when the Doctor produced that second cock from his trousers and, entwining his right hand in her hair, forced her to begin sucking it as a guard straddled her too, keeping her in place with *his* erect cock sticking almost painfully into her back. It wasn't skin-on-skin: the guards straddling her and Edwina frotted themselves through cloth and had to work harder for their pleasure, so that Theodora felt especially helpless, her head seized and controlled by the Doctor, her mouth filled to capacity by his cock, her torso straddled and locked in place by the *frotteur* guard. A confused tangle of fly-buttons and pubic hair filled her eyes; the pubic hair rasped at the delicate tip of her nose as the Doctor forced her head back and forward, mouth-fucking her; the moans and gasps of the Doctor and his two guards filled her ears;

136

the feral reek of their masculine sweat filled her nostrils; and sweat and pre-ejaculate lay thick on her tongue: oh, she had been a feminine pawn in a masculine game, but somehow simultaneously the king too, for without her the game could not have been played.

She stopped whispering to Edwina, swallowing hard and wriggling in the bed at the memory of it as she felt a thread of cunny-juice trickle between her thighs. She reached for Edwina's cunny again, tickling at it to find that it too was trickling. Oh, she couldn't wait. She found one of Edwina's hands and tugged it to her cunny.

'Frot me, darling,' she whispered, 'and I'll frot you as I carry on with the story.'

But, with her mind occupied by the story and by the need to begin frotting Edwina, she had underestimated her own state of arousal: the first delicate tickle of Edwina's fingertips on her clitoris almost made her loins explode and she had to twist onto her side, gasping out as quietly as she could, 'No, darling. Stop. Stop.'

Edwina's breath tickled her ear and she moaned again. All her – what was the name? Oh, yes – all her erogenous zones were dangerously inflamed, keyed to imminent orgasm by her memories of being seized and dominated, mouth-fucked and straddled, in the Doctor's *chambre d'entrevue*. She tried to push Edwina away, but her limbs had weakened, her joints half-melted. Edwina's breath came again.

'What's wrong, Dorrie, darling?'

Theodora struggled to control the sensations in her body.

'I'm ... I'm too aroused,' she managed to whisper back. 'I'm going to come before the end of the story.'

She heard Edwina's low chuckle.

'Well, come then, darling. Here, I'll do it for you.'

But Theodora rolled away from her, locking her thighs to keep Edwina's slim hand from her cunny.

'No,' she whispered urgently. 'I won't be able to control my response: I'll scream, Winnie, I know I will.'

Later, thinking back, she seemed to remember that her heart had begun to pound furiously even before the second voice spoke in her opposite ear, as though she sensed that an extra party had joined them.

'I know a remedy for *that*,' whispered the second voice – *Philippa's* voice – in her ear, and her large soft pillow descended abruptly on her face. She kicked and punched out, but Philippa had lieutenants with her and expert hands seized and subdued her. They must have crept up on Edwina's bed very carefully, crawling over the floor after catching whispers or creaks in the dark. Now she was starting to panic: the pillow was pressed so firmly over her face that she couldn't breathe. She tried to shout through it, but it was no use. She groaned in her throat as her blanket was plucked away and cool air ran over her body. She had a super-abundance of air down there, but none where she needed it: at her mouth. Her lungs were starting to ache and she was still trying to struggle against the strong hands holding her down. Another pair of hands – Philippa's, she was almost certain – were investigating her naked body, rubbing her erect nipples, gliding swiftly downward over her sweat-slicked belly, tickling through her pubic hair.

She faintly heard Philippa again, rapping out an order – the whole dormitory must be awake by now – and her ankles were dragged apart, opening the thighs she tried desperately to lock together and exposing her cunny to Philippa's fingers. Now Philippa was speaking again and Theodora heard laughter. The bitch must be commenting on the *wetness* of her cunny: its wetness, its stickiness, its *smell*. She tried to shake her head beneath the pillow, hearing more laughter through the growing roar of blood in her ears. More faintly heard but incomprehensible words from Philippa and then, with a suddenness that made her stomach lurch and her nipples throb agonisingly with pleasure, a mouth and hot, probing, licking tongue were at work on her cunny.

Edwina told her later that Philippa had pointed out that she wouldn't take the pillow off until she, Edwina, had brought her, Theodora, to orgasm – and that she 'had better be quick about it, before your darling Dorrie asphyxiates'.

'And the way she said it, Dorrie, I thought she really would let you asphyxiate. So I put my best tongue forward.'

Theodora kissed her.

'Your *only* tongue, Winnie. But I wouldn't exchange it for any other tongue in the world.'

Nor would she have done when she was trapped beneath the pillow: no one but Winnie could have brought her so swiftly to orgasm, knowing her cunny and its idiosyncrasies so intimately of old. But it had certainly seemed to take long enough at the time, though Edwina assured her that her cunny was spasming within about half-a-minute.

'You splashed my face like a *man*, darling, you came so hard. Female ejaculate it's called, isn't it?'

'Yes, darling, it is, and I did come hard. Painfully hard.'

It was true: her orgasm had been stronger than any she had known before, swollen and deepened by the emotions and sensations of Philippa's sudden pounce and pillowing. Lungs aching, heart thundering, she had screamed into the pillow as she came, torn at it with her teeth, and then nearly been sick with relief as Philippa pulled the pillow away and she could suck gorgeously cool and refreshing air into her lungs with a whistle that provoked yet more laughter from the girls clustered eagerly around the bed, their faces glowing uncannily in the light of candles being held by two of Philippa's lieutenants. Then Philippa's face loomed over her, looking down with a satisfied smile.

'Was that nice, Dorrie, darling?'

Theodora shook her head, trying to recover from her orgasm, from her semi-asphyxiation, from her rage and humiliation.

'Well, was it?' Philippa said impatiently. 'Hilary, let some wax fall on her cunny. That will get her concentrating.'

'No!' Theodora snarled, managing to raise her head and glare down her own naked, glistening body as Hilary, with a stifled giggle, lowered her candle over Theodora's cunny, still holding it carefully upright.

'No!' Theodora snarled again. 'If you dare do that, Hil—'

'Shut her up,' Philippa ordered and Theodora gagged as a pair of damp knickers were crammed into her mouth. Now all she could do was glare in futile threat as Hilary, shoulders shaking as she tried to control more giggles, held the candle ready.

'Good,' Philippa said. 'Now tip it so hot wax drips on her cunny, which should be especially sensitive after that *gargantuan* orgasm she's just had. But tip it *slowly*, Hilary, very slowly. This is far too good to rush.'

The circle of girls around the bed had gone very quiet, watching with breathless eagerness as Hilary began to tip the candle. Theodora saw that even Edwina, her face glistening with fresh cunny-juice, was watching in fascination for the first drop to fall. Philippa cleared her throat and remarked conversationally, as though the wax-torture of a freshly orgasmed cunny were nothing new to *her*, at least:

'I'd been listening to you and Edwina for ages, you know, and would have happily listened for ages more, but when you complained that you couldn't have an orgasm for fear of screaming and waking the dormitory, I simply had to intervene. After all, the dormitory was already awake, weren't you, darlings?'

No reply from the eagerly watching girls.

'I said, "Weren't you, darl—".'

But now the first droplet of wax, glittering like a tear, fell from the candle and landed on Theodora's splayed and oozing cunny. And as Philippa had predicted, her cunny *was* especially sensitive after her gargantuan orgasm; but fortunately it was also especially *moist*, protecting her from the worst effects of the hot wax, and, though she did not have to feign the knicker-muffled yelp with which she greeted the droplet, she certainly feigned her writhes of agony. Outwardly in severe discomfort, inwardly calm and in near perfect control of herself, she watched the circle of spectators from under almost-closed eyelids, noting expressions and filing away future retribution for those who gloated over her cunny-torture. She hardly dared look at Edwina's face, fearful lest she should see some spark of satisfaction there; and sighed with relief even as another droplet of wax fell from the candle, for Edwina had closed her eyes in horror, unable to watch a moment longer.

The second droplet hit her cunny and she yelped through the knicker-gag again, writhing in simulated agony. But Philippa was calling urgently for a halt.

'No, Hilary, stop for a moment.'

What was up? Theodora wondered as Hilary swung the candle upright and away from her cunny; then she felt her stomach sink as Philippa's next words confirmed that her enemy was as maliciously observant as ever.

'Look at poor Winnie, everyone,' Philippa said, pointing at Edwina as she held her eyes tight-shut. 'She can't *bear* to see Dorrie being tortured like this, the poor tender-hearted little thing. Well, let's respect Winnie's tender-heartedness, shall we, girls?'

Six or seven girls, realising that Philippa had devised a new treat for them, eagerly nodded and voiced their agreement, and Theodora was glad to see that they were exactly those she had already marked down for retribution. She forgave the remainder of the girls, who less enthusiastically, anxious merely not to be the target of Philippa's ingenious cruelty, nodded and voiced their agreement too.

'Good,' said Philippa. 'Then we have a consensus. We must respect Winnie's tender-heartedness and give her a chance to save Dorrie from this most painful, not to say undignified, procedure. Here's the deal, kid,' she continued in her American accent, 'if *you* can take pain *for* her, Dorrie won't have to suffer any more, OK?'

Winnie had opened her eyes now and was gazing fearfully at Philippa, and Theodora's heart contracted in her chest more painfully than ever. Winnie's eyes were gorgeous, glistening blue in the flickering candle-light, swimming with tears she had shed on her friend's behalf. Winnie's mouth came open uncertainly and she quavered.

'I'll . . . I'll try, Philly.'

Theodora was desperately trying to spit the gag out of her mouth, her brain boiling with the angry desire to tell Winnie, *order* Winnie, to refuse.

'Don't do it, Winnie!' she wanted to shout. 'That *bitch* Philippa is going to torture me anyway, and this way she'll get *you* too.'

But even as she managed to get a little of the knicker-gag out, Philippa's index finger was calmly pushing it back in and Philippa was smiling down at her as she responded to Edwina.

'Thank you, Winnie. That is most . . . *philanthropic* of you. Well, dear, this is all you have to do. If you can receive three droplets of hot wax on your bare nip—'

But she had to break off, for Edwina, with a moan of fear, had begun to struggle against the hands that held her in place near Theodora's cunny.

'That's right, girls,' Philippa continued. 'Hold her in place while I finish explaining how she can rescue Dorrie from her pain. Though I suspect, from her reaction, that

142

she is already aware of what awaits her. Here, for the benefit of the rest of you, is the deal again, from the top. If you, Winnie dear, can receive three droplets of hot wax on your bare nipples without crying out, then Dorrie won't have to receive a single further droplet on her cunny. But for every sound you make – no matter how slight – Dorrie will have to receive three droplets on her cunny. Very well?'

But Edwina was incoherent with fear and apprehension, making Theodora feel sicker than ever. She had acted too well during her own torture, making poor Winnie think that the wax hurt far more than it did. Not that it *wouldn't* hurt – sting and burn very cruelly – on bare, unmoistened nipples, but Winnie was worrying more than she needed to.

'I'll take those rather odd noises you're making as a "Yes", Winnie, darling,' Philippa said. 'Though I'm afraid you already committed yourself by promising so sweetly that "I'll . . . I'll try." '

Her imitation of her victim, though far from impeccable, nevertheless caught the hesitation and unwilling bravery Edwina had displayed almost to perfection, and cruel laughter sounded around the bed. Theodora had to force herself not to grind her teeth with rage, and her body streamed and tingled with hot sweat as her head blazed with lurid visions of the vengeance she was going to take on everyone who was enjoying the mistreatment of Edwina and herself. Oh, yes, on everyone, but on smug, cruel, clever Philippa most of all.

'Prepare little Winnie, please,' Philippa said. 'Bend her over backwards, breasts pointing at the ceiling, and light another candle. Hilary can be holding hers ready over Dorrie's cunny – but careful not to drip, Hilary, unless Winnie breaks our little agreement – while we use the new one on Winnie's love— oh, and *aren't* they lovely?'

Eager hands had dragged Winnie to her feet and bent her upper body backwards, readying her tender, pink-nippled breasts for the new candle that other eager hands had already lit. Murmurs of appreciation greeted the sight of Edwina's nipples and Theodora tugged her head furiously against the hand that was fastened in her hair, trying to see them properly too.

'Yes,' Philippa continued, 'Winnie's nipples certainly are lovely, aren't they, girls? So pink, so tender, so ... *suckable*. Yes, so very suckable, and, do you know, I think they will meet that hot wax *much* better if they're well sucked beforehand and well-irrigated with blood. But who is going to prepare them? Dorrie is the obvious candidate, but, alas, she's *hors de combat* at present. Would anyone else like to volunteer?'

'Me, Philippa.'

'Me.'

'Me, Philippa. *Please*.'

'Me, Philippa. I would do it better than *anyone*.'

Eager volunteers' cries and hands went up from half the girls in the room, and Philippa shook her head, tutting with mock disapproval.

'So many of you *want*, no, I can more accurately say, *lust* to suck another girl's nipples? But this is *perversion*, girls. Whatever is young British maidenhood coming to? Well, I cannot make distinctions at such a degraded level. So you'll have to draw straws. Shortest straw wins.'

'But we don't have any straws, Philly,' Theodora heard someone – Jacky? – point out; and from the slight pause Philippa made before replying, Theodora knew that her enemy had smiled for a moment.

'Yes, perfectly correct, darling. But I was speaking metaphorically, knowing full well that we will have to *improvise*. For the degraded, indeed perverted, task of sucking dear Edwina's very pink and very tender young nipples, which so many of you seem so very eager to perform, you will have not to draw straws but *pluck hairs*, darlings. Longest hair wins. Very well?'

144

'Yes, but pluck hairs from *where*, Philly?'

Theodora's heart, suddenly beating faster, knew the answer before Theodora herself did.

'Where do you think? From Theodora's cunny, of course. Longest hair, as I said, wins. Well, get on with it. We haven't got all night. Come on, we'll do it in alphabetic order, by surname. You first, Gwen.'

More giggles, and now the hand locked in Theodora's hair, far from holding her down as she tried to lift her head, was relaxed to let her see what was about to take place further down her body. Another hand slipped between the scantily clad flanks crowded around the foot of the bed, fingers twiddling for a moment before it dropped to Theodora's cunny.

'Urgh,' came Gwen's voice, full of mock-disgust. 'Too low. She's positively *marshy* down there, Philippa.'

'Then select a hair from a less paludal spot, darling. Hurry up, now.'

'All right.'

Theodora tried, almost successfully, to control a shiver of involuntary pleasure as Gwen's fingers slid and tickled their way higher up her cunny, but Philippa's eyes were as maliciously observant as ever.

'Oh, girls, did you see that? The *slut* is *enjoying* it. If Gwen diddles her a *moment* longer she'll probably *come*, just watch her.'

More giggles from the eagerly watching girls around the bed, but Gwen had lifted her fingers away from Theodora's cunny and was wiping them on Theodora's thighs, left and right.

'No, we can't have her coming, Philly. Her thighs are wet too, but it's healthy sweat, at least.'

'Are you sure, Gwenny? I doubt that *anything* coming out of that slut's body is healthy. But come on, pluck a hair.'

Gwen's fingers, wiped mostly clean of cunny-juice, returned to Theodora's cunny, brushing it lightly before settling to her pubes, which they stroked through and ruffled before selecting a hair, taking firm hold of it, and . . . *plucking*. Theodora's body jerked with the pain of it, and her teeth ached from the force with which she was biting into the knicker-gag.

'Excellent, Gwen,' Philippa said. 'Next plucker, please. It's you, isn't it, Jacky?'

Carrying a cunny-hair torn out by the root, Gwen's hand withdrew and was replaced by Jacky's, which darted straight for Theodora's pubes and seized four or five hairs at once.

'Yes, as I was saying,' Philippa continued, 'I doubt that anything at all coming out of this slut's body is healthy. I swear her breath . . .'

She paused with an ill-suppressed chuckle of sadistic pleasure. Jacky had wrenched at the cunny-hairs she held, not tearing any of them up by the roots but making Theodora jerk again and release a faint squeak of pain through the knicker-gag.

'Come, come, Jacky. You're cheating. One hair at a time, not a dozen. Try again, you naughty girl. Now, where was I? Oh, yes. I swear Dorrie's breath smells the same after she's been sucking a cock as it does before. If the boy has *ejaculated* in her mouth it smells, if anything, *better*. So shall we re-christen her, girls? Excellent, Jacky. Now you, Hilary, *n'est-ce pas*? Yes, let's re-christen the slut. From now on, she's "Cock-breath". Excellent, Hilly. That looks a good one. Your turn, Katherine. Are we agreed then, girls? Dorrie's new name is "Cock-breath"? Well?'

But the girls were too excited by the nipple-sucking to respond and only a half-hearted chorus of agreement went up. Theodora's body jerked again as Katherine plucked a cunny-hair from her pubic mound.

'Good, Katy. You next and last, Zoë?'

Et tu, Zoë? Theodora shook her head with helpless anger, glad of the pain as the hand locked in her hair resisted the movement. The large hand of her betrayer pushed its way through the flanks of the girls clustered at the foot of the bed, hovered over her cunny a moment, then descended with artful clumsiness, so that two fingers found its way between her cunny-lips, probing, stroking. Theodora set her mouth, determined not to be softened by Zoë's gesture of reconciliation. Then the tall girl's forefinger and thumb were stroking at her pubes, selecting first one hair, then another, tugging each out, testing it for length and resistance, then plucking one out so swiftly and powerfully that Theodora barely felt the pain. The straight line of her lips relaxed a little. Zoë was ashamed of herself, that was clear, and Theodora knew how much she loved sucking Edwina's nipples. Perhaps she would claim that she acting in Edwina's best interests – shielding her from the possibly cruel mouth of another girl, who would not merely suck and lick but bite, gnaw and nip as well.

But Philippa was speaking again and Theodora pushed the thought of what action she would take against Zoë out of her mind.

'Now, girls, compare cunny-hairs. Hold them by each end and stretch them so we can all see which is longest. Longest wins, remember. Let's see . . . Well, I think we have a clear winner. What do the rest of you think? Marjorie? Daisy? Yes?'

Theodora stopped trying to raise her head. Who had won? Who was going to suck Edwina's nipples? Was it Jacky or Hilary? One of those two would *certainly* put the 'nip' into 'nipple' if she won, and poor Edwina's face would already be streaming with tears before the hot wax began to fall on her glistening areolae and mammillae. So who was it?

'Very well, we seem in general agreement,' Philippa was saying now. 'The winner, by rather more than a short hair, is *you*, Zoë. But I want to remind you, darling, that we don't want any *gentleness* when you are sucking. Edwina must, and will, be made aware that you have *teeth*. I confess that I have been sweating somewhat extravagantly in the past half-hour or so and I am in need of *salt*, my dear Zoë. Salt. Do you understand me? Is my meaning quite clear? Good. Then let sucking commence.'

Philippa's meaning was perfectly clear: she was going to lick Edwina's face when the nipple-sucking was over, and expected to find the younger girl's cheeks wet with tears. Theodora felt tears prick her own eyes at the thought of it and closed them, wishing she could close her ears too and block the sounds now invading her brain: Zoë's eager grunt as she was given permission to commence her work on Edwina's nipples; the kiss she gave first one nipple, then the other; then the slurps and pops, all the more obscene for their gentleness, as she began to lap at them, thoroughly moistening them before she began the sucking proper; the heavy, over-woven breath of the girls who watched, variously envying the girl sucking or the girl sucked; and, heart-piercingly clear and distinct through all else, Edwina's soft, involuntary murmurs of pleasure.

'Teeth, Zo,' said Philippa warningly, and Theodora clenched her teeth at the tiny cry of pain Edwina now released. Zoë had obediently nipped or gnawed at the tender morsel of breast-flesh in her mouth – perhaps both, for now Edwina cried out again with pain, then panted three times before releasing her first true moan of pleasure. Theodora tried to screw her eyes shut, but a treacherous trickle had escaped beneath them, and it was only a matter of time before . . .

'Oh, *look*, everyone,' Philippa remarked coolly. 'Cock-breath's suffering as much as Winnie is. Or . . .' Edwina released another moan of pleasure through the sniggers Philippa had provoked 'rather more, I'd say. I diagnose *jealousy*, my dears.'

148

'Jealousy of whom, Philly?' Jacky asked.

'Well, she can only be jealous of Zoë, I'd say,' Philippa said. 'Our little Cock-breath isn't one for *being* sucked on the nipples, if everything I hear is true. No, she's jealous of Zoë, but jealous in one or both of two possible ways. Zo's not only *sucking* Winnie, but *pleasuring* Winnie as she sucks. Rather too much, in fact!' she went on, raising her voice. 'Hey, Zoë, you're not trying to make the slut *come*, you're trying to prepare her nipples to have hot wax dripped on them. Tenderness is not called for here – we want *tenderisation*. Well?'

Zoë said something Theodora didn't understand, but Philippa evidently understood it well enough, for she snorted angrily.

'Oh, indeed, my girl? Well, you can just get your teeth to work on those tender little breasts or I can see half-a-dozen girls who will be *more* than happy to take your place.'

Zoë grunted something disdainful in reply, but a cry of pain from Edwina showed that she wasn't prepared to disobey. Although her eyes were still firmly closed, Theodora could picture the breast-sucking with more-than-natural clarity: the petite Edwina held firmly in place, looking more petite and delicate than ever by contrast with the tall, sturdily built girl whose strong, almost masculine head was bent over her ceiling-offered breasts, licking, sucking, gnawing, nipping, biting. Theodora's head whirled with her emotions, and certainly jealousy, as Philippa had astutely diagnosed, was a potent ingredient in the mix. But Philippa had been wrong to guess that she was suffering from one or both of two kinds of jealousy. No, she could not disguise from herself that *three* kinds of jealousy were at work: she was jealous of Zoë's sucking Edwina's nipples and of Zoë's giving Edwina pleasure, but also of Zoë's inflicting *pain* on Edwina.

Yes: the pain! The delicious spurts of pain Zoë was exciting in those tender young breasts with her strong white teeth, making Edwina whimper and gasp and cry out, simultaneously protesting at and welcoming the cruelty of her suckstress, for it mingled with and heightened the pleasure of her sucking and licking. But Philippa, somehow contriving, Theodora knew, to supervise the breast-sucking minutely while taking in the reaction of every girl in the room to it, most particularly hers, was not yet satisfied.

'Take her *whole* breast into your mouth, Zoë,' she ordered. 'Or as much of it as you can. Then *bite* into it, *gnaw* it, *nibble* it, working your mouth in a circle. I want to see tooth-marks ringing it *completely* when you take your mouth off to do the same to the other breast.'

Theodora's cunny spasmed in frustrated delight between her thighs and she felt thick dribbles of cunny-juice running over them and down between the cleft of her buttocks. The thought of it: Zoë's large, generous, wide-lipped mouth opening to draw in almost the whole of one of Edwina's small, firm breasts, then Zoë's strong white teeth getting to work again, ringing the breast with tooth-marks. Edwina gasped and moaned: Zoë's teeth were at work already. But what was that other sound? Oh, it was Zoë *humming* as she worked on the breast, pleasuring the nipple deep in her mouth with a tune Theodora struggled for a moment to recognise, then realised was Gilbert and Sullivan's "Tit Willow" from *The Mikado*.

Edwina suddenly gasped on a new note, responding to something someone else was doing to her. But what? Theodora strained her ears for information, unable to prevent the delicious images of Edwina's breast-abuse filling her head, making her cunny throb, her nipples ache with denied orgasm. Someone was pushing through the crowd of girls from near Zoë and Edwina, returning from whatever whoever-it-was had done to

Edwina. Who was it? But she knew before breath puffed at her ear and Philippa's malicious whisper was sewing itself into her vividly infected brain.

'Winnie is *loving* what Zoë is doing to her, Cockbreath. But really, the gasps you can hear from her don't convey this fact as fully as they might. *This* will assist them and help you build up a better picture of how she is *betraying* you.'

And Philippa's right forefinger, heavy with something moist, thick and musky, was rubbing at her upper lip and nostrils, thoroughly coating and clogging them. The forefinger left her skin and breath puffed at her ear again.

'There it is, darling, I mean, Cock-breath. I hope it doesn't make your 'tache grow back.'

Theodora felt a sob of commingled rage, humiliation, jealousy and raw, ravenous lust swell in her chest, heightening the ache in her nipples almost to a sting. She bit it down, refusing to allow it to pass her lips and give Philippa additional satisfaction, feeling her cunny throb and squirm, as though it truly was a second mouth and was chewing eagerly at the rich mixture of emotion in the suppressed sob. She knew now what Philippa had done to Edwina: poked and probed her forefinger into the breast-abused girl's cunny, before carrying away a heavy load of cunny-juice to rub on her, Theodora's, upper lip and nostrils. And Philippa's malicious whisper had been right: the sounds of Edwina's pleasure were nothing to this stark physical symbol of it, redolent of the quantity and aroma of the juice pouring from that well-loved, well-licked cunny.

'The other breast now, Zo,' Philippa drawled, pausing over Theodora's body to deliver a final cruelty. 'And I want to see a complete circle of tooth-marks, remember.'

As she spoke, she tugged and tweaked at Theodora's swollen, juice-slimed cunny-lips and stroked delicately, almost imperceptibly, at the orgasm-famished horn of her clitoris. Theodora's body began to tremble, ready to shake and spasm before plunging into its long-denied climax, but Philippa, with a soft chuckle, had already lifted her hand away.

'Oh, *yes*, Zoë. That is *perfect*. Look, girls: see how Zoë has ringed Winnie's left breast *completely* with tooth-marks. Now for the right breast, Zoë. Set to work, my darling.'

Theodora could barely breathe and felt her heart beating so fast that it seemed to purr inside her chest: Philippa's cunny-tickling, so gentle but so cruel, had promised so much and delivered absolutely nothing. And now the aural torment continued: having to listen to Philippa order Zoë to begin work on Edwina's right breast, then the renewed humming of "Tit Willow", the sound of Edwina's response: her moans, her gasps, her sobs. But then Theodora grunted with triumph: one of the girls holding down her left wrist had been concentrating too hard on the mouthing of Edwina's right breast, and with a sudden jerk, assisted by the sweat that was flowing over her whole body, but especially where skin touched her skin, Theodora had dragged it free and was frotting furiously at her cunny.

'Stop her!' Philippa cried instantly. The bitch was as watchful as ever: noting everything of importance that was going on in the dormitory. Three hands grappled simultaneously for Theodora's, but she smiled mirthlessly: her frotting hand was as slippery as an eel now, coated not only with sweat but also with the juice that was pouring from her cunny, and three hands were too many. They got in each other's way, and grabbed as much, or more, at her cunny as at the hand that was frotting it so hard. Yes, they were *helping* her to her orgasm, just give her another couple of seconds and she would be there . . .

'Here, girls. Let me show you how it's done.'

152

The calm, unhurried efficiency of Philippa's voice made Theodora's stomach tighten with dismay a fraction before, with the same calm, unhurried efficiency, she gripped Theodora by the elbow with both hands and pulled her arm free, dragging her frotting hand inevitably with it.

'See?' Philippa said. 'You were battering on the locked front door when the back door was open all the time.'

Theodora writhed with frustration, feeling pre-orgasm boiling in her whole body but most particularly in her breasts, nipples, inner thighs and cunny. Oh, all she needed was another second's worth of friction on her cunny and she would erupt. Or on her nipples, on just one of her nipples – that would do equally well. But all that touched them now was air and her wrists and ankles were being held more firmly than ever. She heard Philippa's cruel chuckle.

'Careful now, girls. We can all see that Cock-breath, Theodora as she used to be known, is in a most dangerous condition. Think of her as unexploded *gunpowder* – all she needs is a spark and she will blow to Kingdom Come.'

She broke off for a moment as Edwina released an especially loud moan.

'And I suspect she's not the only one. Careful with Cock-breath's little companion too, Zoë. We can't have her exploding either. But I think I have a solution for the earlier problem, that posed by Cock-breath herself. We must draw the *heat* out of her most vulnerable spots, thus reducing their dangerous inflammation.'

Another loud moan from Edwina interrupted her.

'Careful, I said, Zoë! In fact, you can stop now and we'll get ready for the wax-dripping. But first we'll deal with Cock-breath. Volunteers, please, to *blow* on her cunny and nipples. Three girls are needed in all. Right, you three then, Jacky, Hilary and Gwen. But who's

153

going to take her cunny? No, don't try to pretend, darlings, I know you'd *all* like to be blowing on her cunny. I know a way. Where's a coin? Thank you, Frances. Now, choosing one from three fairly with a coin will be a little tricky. Let's think ... Right, girls, what each of you has to do first is make a fist behind your back. If you want heads, push your thumb between your forefinger and middle-finger, like this, see? If you want tails, push it between your middle-finger and your ring-finger, like this. Understood? Good, then do it, please.

'Done? Then I'll toss the coin. Show your fists, please. And ... heads it is. Ah, Hilary, you're out, and I'll have to toss again to choose between you, Jacky, and you, Gwen. Fists behind backs, please, and choose a side. Show your fists, please. And ... heads it is again. Great minds think alike, eh? Fists behind backs, please. Show fists please. And ... heads again. At last. Right, take your positions then and on the count of three, begin. Head ready between her legs, Jacky, you at her left tit, Hilary, and you at her right, Gwen. Good. On the count of three, remember. *Un ... deux ... attendez-vous, attendez-vous, mes petites impatientes ... et trois.*'

Theodora bucked her hips and rocked her shoulders with a snarl of frustration. They had begun blowing on her nipples and cunny.

'Slow but steady, girls,' Philippa ordered. 'Take a lungful of air and *ration* it. But not too slow. There's a delicate balance to be struck and a possibility that Cock-breath, perverted as she is, will learn to take pleasure in being blown upon. That's it. Excellent. Now, carry on while we get Edwina ready for her waxing.'

Theodora bucked and rocked again, unable to prevent another snarl of frustration escaping her lips. Philippa had been right again, damn her: she *had* been beginning to take pleasure in the breath being blown across her left nipple, but now Jacky had lowered the rate at which she was blowing and the pleasure was no longer there. How cruel they were being to her. Bringing her to the point of orgasm, then dragging her back from the brink. But cruellest of all, chief tormentrix, Inquisitrix General, was Philippa, who was now speaking again.

'Ah, so there little Winnie's nipples are. *Look* at them, girls. How they glisten with Zoë's spittle! And they're *stiff* too, look. What an excitable little thing she is, to be sure. But we have a cure for that, in our hot wax. Light the candle again, darlings. But first, as I mentioned before, I need to renew my *salt* and Winnie, most considerately, has shed copious quantities of salted water on her cheeks. Here, let me lick them before we begin to drip hot wax on her nipples.'

Theodora writhed again, picturing Philippa seize Edwina by her hair and pull her face close to begin licking the tears that glistened on her cheeks from the nipple-torture. Yes, from Edwina's squeak of protest, that was exactly what Philippa was doing. Her long red tongue was out, passing up and down Edwina's right cheek.

'Mmmm,' came Philippa's voice. 'Lovely. Little Winnie's skin . . .' she broke off, licking again 'mmmm, yes, little Winnie's skin provides the *perfect* foil for the salt of her tears. It is . . .' another pause, another lick of Edwina's glistening cheeks 'mmmm, it is so smooth, so creamy, so *sweet*. But I must finish what is on my plate and not hold up the nipple-waxing any further.'

Theodora writhed, her inflamed brain manufacturing vivid, tormenting images from the soft sounds of Philippa's face-licking, the murmurs of appreciation from Philippa herself, the murmurs of protest – but also pleasure – from Edwina. Finally, with a gasp, Philippa pulled back.

'Delicious. Most delicious. I can recommend it to *all* of you, girls, if you ever get the chance. Licking tears from Edwina's face is an experience to be treasured.

And I suspect there will shortly be the opportunity for some lucky girl, chosen by a long hair, to experience it again. Is the candle lit? Good: then let the dripping of hot wax on Winnie's nipples commence. And please,' she continued over Edwina's cries of protest, 'you girls holding Theodora down, do not let your concentration lapse as you watch and enjoy the spectacle. She will have another hand free and frotting at her cunny in an *instant* if you do so.'

The grip tightened on Theodora's wrists and ankles and she closed her eyes with a prayer to Our Lady of Tortures. But it was not so much prayer as bargain. Yes, she would endure her own torment, endure the sound of Edwina's torment, but Our Lady must regard it as a payment for a future prize: the uninterrupted and undisputed possession of Philippa's body for as long and as lingeringly as she and Edwina pleased.

Ten

'Théodora,' came the husky whisper from behind her; and Theodora had to clutch at the windowsill to keep herself from sliding with a wail to the floor. Her knees had positively turned to water.

'Turn around, Théodora,' came the whisper again. 'Face your *maître*, you disobedient but, ô, I cannot deny it, most delicious young woman.'

She clutched the windowsill tighter, feeling that she would surely fall over if she released it and began to turn. But there was no disobeying the Doctor; and so, with thudding heart and quavering lips, she released the sill and turned. Somehow her knees held her up, but she could not lift her gaze to meet the Doctor's face as he strode towards her.

'What are you doing here, *ma* Théodora?' he asked. 'And look at me as you reply.'

She swallowed, backing involuntarily against the sill as she lifted her eyes to the cold anger in his face. He stopped and stood a few yards from her, arms folded on his chest. A perverse spark of laughter flashed up inside her, but she forced it down, not wanting to anger him any further.

'I ... I am exploring, Doctor,' she said, suddenly sober again. Her eyes had dropped to his trousers for a moment and she had seen the bulge growing there – the bulge of his two swiftly erecting cocks.

'Exploring? But you have no permission, no right, to explore the *château*. Is that not so?'

She swallowed again.

'Yes, Doctor.'

'Then you must be punished, must you not?'

She opened her mouth but could not speak. She nodded slowly.

'I said, "Then you must be punished, must you not?" Answer my question, Théodora.'

Her right hand went to her throat and she tried to massage away the constriction in it. She managed to swallow.

'Y-yes, Doctor.'

'*Bien.* Then what would be a suitable punishment for you, *ma petite fille?*'

She shook her head.

'I . . . I don't know, Doctor.'

The suddenness with which he strode towards her, seizing her by the shoulder and spinning her to face the uncurtained window again, made her cry out with fright.

'If you do not know,' his whisper came in her ear, 'I have a suggestion. You have taken something illicitly from me, namely the privacy of my domain, therefore I shall take something licitly from you. Very well?'

She was unable to answer.

'I will accept silence as affirmation,' he whispered. 'But first . . .' she cried out again, for he had lifted the hem of her skirt and was sliding a warm hand into her knickers and beginning to fondle her buttocks 'we must get to the *bottom*, my girl, of precisely what your explorations were designed to uncover. Describe to me, *ma* Théodora, what it is you see from the window.'

She shuddered, half-suppressing another cry of surprise and distress, so that it turned into a squeak in her throat. The Doctor's large, warm forefinger had found her bottom-hole and was rubbing at it. She heard him grunt with satisfaction.

158

'*Vas-toi*,' his whisper came. 'Describe to me what you see from the window.'

'I . . . I see a garden, Doctor.'

'And in the garden?'

She shuddered again, unable to prevent herself jerking forward, for now his forefinger was pushing at her bottom-hole, trying to find its way inside. Her mind whirled as she tried to think of a way of escape, but she was trapped against the window and he had her bottom at his mercy. Completely at his mercy.

'Compose yourself, you foolish girl,' the Doctor whispered. 'I am testing a route I will shortly be travelling.'

The scene in front of her – the sun-lit tropical garden dotted with scantily clad girls – went black and she had to clutch at the sill again as her knees gave way completely. A route he would shortly be travelling? Then, dear God, he was going to – what was the word? – *bagger* her.

'Excellent,' the Doctor whispered. He withdrew his forefinger. 'You most certainly still possess the maidenhead of your anus, my dear, and it will afford me the most piquant satisfaction to deflower you there.'

This time she did faint. She awoke with a cry of protest to find the Doctor's hands squeezing her breasts as she hung from two leather wrist-straps on either side of the window. Her consciousness darted into her body, reading what had been done to her while she was unconscious. She was still wearing her dress but her knickers were off, her bra had been levered down over her breasts, and her ankles were strapped wide apart.

'Ah, you return,' the Doctor whispered in her ear, 'and find yourself prepared for your punishment.'

Now she felt something odd about her bottom-hole: it was cool – no, not simply cool, but moist.

'But first you must repair an omission. You have not yet told me, my dear, all it is that you see from the window. "I see a garden", that is all you have told me. But what else do you see, *ma chère* Théodora?'

What had he been doing to her bottom? But a vague dream-memory was surfacing through the darkness of her faint. He had licked her there, moistening and lubricating her bottom-hole in preparation for . . .

'Answer me, my girl. What else do you see from the window?'

She was trembling, her stomach contracted into a ball of fright, but began to gabble an answer as his hands tightened impatiently on her breasts.

'Girls, Doctor,' she said. 'I see naked girls.'

'Ah. So you do, my dear. You see naked girls in the garden. But are they girls you know, my dear?'

His hands left her breasts and she felt him lifting the hem of her skirt, exposing her bottom to the air, making the spittle on her bottom-hole feel cooler still. His forefinger rubbed at it for a moment and he was evidently pleased with what it reported, for she heard him give a grunt of satisfaction. She shook her head, feeling tears begin to trickle from her eyes.

'No, Doctor,' she said faintly, hoarsely. 'I do not know them.'

'Exactly so, my dear,' he whispered, his voice growing fainter as he released her hem and seemed to stoop to the floor. Yes, stoop to the floor: she felt his hands testing her ankle-straps. Then his voice was level again as he straightened to test the wrist-straps.

'You do not know them, but you hoped to know them, did you not? In fact, you hoped to *recruit* them for your little rebellion, did you not?'

She forgot her fear for a moment. He knew! He knew what they had been planning. She was a fly in the web of his spider again: lured on to her doom. He completed testing the wrist-straps and lifted her hem again.

'It was a chimera, *ma chère* Théodora. It is strange, is it not, that not one of those girls has yet noticed what is taking place in the window that overlooks them? That not one of them has noticed the beautiful young woman strapped in the window and waiting in some distress, fine firm breasts on full display, for her condign punishment?'

She cried out. His forefinger had returned to her bottom-hole and was pushing hard at it, trying to slide inside. She shook her head, seizing on his question as a means of distracting herself from his digital assault. Yes, it *was* strange that none of the girls in the garden had noticed what was taking place in the window. There was no curtain in it and a mere glance up would reveal what the Doctor had described: the beautiful young woman strapped in the window and waiting in some distress, fine firm breasts on full display, for her condign punishment.

'Open for me, you slut,' the Doctor whispered harshly in her ear. She tried to obey but her bottom was beyond her control: her buttock-cheeks were clenching hard, trying to shield her bottom-hole from his finger.

'*Non?*' the Doctor whispered. 'You will not allow me to prepare the passage of something much larger? Very well, then. On your own head be it.'

His finger left her bottom and he released the hem of her skirt. She heard him begin to unbutton his trousers, musing aloud as he did so.

'You know, *chérie*, it is one of the many blessings of my double endowment that I can possess a young woman by both lower orifices at once. Even as you yield the maidenhead of *ton cul* to me, you shall yield the maidenhead of *ton con*. But I assure you, my dear, that however frantic your struggles and however loud your cries, you shall not attract the slightest attention from the girls in the gardens ... *Et voilà*, I am ready. Picture them, Théodora, picture the two throbbing shafts that wait hungrily behind you, one eager to possess your *cunny*, the other eager to possess your *bottom*.'

And against her will, Theodora *was* picturing them, and picturing them in the minutest detail: the thick, vein-crawled shafts, the solid purple heads, glowing with heat behind the half-drawn curtain of the foreskins. She moved her lips and tongue uneasily as her mouth remembered the feel and taste of the Doctor's cock, thrust there, cramming it before it spurted the thick, almost scalding load of the three balls he had forced her and Edwina to fondle as he approached orgasm. The monstrosity of his anatomy, which she had managed almost to forget after her second ordeal in the interview-room, struck her again with its full force. Her stomach lurched with nausea and her head swam with unreality. She was trembling, shivering as though with great cold, but her body went rigid as she felt body-warmed air brush her skin from behind. Then she cried out, for the Doctor had gripped her with his left hand while his right presented his cocks, one after the other, to the holes of her bottom and cunny.

'There,' he whispered in her ear, resting his chest against her back. 'I am ready, *chérie*, and thou mayst begin thy futile resistance.'

He thrust at her with a grunt and she came out of her paralysis. By twisting her hands in their wrist-straps, she was able to bring her fingers over the glass of the window and begin to rap on it hard, staring pleadingly down at the girls in the garden. Surely, surely if they saw what was being done to her, in full view, they would rush to her assistance. Another grunt from the Doctor, and Theodora bit her lip, still rapping frantically on the window as the pressure of his glowing cockheads on her bottom-hole and cunny increased yet further.

'I will be up thee in a minute, *chérie*,' the Doctor whispered, his voice hoarser and more sinister than ever. 'But pray continue thy most pleasurable resistance. Overcoming it will add a piquant spice to my inevitable conquest.'

Another grunt, another increase in the pressure on her lower orifices, but not a stir of movement from the sun-bathing girls in the garden. They must be able to hear her, they *must*, it was simply not possible that they were *all* deaf. Her whole body was running with sweat: she could feel it pouring down her spine and between the breasts crushed against the window by the weight of the Doctor's body. Another grunt from the Doctor, another increase in the pressure on her bottom-hole and cunny. She was rapping on the glass so hard and fast now that she hoped it was going to break. Then she gasped with relief and stopped rapping on the window: the cockheads crammed against her lower orifices were suddenly gone and the Doctor's weight eased from her back. She heard him panting with effort and excitement, then swallowing.

'Yes, you are a stubborn one, *chérie*,' he whispered. 'But I have an effective remedy.'

Then his hands were on her again, sliding in the sweat-soaked grooves of her body, fore and aft, then beginning to massage sweat into her bottom-hole and cunny with slow, lingering strokes. His fingertips seemed to burn her, but burn pleasurably, and she realised to her horror that her cunny, at least, was responding, beginning to mingle its own juice with the sweat he was working into its lips and hole. Then she wailed with dismay: her bottom had betrayed her too, relaxing its sphincter sufficiently for the Doctor's forefinger to slide inside her. She tried to clench her sphincter shut on it, trapping it there, but he was too strong for her and the finger slid deeper into her. Now he rotated it and she was unable to resist a shudder of pleasurable surrender. Her whole attention was centred on her bottom, on the sensitive nerves of the sphincter he had penetrated, and she barely felt the fingers still working at her cunny, though her cunny obviously did, for it was gaping greedily and juicily to admit them.

She bit back a cry of disappointment. His forefinger had withdrawn from her bottom and his hand from her cunny.

'Are you ready now, *chérie*?' he asked her. 'But perhaps just a little more preparation *here*.'

He was massaging cunny-juice into her bottom-hole, sliding two fingertips at a time into her treacherous sphincter, lubricating her thoroughly for her buggery.

'*Et voilà, tu es prête.* Brace thyself, slave: I am going up thee.'

His left hand gripped her as before, and as before his right presented his cockheads to her cunny and bottom. But how differently she received them! The remnants of her resistance were like cakes of ice whirling on a boiling flood of lust, shrinking even as they whirled, fragmenting so that they shrank still faster. She tried to start rapping on the window again, but the sound was so feeble, so clearly revealing that she was eager to receive him, that she burst into tears of shame and humiliation. In the next instant he had thrust and his twin cockheads shouldered aside her last efforts at resistance and surged up into her. The sensation was like nothing she had ever experienced, or ever imagined she could experience. Oh, like most of the girls she had experimented with vegetables and other substitute phalluses, pushing them gently into her cunny as she frotted herself with excitement, but the sensation of a shaft of hot, throbbing, all-too-solid flesh sliding urgently into her cunny was of an entirely different and stronger kind.

But even that paled by comparison with the sensation of a shaft of hot, throbbing, all-too-solid flesh sliding into her bottom. The Doctor slowed his thrust, as though catching her thoughts and wanting her to savour the bitter-sweetness of the penetration to the last drop. But what was most bitter about the penetration was that it was also sweet. She choked with near-hysterical laughter at the thought of it, and heard the Doctor laugh with her, softly in her ear.

'You are enjoying it, eh, *ma* Théodora? I – ah – guessed – ah – that – ah – you – ah – *would*.'

He had begun to thrust in and out of her, crushing her body and breasts repeatedly against the window, through which she could still see the unconcerned sun-bathers. How strange it felt to be raped by cunny and bottom in full view of so many and have not the slightest attention paid to the rape. She was starting to float now, lifted on the rhythm of his thrusts, feasting on the double penetration, the double loss of her virginities, and eagerly anticipating the spurting of his semen into her, so that she could compare and contrast the sensations of it. What a very lucky girl she was! If the Doctor had only one cock, she would have to compare cock-in-cunny and cock-in-bottom sequentially, setting reality against memory, but he had *two* cocks, so she could compare them simultaneously, setting reality against reality. She laughed with true hysteria now at the thought of it, drunk on sensation as a maenad from the twin goads of cock-flesh he was wielding repeatedly against her flesh.

The gasps and grunts in her ear, each coming with a gust of hot breath, turned into a long groan: her laughter, shuddering in her body, had evidently triggered his orgasm. Yes, yes, she could feel his semen spurting into her, thick and creamy and boiling. She counted the shafts-fired-from-his-shafts, not wanting them to end: she had a vision of his semen entirely filling her bowels, swelling her stomach, forcing its way up her throat so that, choking, spluttering, she had to let it pour into her mouth and out, flooding over her chin and soaking her breasts, her belly, her legs. But he was a man and not a monster after all, for the force and volume of the semen spurting into her was weakening, shrinking, fading to nothing.

'No! No!' she wailed, splattering the glass in front of her face with spittle. 'Don't stop! Don't stop! Fill me! Swell me! Burst me!'

The Doctor released a last long shuddering groan in her ear, sighed with repletion, then licked and nibbled her ear, rocking his now quiescent and slowly softening cocks gently in her cunny and bottom-hole.

'Ah, if only I could, *chérie*,' he whispered. 'To fill, to swell such a beautiful body as yours with my seed, what finer ambition could there be? But to *burst* you with my seed, Théodora, ah, thereto I cannot aspire, though 'twould be worthy of a place among my great-great-grandfather's incarcerated fantasies. You too – oh, my sweet,' he broke off, 'my sweet, my poppet, my most excellent and enduring *putain*, you accomplish the impossible and already begin to re-erect me.'

For Theodora, feeling an ache of loss at the softening of his cocks in her cunny and bottom-hole, had drawn a deep breath and begun to raise and lower herself on him as she hung from her wrist-straps, trying to tighten herself on his cocks, to squeeze them as they reached their greatest depth inside her. And it was as the Doctor had said: he was beginning to re-erect. She could feel it too, and she delighted in it, gratified not only that her lust had been rewarded but that she had regained a sliver of control over her situation. And more than a sliver: she had demonstrated her power to re-erect her master, to interrupt his discourse and draw praise from him, and the glow of greedy lust in her cunny and bottom-hole strengthened with her self-satisfaction. Could he feel how she glowed? Were his cocks delighting not only in the tightness and friction her cunny and bottom-hole provided, but also their heat?

He grunted, nibbling her ear again, but more forcefully, more dominantly, and now his hands came round her body, pushing between the window and her squashed breasts, taking hold of them, squeezing them fiercely as he responded to her movements on his cocks and began to thrust in time with them.

'Thank you, my darling,' he whispered. 'I cannot hope that I will be able to re-moisten your luscious interior with further shafts of seed, but you provide a most satisfactory accompaniment – ah, indeed you do – a *most* satisfactory accompaniment as I take up my interrupted thread and return to my great-great-grand-father's incarcerated fantasies. Yes – ah, *chérie*, I could swear that your genius for pleasuring an exhausted cock, ah, *two* exhausted cocks, smacks somewhat, *mon Dieu*, of the *diabolic* – but, yes, to return to your request that I fill you, swell you, burst you, the former two tasks I would be delighted to perform, but the last, no, my sweet, I could not aspire to it before and can aspire to it less with every moment that passes. Oh, you possess a cunny and bottom in a million, Théodora, and you bewitch me back through, yes, through time, yes, I believe, yes, *mon Dieu*, *mon Dieu*, oh, *ma petite diablesse*, it is fifteen years and more, I swear it, oh, ah, ah, ah . . .'

Theodora's heart, beating fast and heavily in her chest as she received his thrusts, seemed to throb separately with happiness and pride. She had conquered her conqueror. It had not been *his* choice to begin *fucking* her again, no, not at all, but she had enticed him to it, raising and lowering himself gently on him, making his cocks begin to re-stiffen, re-exciting his lust, re-pleasuring him to the point, the impossible point, as she believed he was trying to tell her, that he was going to *ejaculate* again inside her, as he had not done so quickly with a girl for 'fifteen years and more'. And this time his sexual frenzy was more abandoned: he was thrusting at her more brutally, less scientifically, crush-ing her body against the window as he had not during the first fucking, and his sweat and hers was splattering against the window, running down it, blurring and distorting the girls who basked in the sunny garden outside.

With a last groan and convulsive, almost despairing clutch at her breasts, the Doctor thrust his cocks deep into her – she could feel his pubic hair rasp the stretched rim of her sphincter – and began to spurt again. The first shafts were almost as weak as the final shafts of his previous ejaculation, but they seemed to affect her nerves far more vigorously, to hammer into her more thickly, more creamily, more boilingly, so that she felt as though truly she was being filled, swelled by them, and even opened her mouth with a proleptic belch, expecting her overladen bowels and semen-filled belly at any moment to begin pouring their treasure up her throat. It did not come, but she kissed the window and licked at the sweat trickling down it. The sweat of two bodies: hers and the Doctor's, mingling on the window as their sexual fluids mingled in her cunny. But could she say their sexual fluids mingled also in her bottom?

She pondered the question, wondering vaguely how he managed to keep ejaculating into her before realising that she was mistaking the pulse of her heart for the pulse of his semen: her entire body had been hollowed and sensitised by her second fucking, so that she could not tell, only deduce, where a sensation was coming from, for the nerves of her toes sang with the trickle of sweat down her forehead and her heart seemed to be beating everywhere inside her. The Doctor groaned in her ear, licking it, nibbling it again, and slowly beginning to slide his cocks out of her. She moaned with disappointment, attempting to tighten her cunny and bottom-hole on him, keeping his cocks nailed into her body, but he was whispering urgently in her ear.

'Please, *ma chérie*, do not tempt me to a third invasion of your interior. For your sake I ask it, *ma chérie.*'

She did not obey, trying to clench harder on him, but she was too well lubricated now, her twin lower orifices too semen-slicked and heat-swollen to retain him. But his cocks were not softening: they were sliding out of her as stiff and solid as when they first slid in, as though the pleasure she had given them had broken their mechanism and he would remain henceforward permanently priapic. She chuckled at the thought of it even as she winced and murmured to feel her cunny and bottom-hole deserted – his cocks came out with pops and squelches – and their stretched tissues relaxing. The Doctor pulled his hands from her breasts and she murmured again as they pressed flat to the window, making her feel the imprint of his fingers.

Then she grunted and came partly out of her ecstatic daze. The Doctor's hands, hot and sticky with her breast-sweat, had taken hold of her buttocks and gently begun to lever them apart, sending an arrow of pain through her bottom-hole and into her semen-congested bowels. She could feel his breath on her bottom, on her bottom-hole, exquisitely sensitised by its baggery, and realised he was stooping to examine her anus. He began whispering and she shook her head, trying to clear it so she could understand what he was saying.

'Oh, but my darling, *ma petite*, what is it I have done to you? I should not, I should never have re-invaded a bottom from which I had so recently plucked the flower of its virginity.'

The pain had dissolved now into a glowing warmth, but flared again, piercing the warmth as the Doctor touched her anus, running a finger around its swollen, cockhead-invaded, cockshaft-rasped rim, then pushed the finger inside her. But now the new pain was dissolving into the warmth and she murmured with pleasure, trying to push her bottom out against his invading finger. He withdrew it with a grunt of unease, provoking another spurt of pain that was soon dissolving into the glowing warmth of her violated bottom.

'My darling, I have corrupted you too soon. Your bottom has tasted cock-meat too quickly and is too eager to taste it again. Here, I must lift you down and take you somewhere you can rest.'

She heard a rattle of leather and metal as he began to undo her ankle-straps. *Cock-meat*, he had said. Yes. Her

cunny and bottom had gorged on cock-meat, and were
eager to gorge again. He had converted her from
herbivore to carnivore and she wished to make up for
her years of abstinence. She licked her lips, tasting sweat
on them, and tried to speak. Only a croak came out.
The Doctor had finished undoing her ankle-straps and
was working on her right wrist-strap. She tried again.

'Doctor . . .' she managed to say.

'Hush, my darling.'

He was working on her left wrist-strap now, one arm
supporting her, ready to take the weight of her body as
she sank from the window. She shook her head.

'No, Doctor. Please, Doctor. Bagger me again. Fuck
me again.'

The final strap came loose and she fell back into his
arms.

'Hush, my darling. I must take you to rest.'

'No, Doc—' she began to say, then broke off with a
giggle, drunk on pleasure, drunk on cock-meat, as a
thought struck her. *Actions speak louder than words,*
Dorrie, she told herself. The Doctor had his hands
clasped around her body, carrying her to a rest she did
not want. She shook her head, trying to concentrate as
she clenched and unclenched her right hand, then
reached for him. She giggled again at his gasp, and
squeezed harder at what she had in her hand: one of his
cocks, still semi-erect, still moist with their mingled
secretions.

'Théodora!'

She reached for and seized his other cock with her left
hand.

'Cock-meat. I want cock-meat. Bagger me again,
Doctor. Fuck me again –'

But breath rushed out of her as the Doctor's arms
tightened convulsively on her. Was he angry? Did he
mean to refuse her? Ah, no, no: she giggled again and
gurgled with pleasure. His cocks were slowly but

170

unmistakably re-erecting in her hands. She had successfully aroused him and she opened her mouth again,
urged by instinct to repeat her plea.

'Doctor,' she whispered, for his arms were still
half-crushing the breath out of her, 'bagger me again.
Fuck me again.'

He groaned. She managed to get her feet planted
firmly on the floor again and pushed upward fractionally against him, then lowered herself, then pushed
upward again, then lowered herself, rubbing her body
against his. Another groan from him, and now her
breath *was* completely crushed out of her body, for his
arms had tightened yet further. She could barely whisper now, but still had a request to make of him. But
what for: breath or baggery?

'Doctor, bagger me again. Fuck me again.'

There was a moment, two moments, three in which she
could feel her heart pounding more and more strongly in
her oxygen-starved body, then he groaned again.

'*Noooooooon.*'

She drew in breath with an ecstatic whoop, for his
arms had released her body and he was lowering her
face-down to the floor.

'Release my cocks, Théodora,' he ordered. 'Release
them, you slut. Or I cannot invade you again.'

Now she obeyed after a final squeeze. They were
almost fully erect again, almost ready to invade her for
the third time.

'Bagger me, Doctor. Fuck me.'

She was face-down on the floor, trying to raise her
bottom to him, wriggling it at him as she opened her
thighs, encouraging him on with sight of the two
glistening orifices she wished him to re-fill. She heard
him grunt with lust, and then his hands were on her
body, roughly dragging her over.

'It's "bugger", you ignorant slut. And we'll have you
on your back. Yes, we'll have you on your back and

171

have you on your back. Each cock can taste a different slut-slot.'

She grunted with lust herself now, nipples peaking and cunny and bottom-hole throbbing at the thought that a new cock would be invading it. She licked her lips as she lay on her back and gorged her eyes on the two erect cocks jutting from the Doctor's groin. He was standing over her, straddling her, but making no move to begin.

'Bagger me, Doctor,' she pleaded. '*Bugger* me. And fuck me.'

And then, greatly daring, she issued an order of her own: '*Vite, vite, vite.*'

She heard the Doctor laugh.

'*Patiente-toi, ma sale petite.* I cannot invade your cunny with a cock still dripping with the rich alluvial spoils of your bottom. *Entendrez-vous, mes fils?*'

Running feet sounded on the floor, moving away from them, and she blinked, lifting her head and trying to see who it was.

'*Non, ma sale* Théodora, *ma sale petite, ma sale chérie,* I cannot fuck you with a cock with which I have so recently "baggered" you. Oh, to think that an hour ago you were so ignorant of the procedure that you did not even know its true name. And yet look at you now.'

She felt air move against her breasts and painfully erect nipples as he stooped to her, slipping a hand between her legs and tickling at her bottom-hole with his forefinger. She moaned and wriggled against it, trying to force it up her bottom. With an indulgent chuckle he pulled the finger free and wagged it at her.

'Yes, look at you now, you slut. An hour ago so ignorant, then after two helpings of cock-meat your bottom is ravenous for a third. Ah, here they come.'

Feet were running over the floor again, returning to them. Drops of warm water suddenly hit her face and she blinked up at a servant's hands and arms as they sponged at the Doctor's upper cock, cleaning it so that he could insert it in her cunny. As the sponge came away she saw how it glistened, throbbing slightly from the warmth of the water and the vigour with which it had been sponged. She swallowed, feeling a positive *hunger* in her cunny, a carnivorous craving for her nether mouth to be filled, to be *crammed*, *choked* with cock-meat.

'*Vite*,' she said again, running a too-large tongue around her swollen and aching lips. '*Vite. Vite, maître.*'

'*Patiente-toi, ma sale petite*,' the Doctor said. He said something in French to the servant and when the sponge returned to his cock a male hand had taken hold of the shaft and tugged back the foreskin, fully exposing the huge plum of the cockhead. The Doctor grunted as the sponge set to work on it and Theodora grunted herself, further inflamed with lust at the sight of a male hand on the Doctor's cock. It was so *perverse*, and she wondered whether the Doctor's taste for 'buggery' had ever led him to sample – ah, her stomach rolled at the thought of it, but she felt her cunny simultaneously gape wider and gush more copiously – to sample a *male* bottom. Suddenly she longed to see it, or rather to be near it – sucking herself on the Doctor's lower cock as he forced his upper cock into the tight white bottom of some muscular youth, then tasting the doubly copious gush of his seed as he came.

The Doctor's whisper, harsh with the excitement of having his cock sponged, brought her out of her fantasy.

'Why do you smile, *ma* Théodora?' he asked, brusquely waving the servant away and stooping to seize and position her for his double penetration. 'Do you dream already of my cocks inserted to the full in your tender cunny and bottom-hole?'

She moaned to feel his hands on her body and shook her head, muttering thickly in reply, then shuddering as he laid first one, then the other, of his cocks to the orifices that awaited them.

'What is that, *ma* Théodora?' came his whisper again. 'You do dream of this? Then . . .' he thrust and they issued a simultaneous groan of pleasure as his cocks slid into their sheaths 'then, *ma chère*, tell me, tell me as I tup thee – ah – tell me what it was that brought thee to smiling as thou layst there whilst I was prepared for thee.'

He had pushed himself into her as he spoke, forcing both of his cocks up her to the roots, stretching and tightening the already-sensitised tissues of her cunny and bottom. She tried to savour the sensations of the double penetration, but they were too strong: he was fucking her again too quickly, giving her too little time to recover.

'Tell me, thou slut,' he whispered. 'Or I shall *not* tup thee.'

She had been struggling to breathe; now the threat made her gasp with anxiety, fearful that he would fulfil his threat – that he would withdraw from her, leaving the sheaths of her cunny and bottom collapsed on themselves. She shook her head, trying to focus up at him.

'I . . . I was fantasising, Doctor.'

'Ah.'

His hands tightened on her body and he rewarded her with a half-thrust, sending a bolt of mingled pain and pleasure through her body.

'Tell me more. Of what were you fantasising?'

'Of . . . of you, Doctor.'

'Yes?'

Another semi-withdrawal and another vigorous thrust, another bolt of pain-and-pleasure through her body.

'More. Tell me more. And I will reward thee with the most energetic yet of my tuppings.'

She swallowed, trying to gather her thoughts. What had she been fantasising about? Oh, yes, it had been . . .

'I was fantasising about *sucking* you, Doctor while ...'

The Doctor grunted and she shuddered to the bolt of a three-quarters withdrawal-and-thrust.

'Yes. Go on,' he whispered thickly. 'Thou wert sucking me as I ...'

'As you bugger ...'

She gasped again, for the mention of buggery, like the mention of sucking, had sent the Doctor's cocks almost automatically pistoning in her cunny and bottom.

'Yes?' he whispered impatiently. 'More, thou slut. Thou wert sucking me as I buggered ... whom? Whom, thou slut? Tell me.'

'A *youth*, Doc—'

She gasped to the strongest of his thrusts yet.

'A youth, thou slut?' he whispered. 'Thou fantasisedst that thou wert sucking me as I buggered ... a youth?'

She gasped twice as he spoke – he seemed almost to be punishing her with his thrusts, knowing how tender her cunny and – especially – her bottom-hole was, after the two vigorous pokings each had already received.

'Y– ah! – yes, Doctor. A youth, Doctor. I fantasised that I was sucking you as you buggered a y—'

The Doctor snarled with lust and began to fuck her in earnest for the third time, whispering furiously in between the quickening rhythm of his thrusts.

'A youth, thou slut? Thou fantasised thus, didst thou? Well, then thou hast read the fluid aright that I have pumped into thee so copiously *par con et cul*. In its heat and thickness you read the family secret, transmitted doubtless from the dark and salty wells of my blood. I *do* bugger youths, my sweet, and one day thou shalt watch – watch, my sweet, as thou suckst – watch me slide my cock home into that twice-nefandous sheath: the male bottom. But I misdoubt me, truly I misdoubt me, that any male bottom could ever offer me delights to approach, let alone match, those that *thy* bottom

175

offers me. Yes, my sweet, for tightness, for heat, for smoothness and depth – ah, but I must not dwell on its superlatives, or I shall spurt prematurely, drained though my balls already are. And when thy bottom is coupled – coupled, I say – with the slickness and softness and *squeeziness* of thy unsurpassable cunny – oh, *Zeus Paiderastes* himself never knew transports such as mine, my sweet, I promise thee, I swear to thee, though Ganymede writhe as Ganymede never writhed.'

She could barely understand him: he was flinging his whispers at her brokenly, in an accent that had thickened with the speed and strength of his thrusts, and she could not have said for certain afterwards whether he spoke in French or English or in a mixture of the two or neither at all. But even if he had been speaking clearly, crisply, loudly, in accentless English, she would have had great difficulty in catching his words, for she was overwhelmed with the sensations of her third double-fucking, falling deeper second by second into a bottomless pit of painful pleasure and pleasurable pain. Her bottom was burning more fiercely with every thrust of the cock inserted into it, as though he was stoking a fire there, shovelling harsh-burning coal into a squat, thick-walled furnace; but the more fiercely her bottom burned, the more greedily and moistly her cunny accepted the cock's twin: the pain fed the pleasure and the pleasure fed the pain, till she could not tell what delighted or agonised her more, the buggery or the cunny-tupping.

In the end, as the length of the fucking matched twice that of the first and stretched beyond it, she began to hallucinate with ecstasy. The feral musk of her own and the Doctor's sweat, mingled each with each and with the splashing juice of her cunny, seemed to be stabbed with a reek of burning, as though her bottom really was on fire. Then, halting her for an endless moment on the brink of a precipice that opened within the pit into which she had been falling, the Doctor thrust both cocks to their fullest extent into her with a groan of exhausted triumph, and began to spurt, dousing the fire in her bottom as she fell from it and from her body through the floor and down towards the centre of the earth. She wondered vaguely if she would ever be satisfied by sex again after the poking she had just received, or ever be able to have sex again: had he not converted both her cunny and bottom-hole into gaping, slack-mouthed pouches that could not tighten again on a cucumber, let alone a cock?

She did not have long to wait for her answer: the Doctor, having luxuriated a minute in the depths of her semen-flooded holes, groaned again and began to struggle free, almost having to drag his cocks forth from the orifices into which he had plunged them so deeply. Theodora smiled sleepily to herself, neither resisting his efforts nor trying to relax. Her cunny and bottom had wills of their own and they evidently did not wish to let what had pleasured them so well to leave.

'Slut,' she heard the Doctor whisper thickly. He grunted and she gasped in response, struck by a shaft of pain-pleasure from her bottom as his cock slid out an inch. The sounds still seemed to be coming from far above her, but she was slowly beginning to rise from the depths to which she had fallen.

'Slut,' he repeated. 'Release me, thou slut. Or should I say "thou witch"? Thou keepst me as stiff as ever and squeezest thy cunny and bottom-shaft as tight as ever on me, in contravention of plain physiological law.'

Another grunt, another gasp.

'Hast thou bewitched me?' he whispered wonderingly. 'Bewitched my cocks? Release me. Ah.'

Another grunt, another gasp. But now she had almost returned to her body from the earth's depths – orgasm was fading at last in her body, loosening the tightened strings of her cunny and bottom and allowing him to

177

finally begin sliding his cocks out of her. The squelches and pops, the cunny-farts, as his thick moistened man-meat slid from her slick moistening girl-meat, were now sounding only a yard or two above her, and in another moment she would be back in her body. There: with a slight jolt prolonged by the shock as his cocks popped finally free, she was back, listening in puzzlement to a loud, moist sound that she suddenly and blushingly (think of the servants listening too!) realised was her bereft bottom blowing a lament for its departed buggerer.

Eleven

Luxuriating in the bath she had been ordered to take by the Doctor, Theodora sighed happily and began to turn over the events of the past hour in her mind. Under the water she ran her hand gently over her cunny and down over her perineum to her bottom-hole. They were gaping in the warm water, as though to suck it in and soothe their battered tissues. She slowly pushed a finger into her bottom, rotating it as she pushed it past the first and second knuckle. Yes, it was a little sore, a little bruised, but what a privilege the Doctor had granted to her! She was truly a woman now, having lost the virginity of her cunny and bottom simultaneously in a way almost no other women on earth ever had and ever would. For surely the Doctor's double cock was unique? She moaned slightly at the thought of it, at the thought of them, shifting in the water, and her other hand seemed to slip of its own accord between her thighs, beginning to rub and squeeze at her cunny-lips and the stiffening nub of her cunny-horn.

But suddenly she splashed back to attention, pulling her hands from her lower orifices and shielding her breasts. She had seen in a clear patch of the steam-misted mirror at one end of the bath that the door of the bathroom was open. She turned her head, crying out a little in surprise as she saw that one of the Doctor's young servants was standing behind her, holding out a yellow silk dressing-gown. How long had he been there? Had he watched her as she began to frot herself?

'What do you want?'

The youth said nothing. She licked her lips a little, recovering fast from her fright.

'Does the Doctor want me?'

After a moment's pause, the youth nodded slightly. Her eyes dropped to his groin, reading the bulge there, estimating the size of his cock. She sighed and dropped a hand from her breasts, sliding it back between her legs. Why did she care if he had seen her frotting herself? She was the Doctor's captive, he the Doctor's servant. Was there such a gulf between them? She licked her lips again.

'Co—' she had to swallow away the tightness in her throat 'Come here.'

The youth blinked but did not move. Theodora narrowed her eyes, reading more of the expression in his face. Perhaps there was a gulf stretched between them – but she was on the Doctor's side of it. Her heart had started to hammer in her throat, but when she spoke her voice was calm, unquavering, authoritative.

'*Viens ici.*'

He blinked again but this time he obeyed. Ah, so she had been right. She had some special relationship with the Doctor now, some relationship that his servants recognised as placing her above them. Above them and able to order them to come and go. And come. The hand shielding her breasts flashed out, leaving them bare, as the servant came within range and she could seize his crotch. She smiled broadly, opening her thighs wider beneath the water, allowing her frotting hand easier access to her re-excited cunny. Wholly confident now, she looked up at him, squeezing the stiff cock she had found in his trousers.

'*Dites-moi*, has the Doctor buggered you?'

'But of course, *ma* Théodora,' came a whisper from behind him through the whisper of the silk dressing-

180

gown sliding from the servant's arm. The servant's cry of surprise and her own were simultaneous, and she heard vertebrae crack in the servant's neck as he turned his head to look behind him at the tall figure in the doorway. Theodora felt her thighs close, trapping her frotting hand between them, futilely trying to shield something of herself from his wrath, as the Doctor walked forward into the bathroom. Her other hand had tightened convulsively on the servant's cock too, surely hurting him, but he did not seem to notice.

'*Maî*—' he started to stammer, breaking off with a gasp as the Doctor seized him by the shoulder and shook him. But not angrily – paternally, avuncularly, Theodora suddenly realised.

'*Silence*, Louis,' came the whisper. 'I forgive you freely, have no fear on that account. You have been tempted and – unhand him, you slut – have fallen.'

Theodora released the servant's cock as the Doctor slapped at her hand and watched, her nipples aching with a strange mixture of pleasure and disgust, as the Doctor expertly loosed the servant's trousers and freed the stiff member therein, which Theodora saw with an unmistakable pang of disappointment was beginning to soften.

'But have I not fallen thrice myself today with the same slut?' the Doctor continued conversationally, taking firm hold of the cock and beginning to frot it back to life. It sprang back to full stiffness with what Theodora thought was astonishing speed. The Doctor grunted sardonically.

'Ah, but he is an excitable one, *mon jeune* Louis. Large enough, you no doubt conclude, to satisfy you, but not, alas, continent – Ah, what did I tell you?'

Theodora's left eye was suddenly stinging furiously, distracting her so that it took her a moment more to realise that the servant was ejaculating thickly over her as she sat in the bath.

'Forgive me, *ma chère*,' the Doctor whispered as she tried to knuckle her eye clean and wipe more semen off her cheeks and lips. 'But a practical demonstration, as you see, was worth a hundred admonitions. Louis, if you follow the pun, is the boy who put the "cock" into "praecox". One barely sets hand to the pump and it responds in torrents.'

Theodora could certainly agree with that. The servant had positively drenched her – his semen was dripping off her into the water with heavy minute *spluts* and *splinks* that sounded clearly through the subsiding gasps of his orgasm.

'*Oui*, in torrents,' the Doctor continued, shaking final drops off his servant's cock into the bath, 'but they seem almost desiccated by comparison with what he can produce when a cock – my cock, *ma chère* – has been inserted into his rectal chamber and tickling his prostate a minute or two. He could have inundated your delightful breasts too, in that case, *ma chère*, with sufficient remaining to write his initials on your belly. But stop that. There is a much more effective means of freeing yourself of his sticky tribute than that, eh, Louis? Lower your hand, *ma* Théodora, and close your eyes. At my direction Louis will piss you clean.'

She had been lowering her hands, glad that the Doctor knew a better way to free her of the servant's semen, which was especially thick and clinging, for all its copiousness; but now, as the meaning of the Doctor's final words sunk in, she raised them again with a cry of disgusted protest. The Doctor grunted with impatience.

'Lower them, I say. You must rid yourself of all your *bourgeois* prejudices, *ma* Théodora, if you wish to occupy the post I have in mind for you. Obey me. Lower them. That is a good girl. And close your eyes. *Bien*. Now, Louis, piss on her.'

Theodora was still watching through slitted eyelids, heart pounding again. The servant's large cock was still stiff, pointed directly at her face by the hand that encircled it, and she stored away the fact that men could piss through a stiff cock. How much she still had to learn! She gasped a little with shock: yellow had suddenly exploded against her eyes and she closed them tight, feeling a warm, thrumming stream of urine hitting her face, washing away the traces of semen that still clung to it.

'Excellent for the skin too, *ma* Théodora,' the Doctor said. 'But it is possibly enriching the water in your bath to excess, after all you and he have already deposited in it. Pull the plug, please, that you may sluice yourself thoroughly before you emerge and I take you into the garden. I wish you to meet those mysterious girls you saw earlier, through the window.'

Keeping her face carefully in the servant's piss-stream, for she had begun to enjoy the sensation, Theodora obeyed, groping underwater for the plug of the bath and tugging at it. Was piss really good for the skin? She felt a sudden current on her legs as the water began to drain. The piss-stream was beginning to weaken now, but what an enormous bladder the servant must have! Much larger than her own. But then she thought back to listening to her father and some of his friends visiting the lavatory on a bridge night. Men did have large bladders. And could release them even through a stiff cock, dear Diary.

'*Là*,' the Doctor whispered as, with a few last spurts and sputters, the servant exhausted his bladder on her and stopped pissing. 'He has finished and your face is returned to its usual shining smoothness. Sluice yourself as I have ordered and then Louis will bring you to me in your dressing-gown.'

The Doctor turned to leave, but paused a moment, as though aware that Theodora was wondering apprehensively where he would be waiting for her and what he intended to do with her when she arrived. But the words

183

he threw over his shoulder merely increased her apprehension.

'*Et ma chère*, please prepare yourself for further vigorous sexual activity. Louis, you are under strict orders not to tire the slut or allow her to tempt you. *Oui? Alors, bien. Au revoir, ma* Théodora.'

Then with his faint wheezy chuckle he left them. Theodora began to sluice herself as she had been ordered, stomach loosening and tightening alternately as she thought of what he might have planned for her next.

Tying the cord of the yellow silk dressing-gown, she followed Louis from the bathroom, feeling her cunny and bottom begin to throb harder with every step she took. For was not each step carrying her nearer the Doctor? And had he not warned her to prepare for more 'vigorous sexual activity'? But perhaps not with the Doctor himself. Was he not exhausted by now, having fucked her not once, not twice, but thrice? And with two cocks! She licked her lips, wondering whether she should ask Louis what the Doctor intended, then shook her head, struck by a new thought. If the Doctor himself was not going to fuck her, perhaps he intended Louis – and another servant – to fuck her, one by cunny, one by bottom. Oh, and one by mouth. Would the Doctor not take great pleasure at the sight of three lusty young servants plying their cocks in her three orifices?

But it was not the thought of three servants at work on her that made her knees suddenly weaken, so that she nearly staggered. No, she had been struck by a further thought, as deliciously dark as it was darkly delicious. Why should the Doctor stop at setting three servants to work on her? There were her arm-pits too, and the hollows behind her knees, and her hands and feet. Each could accept a cock or at least have a cock rubbed on it, so that *eleven* young servants could work

184

on her at once, crowding around her like – a memory occurred to her from her childhood – yes, like ants manoeuvring a particularly toothsome morsel of food toward their nest. But the servants – and why should there not be an outer circle of servants too, masturbating furiously as they watched and envied the inner circle? – no, the servants would not be clustered on her in order to eat her, but in order to *pleasure* her, and then *flood* her, *soak* her, from head to foot with their s—.

She broke off her train of thought guiltily, for young Louis was opening a door for her and bowing her through it. Her eyes flew to his groin again, trying to detect whether it was bulging as it had bulged before, signalling his excitement at the coming cockomachy. She licked her lips involuntarily as she saw that it was, but then was struck by a dismaying thought. Perhaps he was not to be part of the cockomachy, excluded because he had come too recently or because the Doctor resented the way he had succumbed to her temptation in the bathroom. Oh, she would beg the Doctor to include him if that were the case, indeed demand that he be included and set to work in a place of central honour, thrusting into the smooth depths of her cunny or bottom. She stepped through the door, lifting her eyes coquettishly to his as she did so, and suppressing a smile at the lust that flared up in the clear green eyes meeting hers as she almost imperceptibly quirked her eyebrows.

Then she was through, stepping onto a creeper-shaded walkway at whose far end she could see a rectangle of brightly lit garden. The door closed behind her with too great force and she glanced back over her shoulder, smiling openly as she felt the glow in her cunny and bottom strengthen almost to pre-orgasmic strength. Yes, the poor servant-boy was excluded from the cockomachy and yes, he was lusting for her, having been, quite naturally, entirely unsatisfied by the mere act of squirting semen over her as she sat in the bath. That

185

had merely stoked his lust, made it more urgent, and now she had flung another heaping of coal on the fire, so that he was like a train whose boiler was being kept at high pressure while its brakes were full on and it waited in the gloom of a station, throbbing and trembling with the need to burst into the sunshine, shining steel pistons pumping indefatigably in their well-lubricated . . .

'Why,' came the whisper from her left, 'do you smile, thus, *ma* Théodora, like the cat that has got the cream?'

She had reached the end of the walkway and was about to descend the three steps that led to the garden. Now her hand flew to her mouth with a soft scream of surprise, for the Doctor had been waiting for her, deliberately standing back a little beside the creepers so that his whisper would shock her. A strong hand seized her upper arm and she was lifted bodily down the steps, heart pounding harder, cunny and bottom-hole flaring as she again realised his implacable masculine strength.

'Is it because you have been teasing poor Louis?' he whispered, stooping to place his mouth directly against her ear. 'Ah, do not answer, for I see that it is so. You have been teasing the poor fellow with promise of the delights you so barely conceal beneath your dressing-gown.'

He began to pull her along a path whose smooth and sun-warmed marble treads, inlaid with fish and other marine images, almost scalded the bare soles of her feet. The path twisted and turned to pass beneath first one extravagantly flowering tree, then another. The scent of their blooms was shockingly sweet in her nostrils and she realised that her senses were sharply heightened, recording the world's impressions with a strength that was now beginning to frighten her. But then what would the cockomachy be like? Would the sensation of eleven cocks at work on her body be too powerful, so that she fainted from the pleasure of it?

She shook her head slightly, reassuring herself, and remembered that she was to beg for Louis to be included, yes, and in a place of honour, thrusting into her cunny or bottom. She cleared her throat and glanced sideways and up at the Doctor.

'Doc—' she began to say; but he shook her arm impatiently and dragged her to a halt.

'*Voilà, ma sale petite*,' he whispered, stretching out a long arm. 'There they await you.'

She followed his pointing finger down the slope ahead of them and all thought of Louis and the cockomachy flew from her head. The path had brought them back to the house – back to overlook the sun-lit spot she had seen from the window as the Doctor took the maidenheads of her cunny and bottom – back to observe the group of oblivious, sun-bathing girls. They looked more beautiful than ever from where she now stood: long black hair glistening as they moved occasionally, presenting some new section of their firm, deliciously rounded bodies to the golden rays of the sun. But she was struck by something uncanny about them, some strangeness beyond anything she had encountered before.

'What do you think of them, *chérie*?' the Doctor whispered. Theodora narrowed her eyes, staring harder and opened her mouth to speak.

'Are they . . . are they all blind, Doctor?'

'Yes, *chérie*, all blind. And all deaf, as you will remember from your efforts to attract their attention while you hung strapped in the window. But there is something more than that, is there not, *chérie*? Observe them closely and tell me what it is.'

Theodora stared, forgetting to breathe for a moment.

'It is their . . . their skin, Doctor.'

'Yes? What is it?'

'It is strangely pale, Doctor, and I could almost think . . .'

'Yes? You could almost think what?'

187

'That . . . that it has a . . . a *greenish* tinge.'

The Doctor sighed happily and stepped behind her, seizing her in his strong arms.

'Ah, yes, *chérie*,' he breathed into her ear, 'their skin, it does have a greenish tinge. You see it clearly now, do you not, now that I have confirmed it to you?'

He kissed her ear, then nuzzled her neck.

'Yes, Doctor,' she said.

His mouth was back on her ear, licking at it, nibbling the lobe.

'But there is more still, is there not, *chérie*? Their blindness, their deafness, their green skin, these three are not all that strikes you with a sense of . . . uncanniness.'

More licking and nibbling at her ear. Her cunny had melted, streaming juice down her thighs, and if the Doctor had not been grasping her so firmly, holding the cheeks of her buttocks together, she felt sure that her bottom-hole would have signalled its desire to be re-penetrated with a long, relaxed fart. But what did the Doctor mean to do with her? Fuck her again as the girls sun-bathed as obliviously as they had before? Or would he signal young servants out of the bushes and watch the cockomachy she had guessed was awaiting her? No, it was something involving the girls beneath them more . . . intimately. She strained her eyes staring at them, knowing that the Doctor spoke truly when he said there was some extra strangeness about them, beyond their blindness, deafness and green-tinged skin.

'Yes?' the Doctor whispered, withdrawing his lips from the cheek, which he had been kissing and licking as he awaited her reply. He had read the movement of her jaw there and knew she was about to speak again.

'It's . . . it's their bodies, Doctor,' Theodora said slowly. 'From the way they move, their bodies seem lighter, somehow, than they should be. As though . . .'

'Yes? As though what? No, do not shake your head. Speak your thoughts to me, however extravagant, however *insane* they may seem to you now.'

'But ... but it *is* insane, Doctor.'

'No. Observe them, *ma* Théodora, and report to me.'

'Then ... their bodies, from the way they move, it seems as though ... as though their bodies have no ... no *bones*, Doctor.'

She jerked a little in his arms, so loud was the gasp of pleasure he now released.

'Oh, my observant little pleasure-doll,' he whispered. 'Yes, I will make a scientist of you yet, *chérie*. They seem, you say, these blind, these deaf girls, to have no bones in their green-skinned bodies. And it is precisely so, *chérie*, no bones do they have, these blind, deaf, green-skinned girls. For in fact they are not ...'

With blood pulsing and buzzing in her ears, for she had caught his excitement and her heart was pounding with it, she daringly interrupted him.

'I think I know, Doctor. I think I know what they are *not*. Though I don't know what they *are*.'

'Then tell me, *chérie*, tell me what they are not, and I shall tell you what they *are*.'

She swallowed, opening her mouth to speak.

Twelve

'There, *ma petite.*'

She gratefully accepted the glass of hot wine from his hand, still shivering a little from the rescue. But as she was about to drink he slipped the hand under her chin and tilted it upward so that he could look down on her. After a moment in which their gazes contended, his striving for dominance, hers half-seriously, half-coquettishly resisting, his lips quirked and he smiled.

'I begin to believe you truly are worthy of the position I have in mind for you, *ma* Théodora. Ah, *non,*' he shook his head, smiling again 'it is not *that* position I speak of, or rather, not *those.* Those positions you have already occupied, *chérie,* and will surely occupy again. No, I speak of something other. I am pondering whether to offer you a position of . . . well, can you guess? Yes, can you guess? Here is another one of the tests by which I shall see whether you are worthy.'

She blinked and dropped her eyes, unable to concentrate when their gazes were locked. What position was he pondering whether to offer her? 'A position of . . .' That was what he had said. She lifted her eyes to his again, moistening her lips with her tongue before she answered. She opened her lips, pausing a moment, seeing his eyes narrow involuntarily with lust and knowing that she had stiffened his cocks again.

'A position of power, Doctor,' she said softly. His

chest swelled and she saw his nostrils flare. He released his breath in a long sigh, eyes almost closing.

'You have provoked me, *chérie*, almost to immediate rape, heaping such quickness of wit on such *coquetterie*. Yes, you have guessed right. I am pondering whether to offer you a position of power here on my island. A position of power over your schoolfellows. Over Edwina. Over Marie. And over . . . Philippa.'

She had guessed what he was going to say, had known he was watching her hard to see how she reacted to it. But she was unable to conceal the greedy delight that sprang into her face. He nodded with satisfaction.

'Yes. A position of power over Philippa. And you would give very much for that, would you not, *ma petite*? But come, sample your wine and I will speak of other things while you absorb the news.'

She had almost forgotten the wine-glass in her hand; now she raised it to her lips and sipped, feeling the shivering, almost forgotten too, strengthen again in her body. The Doctor stooped to her, sliding an arm beneath her thighs and another around her neck, lifting her off the chair so that he could sit there instead, holding her on his lap.

'Take another sip, *ma petite*,' he ordered. 'It will warm you as I speak of somewhat chilly scientific matters. For you know, as yet, very little of me, *n'est-ce pas*? Good girl. And are you comfortable?'

Emboldened already by the wine, she rocked on his lap as though testing it for comfort, and replied: 'No, Doctor. Your cocks are sticking into me.'

He snorted with laughter.

'Then I give you leave to adjust them, *ma petite*. But adjust is all you must do, for I will not have you distracting me as I prepare to begin my story.'

She felt a thrill of surprise and excitement run through her and pushed himself up a little, putting her free hand beneath her as she held the wine-glass out a little, safe from upset. She rummaged for a way into his trousers, found one, and slid her hand inside for his cocks. They felt stiffer and huger than ever, as though their repeated insertions into her body had nourished them, made them swell in anticipation of further insertions, of further doses of pleasure from her willing flesh.

'Careful, you slut,' came his whisper, suddenly less gentle. 'I warned you to try no tricks, simply to adjust them ... Yes, that is better. Now, are you ready to sit quietly and in comfort while I speak a little of my career to date? Then that is good. Another sip from your wine, *chérie*, and I shall begin.'

She took another sip from her wine, almost laughing at the thought of what she had done. She had not adjusted his cocks to make herself more comfortable at all – no, she had adjusted them so that she felt them more than ever, boring into her back and buttocks. She rocked on them a little, vowing to herself that she would keep them stiff right through the story.

'Ah, if you intend to provoke me so, *ma petite*, then I will have a sip of your wine also, to give me the strength to resist, for your sake, that urge of which I spoke earlier. To rape you, my dear.'

More clumsily than she needed, she twisted on his lap, pressing and rubbing on his cocks again with her buttocks, to present the wine-glass to his lips. He took a sip, licked his lips, and then grunted to indicate that he wished for another.

'*Merci, ma petite*. And now I think that at last I can begin. Settle yourself, you slut. And do not wriggle thus or I warn you, the rape of which I spoke will commence forthwith. *Bien*. Now, listen. I am Doctor Julien de Sade, Théodora, direct descendant in the male line of the most illustrious Marquis de Sade of blasphemous memory. But I fear that for many years I was unworthy of him, *ma* Théodora. Indeed, I would have denied him thrice both before and after cock-crow, claiming to be of a mere cadet branch of the family and to be able to spare not the slightest interest in him from my scientific work, the all-consuming, all-important passion of my life. But tell me, *ma* Théodora, can you guess what my scientific work was? And, of course, what my scientific work remains?'

He spoke with apparent casualness and Theodora, her head beginning to spin pleasurably from the wine, was about to answer him casually when something warned her to pause. Here, perhaps – no, here for sure, was another test, to see whether she was worthy of the 'position of power' he was pondering for her.

'Well?' the Doctor said when she remained silent; and she smiled, realising that she had been right. But the answer that she would have given casually was the same as the answer she gave now.

'Botany, Doctor. Your scientific work was, and remains, botany.'

'Exactly so, *ma petite*,' the Doctor whispered. '*La botanique, reine des sciences.* Botany, queen of sciences, whom I wooed long and finally won, I will boast, on the occasion of my being awarded the Nobel Prize for Medicine in 1907 in recognition of my work on certain . . .'

Theodora had been taking another and deeper sip of wine as he spoke; now she choked on it, feeling her sinuses burn as some sprayed there from her throat.

'But what is wrong, *ma petite*? Do you doubt my word?'

She shook her head, feeling his erect cocks more clearly than ever in the soft flesh of her bottom. Had they hardened even further as she choked with surprise? Or was she simply more aware of them?

'No, Doctor,' she said. 'I don't doubt you, it's just that . . . it seems impossible.'

'What?' he whispered. 'It seems impossible to you, you arrogant child, that I could have won the Nobel Prize?'

'No, Doctor,' she began to say hastily; but broke off as she felt him laughing and realised he had been speaking with mock anger.

'Ah, my apologies, *ma petite*, for teasing you so. No, do not roll your delightful buttocks on me as you are doing, *ma petite*, for my threat still stands as firm as my cocks. That's a good girl. A wise girl. But where were we? Ah, yes, I quite understand what you meant to say. It seems impossible, does it not that I could have won the Nobel Prize so long ago, for I must have been at least thirty, more probably above forty, most probably above fifty, when I did so, which would put me now at – what – sixty, seventy, eighty?'

'Yes, Doctor.'

'Well, *ma petite*, your reasoning was quite correct. Indeed, it did not go far enough. I am eighty-three, my sweet morsel of girl-flesh, eighty-three and seven months. My researches, you see, have taken me far beyond that advance which won me my Nobel. Ah, come now, you have provoked me sufficiently. Off onto the floor with you, and you can service me while I continue my story.'

He half-rose in the chair, spilling Theodora from his lap onto the floor, where she sprawled a moment before his strong left hand gripped her firmly by the neck while his right hand was busy lifting first one cock, then the other, from his trousers.

'You can take two at once today, *ma petite*,' he whispered, taking hold of the two shafts in one hand with some difficulty and forcing them together. 'Tilt your head thus' – he tugged at her neck – 'and open your mouth to its widest. Come, girl, open. Open for your master. Good girl.'

He was cramming his two cockheads into her mouth, mastering the tremor that weakened his voice for a moment, and pulled her nearer, pushing his cocks deeper into her mouth.

'Now, that should keep you quiet. No! No complaints, if you please. I know your jaw has already begun to ache, but that is what you must expect when you have two cocks in your mouth. No complaints, I said, and do not make those beaten-puppy eyes at me. You were warned quite explicitly, my dear, of what would follow if you continued to provoke my lust, and you can consider yourself lucky that I have not fulfilled my threat to the letter. You are not being raped, you are only being required to suck me. Suck me simultaneously, it is true, and swallow the double load that I will sooner or later deliver, but that is less than you deserve. Now, suck and listen in silence. The ache in your jaw will wear off presently, or so I have been told. Good girl.

'Very well, then, to recommence my tale. Hard though it may be for you to believe, as you kneel there and suck those two splendidly youthful phalluses, which have already been so active so often earlier in the day, I did win the Nobel Prize for Medicine in 1907, at the age of fifty-two, and I *am* eighty-three today. Ah, yes ... Excellent, my dear ... Excellent ... And if you could hum too, please. *La Marseillaise* is what I request most often on these occasions, as I wallow in nostalgia, for after all, did I not do what I next proceeded to do, having won the Prize, for the greater glory of France? Little dreaming – ah – that my patriotic endeavours would lead me to follow in the footsteps of my then-despised, now-venerated, forebear, the Marquis. Thank you, my dear ... But perhaps a little louder, and with a little more – *ô, quelle sagesse*, you anticipate the request before I make it.

'Yes, think of me then, *ma* Théodora, standing astride the world of botany like a colossus but restless to expand the horizons of that world. And your soft hands on my balls now, if you please. Squeezing them. Ah, excellent. Excellent. But not to excess. Yes. Massage them. The more slowly you bring them to the boil, the more copiously they will overflow. Yes. Ah. Excellent. I had chosen a new field to explore: that of the *orchidées-abeilles*, the bee-orchids, my dear. Ah, you have found that exact conjoint rhythm of mouth and hand that most satisfies me while delaying longest my *paroxysme*. Ah. I treasure you and your orifices more with each passing moment, *chérie*. Yes, I had chosen a new field to explore: the bee-orchids. But what do you know of them, *ma* Théodora? Lift your eyes to me and wink – no, squeeze my balls tighter in your right hand for a moment if you know of them but tighter in your left if you do not . . .

'Ah, so you do not. Just as you do not know how appropriate it is that you have three fine balls to play with as I discourse to you of orchids. For they are named, *chérie*, from their resemblance – that of their bulbs, *on dit* – to testicles. No, I do not jest with you: it is plain philological fact. Orchids are named for their resemblance to balls – *orchis* in Greek, my dear, with genitive *orchidos*. But the bee-orchids take this sexual – this genitive – theme a step further in their flowers, which mimic the bodies of female bees. No, again I do not jest. When I have thoroughly filled your mouth with the semen that your untutored but innately skilled mouth and hands are encouraging to build in my own orchids, I will send you to fetch a book wherein you can see the truth for yourself. The bee-orchid flower does indeed mimic the body of a female bee, enticing the male of the mimicked species to a futile copulation. Futile, that is to say, from the bee's point of view; from the orchid's, it is the very means of continued existence. After one pseudo-copulation, the male bee flies away laden with pollen for another pseudo-copulation, and thus the orchid is pollinated.

'But you will see when you fetch the book – which will not, I promise, be long delayed – that the mimicry employed by the flower is somewhat crude. They are no

Caravaggios, no Titians, no Velasquezes, these deceptive flowers, reproducing exactly the lineaments of desire – they are impressionists, rather, or even modernist daubsters, who merely *hint* at the reality of apian pulchritude with a hairy outline and a perfunctory sheen approximately where the wings would be. Thus they appear at least to our human eyes, we botanists had – *ah* – long suspected that the orchid deployed something ... *ah, je viens, chérie, je viens.*'

Kneeling on the floor as she listened to his lecture on bee-orchids, mouth crammed with his cockheads and an increasing part of his cockshafts, hands busy on the three large balls that hung beneath the same, Theodora had been dizzy, almost dreaming, with sensation and ideas; now, as his cockheads throbbed and began to spurt, she was dragged brutally back to reality: his semen was too thick, too hot, too salty to be part of a dream and she was forced to concentrate hard lest it choked her as it hosed into her mouth. She gulped at it, swallowing it dutifully, obediently, she told herself, but the leaking slit between her thighs, its tender lips aching anew with the blood that had swelled and parted them, told its own story. Her submission to the Doctor, her humiliation by him, her powerlessness in the face of his masculine strength and pride, excited and satisfied her more powerfully than any power she had exercised over her own sex. But somehow it increased her longing for power over her own sex, as though the glowing mass of semen she could feel sliding finally down her throat to settle in her gut, was granting her feudal power, making her queen of some part of an empire ruled by the Doctor.

'Thank you, my dear,' came his whisper, 'now, if you'll just let me get my cocks out of your ... Good girl. Yes, kiss them if you like. They'll soon enough be back, my dear. I believe they would tear themselves from my body and come crawling to you if I tried to deny them.'

He broke off with a smile. She had belched genteelly, rubbing at her flat stomach between the flapping-open halves of her dressing-gown.

'Ah, *ma petite*, such a graceful compliment you pretend to pay me! But let me . . .'

His strong right hand came out, taking her by the jaw, gently but firmly squeezing to open her mouth and allow him to sniff her breath. He released her and drew back, shaking his head.

'Yes, a flattering pretence, but a pretence all the same. I have not swollen your tender stomach so quickly and so densely with semen that you need to relieve the pressure with a belch. Your breath does not smell strongly enough of me for that. So, *ma petite trompeuse*, my little deceiver, go and fetch that book I told you of. Louis or whoever it is lurking behind that curtain over there, having frotted himself as he peered on your servicing of me, will guide you to it. But tie up your dressing-gown before you go to him, *ma* Théodora, for I will not have you enticing my staff with glimpses of your firm young flesh. Tie it up, I say, and fetch that book.'

Theodora stayed on her knees a moment longer, trying to provoke a genuine belch from her semen-warmed stomach. The Doctor wasn't entirely right: she hadn't just been trying to flatter him, her stomach had felt full, even distended with his semen. But she supposed that the very fact she had felt the illusion was a compliment to him: her subconscious mind was so eager that she should accept the salty load of his balls that it manufactured sensations to convince her that she had received even more than she had. Abandoning her attempt to belch in earnest, she pushed herself upright, re-fastened the cord of her dressing-gown and went to fetch the book he had ordered her to bring. A servant was hiding behind the curtain as the Doctor had foretold, shamefacedly trying to pretend that the large

198

bulge in his trousers had not just been folded away there.

'The book, please,' she whispered to him, daringly reaching out to grasp and squeeze the bulge. A heavy foot stamped on the floor behind her and she hurriedly released her grip, realising that she had not disguised the movement of her back and shoulders sufficiently. The servant swallowed, eyes flickering between her face and the Doctor, then bowed his head and held the curtains open for her, jerking his head back to indicate the door concealed behind them. But another stamp sounded on the floor and before she could move forward to the door, something hit her between the shoulders and fell away, rattling a moment later on the floor. She turned and saw a paper-plane that had evidently just been folded and thrown by the Doctor, who was glowering at her from the chair.

She stooped and picked it up, unfolding it to read his bold scrawl: *If you delay thirty seconds longer than I expect, I will know you have been sucking him. And this time my punishment will descend with full force. On both your heads – and elsewhere.* Now it was her turn to swallow. She nodded and flapped the paper at the Doctor, feeling foolish the moment she did it, then turned back to the door. But yet another stamp sounded on the floor, and she looked back to see the Doctor stabbing his forefinger at the servant. Ah. She handed him the paper too, watched the look of fear that came into his face as he read, and the nervous glance up at and nod to the Doctor, and then hurried to get through the door with him and fetch the book with the minimum of delay, her cunny and bottom aching again with flesh-memories of what they had endured from the Doctor already that day.

When two minutes later, flushed and panting, she returned with the book, the Doctor nodded silently and took it from her as she climbed again onto his lap, instantly aware that his cocks, so recently sucked to orgasm, had hardened again. Then he handed the book back and she began to leaf through it, looking for the bee-orchids he wanted her to find. It was a large and beautifully produced botanical text-book in French, and she found herself pausing at some of the other illustrations. She felt the Doctor shake his head.

'No, it is the bee-orchids that concern us now, *ma* Théodora,' he whispered. 'There will be time for all that later. Look in the index under *orchidées-abeilles*.'

She reluctantly turned to the index and found the entry for *orchidées-abeilles*. Page 293. When she tried to find the page the book fell open there as though anxious to help her, but then she felt a pang of jealousy as she realised what must be the truth. Other girls – many other girls – must have sat on the Doctor's lap and opened the book to that page too. And had they sucked him? Had their bellies been full of his semen too as they began to read?

'See, *ma* Théodora.'

A blunt forefinger tapped one of the illustrations on a page: a plump, vaguely apine orchid labelled *Ophrys apifera*.

'They are not so convincing, are they, as simulcra of a female bee?'

She nodded slowly, examining the illustration.

'No, Doctor,' she said. 'If I hadn't known what it was supposed to be, I should never have guessed that it was what it is.'

The Doctor laughed in his papery fashion.

'Exactly so, *ma* Théodora. One would not know unless one knew. But of course, there is more to the bee-orchids than meets the eye. And more, indeed ...' he playfully caught Theodora's nose between the knuckles of his forefinger and thumb, tugging on it almost hard enough to make tears come to her eyes 'than meets the nose. Or than meets your pretty little nose, *chérie*, and mine, and those of all others of our distressingly coarse-sensed species. Even the uncorrupted cannibals of Amazonie or Papouasie, trained to sensual acuity by their manner of life, would find nothing particular to remark in these flowers, *chérie*. Yet they deceive their bees by two routes: that of the eye and that of the nose.'

Theodora suppressed a yawn. The room felt hot, despite the looseness and lightness of her dressing-gown, and the feeling of the Doctor's hard cocks beneath her bottom had a curiously enervating effect on her. He could quite easily fuck her again, it seemed, but she wasn't at all sure that she would be able to raise the energy to respond adequately, for all the difference in their ages. Even the Doctor's next words barely roused her interest.

'For the orchids release a special sexual scent, you see, *chérie*, mimicking a sexual scent of the bees. It is a marvel of natural selection – of the tirelessly patient, endlessly winnowing hand of *Dame Nature*. And after my Nobel Prize, *chérie*, I threw myself into investigating the phenomenon, into discovering precisely the structure of these oh-so-enticing chemicals, to the nose of a bee. There was scientific gold a-plenty for me to mine in this seam, but great commercial possibilities too, I confess. The apiculturists of Europe and America, what would they not give for the key of controlling more precisely their hives? Farmers too, think how they might direct the pollination of their crops. And beyond that, my research might unlock a door leading to a door behind which lies the key of control over pests. Ah, and there would lie boundless riches, *chérie*, which, unimportant to me in themselves, would nevertheless allow me to pursue my scientific interests to my heart's content.'

Theodora farted softly on his lap, smacking her lips a little as she began to drift into sleep. The Doctor, lost in his reminiscences, barely noticed, though his nostrils, more alert than he, flared as the spermy scent of her fart drifted to them.

'But in these prospects, alas, lay my downfall,' he continued. 'I threw myself too wholeheartedly into my pursuit of the secrets of the bee-orchid. There were too few hours in my day, though I rose with the sun and did not retire till long past midnight. Accordingly, I drew on my chemical expertise and brewed myself ever-more potent soporifuges, till I was working two and three days at a stretch. I see now how foolish I was, for I was seeking to do the impossible: to cram a year into a month, a month into a week, a week into a day. Better by far to have worked with excessive slowness than with excessive speed, for the crash, when it came, was deadly, and I lost many months in my recuperation. But I might have lost more than that – my sanity for good, even my life. Yet in the end, it was, as you say, a "blessing in disguise", *ma* Théodora.'

Theodora murmured, releasing another spermy fart as she sank fully into sleep, but once more only the Doctor's nostrils detected her insolence.

'For one day I sat in the sanatorium musing on my bee-orchids and a strange thought struck me. When I say that I might have lost my sanity, perhaps I was wrong. Perhaps I did lose my sanity in the crisis, for the thought was certainly not one that I might have ever entertained before. In brief, it was this: we have seen, in the bee-orchids, how the Vegetable Kingdom plays a sexual deception on *one* order of the Animal Kingdom, but why should we suppose it does not play a similar trick on *another* order of the same? And why not – and here, I believe, lay more than a hint that I *had* been driven insane by my crisis – on the class Mammalia; the order Primates; on the species *Homo sapiens*? That is to say, what I pondered, *ma* Théodora, was the question of whether there existed *human* bee-orchids.'

The Doctor paused, breathing heavily in his remembered excitement, and Theodora, her bottom-hole stretched by his repeated penetrations and still recovering its youthful elasticity and tightness, murmured and farted for a third time, longest and loudest of all. The Doctor's nostrils flared to accept its spermy bouquet and his mouth was touched with a smile of reminiscent pleasure, but his eyes were wide and unaware, staring down a time-shadowed avenue of his past. He nodded slowly and resumed speaking.

'Yes, human bee-orchids, *ma* Théodora. That is to say, orchids that had adopted the form of human beings in order to better spread their pollen. The idea may seem to you lunatic, and perhaps it would have seemed to me equally lunatic, had I not been in that fragile mental state, brought on by my breakdown, in which the boundaries of dream and waking were permeable, even non-existent. So I did not dismiss the idea when it occurred to me. On the contrary, I pondered it by the hour, by the day. I could quite easily imagine a means by which this sexual chicanery might arise. Suppose, *chérie*, that some large tropical orchid, by chance mutation, had come to have a passing resemblance to the *pudendum muliebre* – the female genitals, *chérie* – perhaps accompanied by a certain *muskiness* of scent. Not so unlikely, after all. Then suppose that men of the region begin to pay certain attentions to the orchid. Given the polymorphous perversity of my sex, that is not so hard to imagine, eh?'

Theodora woke with a start, for the Doctor had jocularly but rather cruelly squeezed one of her thighs, his fingers probing for a moment into her cunny-hollow.

'Yes, not so hard to imagine at all. So, with the orchids pollinated for free by the pokings they receive, we see immediately how natural selection might begin to take place. The more the orchid came to resemble the female genitals, the more pokings it would receive and the more widely its pollen would be spread. But with human beings, the mimicry could be refined far further

203

than among the bee-orchids. The race for survival of the fittest would carry the orchid beyond a simple resemblance to a fine pair of cunny lips, a tight cunny-throat, and a richly enticing cunny-aroma. It would add thighs. A belly – a pair of breasts, a head, and sculpt each more and more finely, till the resemblance to a beautiful young woman was more and more complete.

'And what if man himself took a hand? What if the orchid came to be regarded as sacred – remember the temple prostitutes against whom the Hebrew prophets so often railed, *chérie* – and to be grown in the precincts of some prehistoric temple. For all this is taking place long, long ago, *chérie*, many, many thousands of years ago, and perhaps the men who originally persuaded the orchid to take its first steps down the path I have described were not men as we would recognise them. But in the end the orchid would be satisfying true men by its resemblance to true women – or by its more-than-resemblance. Imagine that, *chérie*. For after all, the evolution of true women, such as yourself, has not been devoted solely to satisfying the sexual appetites. Your luscious cunny ...' he squeezed Theodora's thigh again and tickled at her cunny-hollow with his fingers 'is designed not only to admit and pleasure the penis, but also to release the nine months' fruit of that pleasure. It is a birth-canal as well as a sex-canal and there is a mechanical, a physiological, limit to the pleasure it can evolve to give.

'But a human bee-orchid, *ma* Théodora, would have no such constraints on its pseudo-cunny. It could evolve solely to give pleasure, once the mechanically trivial task of loading the genitals of its copulator with pollen were solved. Perhaps the pollen was deposited on the pubic bush of the copulator as he gripped the pseudo-body and thrust into the scented flower-throat. That would scarcely interfere with the pseudo-cunny's ability to evolve for pleasure, would it? Yes, I fancy that in the end the orchid would leave its human model behind, perhaps far behind, to encourage future copulation. Yes, this far I pondered, but then a further consideration entered my mind.

'My putative orchid had evolved in response to human concupiscence, but what of human superstition, human resentment? Would the women of the region take kindly to this competition? Would the increasingly uncanny resemblance of the orchids to human females fail to arouse a religious aversion at some stage? Ah, I thought not, and I hypothesised a further stage in the evolution of the orchid. From lying in the jungle and awaiting a chance encounter, whether for good or ill, what if it began to walk abroad?'

Theodora, drifting off again, murmured sleepily at this point and the Doctor, misreading her intent, shrugged and pouted with characteristic French irony.

'Ah, so you grow sceptical, *ma* Théodora, and can I say that I blame you? No, I cannot, for I place myself in your position, as a luscious but otherwise unremarkable schoolgirl who does not understand that one must make these leaps of the imagination if one is to make the great discoveries, the great advances, that truly mark one out among one's scientific peers. Yes, so I made the leap of imagination beyond those other leaps, and hypothesised that my orchid evolved the ability to walk, coupled with a rudimentary but ever sharpening awareness of its surroundings. Not an awareness of hearing or sight, *chérie*, for it would indeed be fantastical to suppose that an orchid could evolve those, but certainly an awareness of *smell*. The scent of male sweat, for example, might easily enough trigger a chemical response in the orchid, causing it to put on a sexual display to accompany the strong sexual scent of its own.

'So see, *chérie*, where my lunatic reasoning had brought me: to the hypothesis that in some tropical region of the world there existed a species – or perhaps more than one species – of gynaecomorphic orchid that owed its continued survival to copulation with male human beings. I even began to wonder what name I would give it. *Megalophrys sadica. Pseudophrys gynaecomorphica.* Or some such. I burned with the desire to undertake an immediate search for my hypothetical orchid, but I was too soon recovered from my breakdown even to consider such a course. I had no energy, whether physical or mental, to spare and so I threw myself into research, consulting the anthropological literature for folk-tales and mythology that might support my hypothesis. The dryads of Greek myth no doubt occur to you at once, *chérie*, as they occurred to me. Were they some rumour of my hypothesised orchid reaching the West? Or – and at the thought I confess I almost wept with excitement, such was my emotional lability and the psychic investment I had already made in my hypothesis – had the orchid existed within Europe also? Did it still exist there?

'For I had decided that at some stage of its evolution it would surely come under *commercial* selection – that is to say, it would be recruited for service in *brothels*. Such a perfect environment for my orchid: endless copulation, endless opportunities for pollination, and it would be greatly prized by any madam or pimp for whom it worked, for it would not, of course, be subject to tiring or venereal disease or show any rebellion at the length of its hours. It would strike its madam or pimp as some dream-whore – the mind of a docile imbecile within a beautiful, lust-provoking exterior. Ah, so many speculations, with, as yet, so little evidence pointing the way to their truth. In fact, to be frank, no solid evidence at all. But I read my literature, making careful notes on all beautiful forest-spirits and flower-maidens, and began to sketch out my expeditions of discovery, little guessing that my scientific quest would take me to a new appreciation – nay, to my first appreciation – of my illustrious forebear the Marquis.

'For you will have guessed already how I planned to spend part of my time, *ma* Théodora: yes, in visiting the brothels of likely regions, sampling their wares, and questioning those who ran and supplied them. Hitherto, I confess, matters of the flesh had been of little moment to me – my scientific work had absorbed me and I lived an austere, even monkish life. Indeed, at first I approached my quest in a scientific spirit, visiting my first brothel with little enthusiasm, but I soon found a new world opening to me, literally so, *ma* Théodora, in the orifices of the whores with whom I coupled by mouth, vagina and anus. My desired destination was unaltered and my determination to arrive there unquenched, but now I cared not that the journey was prolonged a little through this new world of women. And this was, you understand, before I had set foot outside France! Yes, precise as ever, I sought to *practise* on the whores of my natal realm, that I might familiarise myself with the procedures common to brothels before I travelled overseas.

'Annette . . . Giselle . . . Bernardine . . . Véronique . . . I recall their names even now, those girls who initiated me. Run-of-the-mill whores they might have seemed to experienced *roués*, *ma* Théodora, but I was no experienced *roué* and they struck on my famished senses like Venus herself, and struck all the harder for the fact that I had had no inkling that my senses *were* famished. But it was so. My absorption in botany, rich as the satisfactions were that it brought me, had starved another side of my nature and I realised on a sudden that a germ had been transmitted faithfully to me down the generations from my ancestor the Marquis – the germ of a ravenous sensuality. Aye, it had slumbered long in me but that first visit to a brothel, that very first visit, had wafted richly spiced meat before its nostrils and now it woke ravenous and prepared to gorge till it burst.

'I had two whores on that first visit, *ma* Théodora, and though I liked to fancy that I left each of them weak and sore-cunnied, rather' – again he squeezed her thigh and tickled at her cunny-hollow – 'as I have left you, *chérie*, I soon knew it could not be so. They were too well-accustomed to the venerean joust for a no-more-than-moderately-equipped patron to cause discomfort, vigorously though he coupled with them. Today I flatter myself I would do rather more to impress myself on their memory, but that first visit was long before I acquired my second penis.

'Ah, can you feel how I swell and harden at the mere memory of my first visit, *ma* Théodora? Their whorish tricks, their well-honed coquetries, all were new to me and inflamed me like *absinthe*. I was drunk on female flesh, *chérie*, and threw myself further into the delirium of intoxication with the delicious realisation that I would have no fee to pay on the following day – no hangover, no crapulous vomiting, nothing but a raw cock and a teeming headful of fresh memories. And that is exactly how I did wake, but raw as my cock was, I seized it lustily and strummed out an orgasm in tribute to those fresh memories, being too impatiently aroused to hurry around and quench my lust at the brothel I had visited. But I was puzzled by the name I gasped in the throes of my paroxysm. Not, as you might expect, Annette or Giselle, the girls who had given me those oh-so-arousing memories, but – can you guess? – *Alphonse*.

'Ah, it was a message from my subconscious, a command to seek out and study the Scriptures I had neglected, or rather disdained: the Marquis's blasphemous *œuvre*. Do not mistake me, *ma* Théodora, I did not – but I forget, you and your young companions know nothing of that *œuvre*. Well, suffice it to say that it embodies the most monstrous day-dreams of frustration – the frustration of a sensuate unjustly imprisoned within a literal gaol of stone and a metaphoric gaol of impotence, out of both of which he seeks to escape by stimulating his sexual imagination to heights never before or since equalled. But I had no need to imitate the sexual atrocities he described to discern the lessons he hid in the descriptions thereof. The Marquis was an Evangelist of the Flesh and its Pleasures – *et moi*, I was soon his ever-more-eager disciple. So eager, indeed, I found myself reluctant to leave France and begin my quest in the tropics, for thought of the deprivation it would entail, as I travelled aboard ship without a trained whore to minister to me.

'That difficulty was soon solved, *chérie*, for I hired two whores to accompany me on that voyage. One would not have been sufficient, and I was well enough versed in my Sadean Scriptures by then to describe them, when I purchased the tickets through my secretary, as my *nieces*. Both were of exceptional beauty and futuibility, but one was selected also for the size and firmness of her breasts and buttocks, and the tightness of the hole she held between the latter, and the other for the expertise with which she fellated. Oh, that girl could have collapsed a water-spout by sticking a straw into the sea and sucking a moment in reverse. And thus I travelled to conduct my botanic research in the tropics, well-tended by my two nieces.

'Too well-tended, in fact, for I tired of them in the end and when I arrived in Bombay, my first port of call, I quickly dispatched them home with their wages. By then I was already sampling the brothels of the city and probing both literally and metaphorically for the orchid-girls of which I have spoken. But the Indian and Eurasian girls I fucked by all three orifices, delightful though they were, and doubly so by contrast with the six unvarying orifices I had been penetrating several times daily since my departure from France, were all too obviously human. I soon moved on, travelling overland to Burma as I perfected my techniques of interrogation and settled on a suitable translator, an Armenian by the name of Krikorian. He is with me yet, *chérie*, overseeing my correspondence and translating scientific journals for me, and you will meet him in due course. I think, though, that I would happily keep him in a sinecure till the end of his days, for he it was who set me finally on the trail of my orchid-girls.

'We were in Burma by then, near the border with Laos, and I was taking a day of rest from my priapic labours and turning over the pages of *Juliette* – one of the Marquis's finest works, *chérie* – when my indefatigable little Armenian rapped on the door and, at my permission to enter, tumbled in to tell me that he had picked up a scent whilst gossiping in the market. We were on our way to Laos after an hour, for my drooping *membrum virile* was quite restored to life by the prospect of success and I had first to quench its ardour with two Burmese girls. Perhaps if it, and I, could have foreseen that success was not so close at hand as Krikorian's tale led the two of us to believe, it would not have erected and throbbed so strongly. Or perhaps it would. There is a certain capriciousness to the tides governing the phallus, *chérie*, as you are no doubt already discovering, and they may surge quite as powerfully out of promise of frustration as out of promise of fulfilment.

'For, yes, I had to fuck my way through Laos a fortnight before that final, fateful encounter in a brothel I visited high in the hills, when the scent that filled the cubicle I entered almost made me faint, so quickly and thickly did it fill my penis with blood. Ah, and the girl that stirred on the pallet therein, the source of that too-delicious scent, she at last fulfilled the criteria of my search. She was obviously blind, *chérie*, but of a surpassing beauty and with flesh unmarked, so far as I could see, with any trace of sweat, despite the oppressive heat and humidity. As my fresh male odour reached – well, not her nostrils, but that term will pass – she responded with reaching arms and wide-splayed thighs and I threw myself on her with an eagerness I had not shown since the earliest days of my sensual apprenticeship.

'Oh, and the first contact I made with her skin told me in a brain-splitting, heart-twisting, cock-swelling flash that I had reached the end of my quest. Her skin was cool, *chérie*, and smooth in a way no other girl's – no *human* girl's – could ever be. And when I seized and gripped her, almost babbling with frustration at the momentary delay of penetrating her, I found that she was weightless in a way no human girl of comparable size and muscularity could be. Then, with a grunt that must have echoed throughout the entire brothel I was patronising, I plunged my blazing sword into her thigh-borne sheath to the root. Here again I found an immediate difference: her pseudo-vaginal canal, which was trembling and flickering with what promised, and indeed proved, to be much greater vibratory power, was *grooved* in a most peculiar but most cock-delighting fashion, and the lubricant that slicked it *stung* my cockhead and cockshaft in sharp but delicious ripples, screwing their sensitivity to a pitch of which I had never thought them capable.

'But I had no inkling of the storm that was about to fall on me, *chérie*. The light and seemingly fragile girl lying beneath me accepted the full length of my cock without a murmur and indeed with scarcely a movement. Her head arched back a little, allowing me to see that her perfectly sculpted nostrils were *culs-de-sac* ending perhaps a knuckle's-length into her head, and she seemed to await my first withdrawal and thrust. I was reluctant to supply it, revelling in the sensations afforded my cock by the pseudo-vagina it had penetrated, but my hips were, it seemed, eager for me to undertake the journey to orgasm and withdrew me without conscious command. Within two seconds I felt

211

as though I had stuck my cock into a hurricane or tornado: that first strong thrust into her sheath must, I concluded later, have triggered some pseudo-muscular mechanism. Her arms enfolded me with serpentine tightness and strength, her slender thighs locked around my waist and her velvety heels arched to lodge in the small of my back.

'Then she exploded into activity and I, outweighing her vastly, was barely able to retain my place atop her. She clung to me with all the tenacity and strength of ivy and thrust against me like one demented, her vibratory pseudo-vagina tightening and loosening and positively *rotating* on my poor cock, which, veteran of a thousand venerean encounters though it already was, felt as though it were about to be torn out by the roots. Her sexual scent had increased in strength so enormously that I felt as though my nostrils had assumed the size of saucers, sucking it directly into my brain, where it maddened and excited me half-way to delirium. I felt, *chérie*, as though every member of my body, every extension of my body, no matter how slight, was erect and ravenous for sexual pleasure. Most especially my cock, of course, which seemed to be doubling in size by the second, but also my arms and legs, my fingers and toes, my ears and nose, my ankles, my knees, my ear-lobes, my lips, my shoulders, my shoulder-blades – ah, the whole of me, my entire body was converted to a cock caught in the tightest and greediest and most delightful of cunnies.

'Yes, even her pseudo-labia had new tricks to play, engulfing and fluttering and even vibrating on my balls. By then, perhaps two seconds into my penetration of her pseudo-vagina, I had indeed lost my place atop her and she was almost throwing me about the cubicle with the vigour of her fucking. A hurricane or tornado, did I say? Nay, it was like fucking a maelstrom full of octopus and jellyfish, for beside the vigour of the

212

movement there was the *moisture* and the *suction* and the *stinging*. Yet the maelstrom was scented also, *chérie*, affording a universal feast of sensation that my senses gorged on and vomited up in the same instant. I believe that the overwhelming nature of her venereal assault, so shocking and surprising as it was, delayed my orgasm, but it arrived, in unprecedented strength, length and copiousness, at the end of the half-minute.

'The thick and salty drenching of that astonishing pseudo-vagina thereupon triggered some other pseudo-muscular mechanism, for the frenzy with which she had provoked me to orgasm instantly fell away into the gentlest, most soothing, most quickly erection-renewing sexual languor, in which her movements were barely detectable, seeming to accuse me of brutalising her, a tender slip of a girl. Had I not the sweat and bruises to testify to it, and had my cock not still been buried in that most peculiar and satisfying of pseudo-vaginas, I could scarcely have believed that this same girl had been fucking me hither and thither about the cubicle a few moments before. Her gentleness and the implicit accusation of rape, began to re-erect me, of course, Sadean disciple as I was, and the re-erection was evidently reported by the sheath in which it was buried, for in one breath she was stirring languorously beneath me and in the next she was the scented maelstrom full of jellyfish and octopus again, flinging me about the cubicle as before, or even more vigorously perhaps.

'Do you know, *chérie*, that I positively began to fear for my life during that second bout? Would I emerge from it with a working penis, with all my limbs intact and a whole skull? For, having so recently and so heavily spurted within her, I knew I would be unable to muster another orgasm quickly, and what but orgasm would calm this vegetable maenad? She was deaf to pleas, blind to the panic that I am sure showed in my face, and could achieve no orgasm of her own, indeed gained no pleasure of her own in the fucking. She was inaccessible, running on automatic mechanisms forged, or better say woven, in lost millennia of evolution, and all I could do was cling to her and hope. But I was wrong, *chérie*, in dismissing my chances of mustering another orgasm quickly. That vagina of hers, oh, it was the eighth wonder of the world, and during our second bout it was rotating on my cock as it sucked and vibrated on me, rotating a full three-hundred-and-sixty degrees, I could have sworn and have since confirmed it by direct observation, but that was not all, for now its *teeth* came into play.

'Aye, 'twas a true *vagina dentata* that was no true vagina. A *vagina dentatissima*, rather, for the teeth, blunt but hard, seemed to number in thousands – I have since discovered that they average between five and seven hundred – and chewed and munched most vigorously on my cock, simultaneously injecting into the microscopic abrasions thereby caused some new chemical of arousal. My fear that I would *lose* my cock to these teeth was not calmed by my theoretic knowledge of the orchid-girl's evolutionary history, which could never have stretched so long if her ancestors had castrated their copulands, but my fear perversely heightened my pleasure and that newly injected chemical caused my cock to swell and delight in her pseudo-vagina even further. You will remember, *chérie*, that my first orgasm had taken half-a-minute to arrive; my second was there within one, and as before my spurting within that astonishing sheath brought her instantly out of her frenzy and back to that most provoking languor.

'I first guessed then what I later confirmed by more direct investigation: that the orchid-girls *feed* on semen in some fashion, provoking its more copious flow in order to nourish themselves on the cocktail of chemicals it contains. So it proved: for each pseudo-vagina of the species culminates in a pseudo-cervix, which sucks the

214

semen most efficiently through to a pseudo-uterus, where it is absorbed into the peculiar bloodstream of these delightful but not undangerous creatures. For did I not lie there more heavily bruised than before, and praying to Venus, at most in quarter-jest, that I would not erect again? For I struggled, I swear to you, *chérie*, I struggled to release myself from my orchid-girl's grip both of body and of vagina, but her languor was a velvet glove on an iron hand – or rather, a velvet veil on steel arms and legs, for she gripped me still with those members and my bewildered cock was not released from the sheath into which I had plunged it so eagerly and so ignorantly barely two minutes before.

'Minutes? They seemed like hours. Oh, and the cubicle echoed to my groan as I felt myself, against my will, against my petition to Venus, began to re-erect again inside her. I felt like a mountaineer who has survived one avalanche only to stumble directly into a second and now, having staggered forth from that, feels the slope tremble beneath his feet and knows that a third is about to descend about his ears. So it proved, *chérie*, but to tell you the truth I remember little of that third venerean bout, that third sexual avalanche she sent crashing and roaring over me. I was too exhausted in body and mind, had discharged my balls too heavily not once but twice, and when my re-erecting cock re-triggered her frenzy, I seemed to pass into a trans-copulatory daze, a kind of sexual shell-shock – cock-shock, shall we say? – in which what happened to my body did not seem to be happening to *me*.

'I believe more by exercise of my reason than by true memory that I achieved a third orgasm with a speed I should have once thought impossible for a first, and that my partner, sensing no doubt through her pseudo-vagina that my cock was finally exhausted, released her grip on me and allowed me to crawl clear of her, as though of a loudly ticking bomb. But if bomb she was, she was of a kind that could explode repeatedly and remain intact to explode again. Then, collapsed and feebly groaning on my back, I vaguely remember the brothel-keeper supervising two underlings as they carried me from the room for a bath and massage, while the orchid-girl, I later discovered, was carried in a similar state of collapse to the roof, where she absorbed the sun while her alien chemistry assimilated the semen I had so pleasurably but so exhaustingly spurted into her.

'Krikorian later told me that during my massage he was sent for to translate a peculiar string of phrases I was mumbling in a manner that suggested they were of great urgency and import. To his surprise and chagrin, my faithful Armenian found that he was unable to do so. For I was rehearsing the scientific name of my orchid-girl, *chérie*. *Pseudophrys futuens*, should I call her? That is to say, "the false *Ophrys* that fucks". Or *Megalophrys futuens*, perhaps, "the great *Ophrys* that fucks"? *Colporchis odoratissima?* Which is to say "the most strongly scented vagina-equipped orchid" . . .'

Theodora murmured and farted again, slipping deeper into sleep and dream.

Thirteen

She was dreaming of what had taken place earlier in the day, when, folded in the Doctor's arms, she had overlooked that sun-bathing group of blind, deaf, green-skinned girls. She was to tell the Doctor what she thought they were *not*, and he had promised, in return, to tell her what they *were*. So she had swallowed and said:

'They . . . they are not girls, Doctor.'

Theodora murmured again in her sleep, re-living the moment at which, in his excitement, his arms had tightened painfully on her body. But then they loosened as he heard her groan of pain and whispered his reply:

'Precisely so, *ma petite délicate*. They are not girls, no, not at all. But then shall I tell you what they *are*?'

She swallowed again, feeling as though she were blindfolded and about to leap into space, not knowing how long she would fall or what she would fall into. Rose-petals? Thorns? Something unguessable?

'Yes, Doctor. Please tell me.'

'Then I will tell you, *ma* Théodora. They are *flowers*.'

Another murmur from the sleeping girl on the Doctor's lap, unnoticed by the Doctor himself, for he too was lost in a dream – a dream of his past, of that first encounter with an orchid-girl in a Laotian brothel. How Theodora's head had swum as the full meaning of his words had been absorbed by her brain. *Non filiae, sed flores!* Not girls, but flowers! The Doctor's arms tightened again on her body, reading the tremors that shook it, controlling them, calming them.

'No, *ma* Théodora, do not be afraid. I am not mad, nor are you dreaming, and I speak nothing but the truth. They are flowers, *chérie*, as you can see for yourself. Their blindness, their deafness, even their green-tinged skin might not be sufficient to mark them out as unhuman, but you have observed something beyond those things, something that can by no means be reconciled with membership of the human race. Their bonelessness, *chérie*. They have the shape, the grace and the beauty – or more than the grace and beauty – of human females, and yet they have no bones. How can this be, if they are human? How can it be? The answer is quite simple, *chérie*, quite, quite simple. It *cannot* be. Cannot be if they are human. But then they are *not* human, but flowers.'

'*Non filiae, sed flores*,' she had murmured, and the Doctor had grunted, not understanding her.

'What was that, *chérie*?'

'It's . . . it's just something I thought of a little while ago, Doctor. You know, like the pun Pope Gregory made when he saw the English slaves. *Non filiae, sed flores*.'

'Ah. I see. *Non filiae, sed flores*. Yes, that is very clever, *chérie*. I wish I could reward you for it, but alas, I could add nothing greater to the reward I already have prepared for you.'

She had felt one of his arms release her and glancing sideways had seen him gesturing to a nearby bush. She heard running feet on the grass and then two servants were in front of them, one of whom, oddly, continued to run on the spot at a further signal from the Doctor. The other carried a leather case that was just a little too small, she thought, to be contain a violin.

'Yes, *chérie*,' the Doctor continued, 'I have a great

reward prepared for you. Please throw off your gown and let Henri here equip you to receive it.'

The Doctor released her, stepping back and watching her, she saw as she glanced uncertainly over her shoulder, with a paternal smile.

'Come, *chérie*,' he whispered through the puff-and-pant and softly thudding footsteps of the running servant. 'Strip for Henri.'

She looked in front of her now, trying to read the expression in Henri's eyes. But he was staring straight ahead and keeping his face carefully expressionless. She swallowed, glanced back over her shoulder at the Doctor again, who nodded and smiled, then undid the belt of her dressing-gown and, with a sudden rush of bravado, let it slither from her shoulders and down her body to pool on the grass. She shivered slightly at its caress, distracted for a moment from Henri's face, so that she could not be certain whether his eyes widened fractionally with interest – or rather, with *lust*.

'*Excellent, chérie*,' came the whisper from behind her. '*Et maintenant, équippez-la*, Henri.'

The servant nodded, then went down on one knee, using the other knee to prop the case up as he opened it. The catches flew up under his strong thumb with bright metallic clacks that made Theodora twitch in her suppressed excitement, then with one hand he was lifting forth what the case contained and with the other slipping the case off his knee and laying it on the grass. Then, resting now on both knees, he shuffled forward to Theodora's groin. For a puzzled instant she did not understand what he had lifted forth, but then she understood. It was a double-shafted ivory dildo, with leather straps and an enormous pair of balls dangling between the two shafts, one of which, she was glad to note, was much shorter and much less thick than the other.

'*Préparez-la d'avance*, Henri,' came the whisper from behind her, and the fractional delay in which her brain translated the Doctor's words heightened the shock with which she felt the puff of breath on her sore cunny-lips before the young servant's lips and tongue were pressed there and working hard to moisten and dilate her for the dildo to be inserted. She responded quickly, gushingly, blushingly, for the other servant, still running on the spot, was remarking the cunnilingus with a strong erection that she could see bulging in his trousers.

'*Assez*, Henri,' came the whisper from behind her. '*Équippez-la.*'

She grunted with disappointment as the young servant's mouth left her cunny, then murmured with pleasure again as his hand replaced it, fingering her cunny-lips wider apart before he presented the smaller shaft of the dildo to her passage and gently, rotating it slightly left and right, began to slide it inside her. Suddenly, with a shiver of broken concentration, she smiled and snorted. The other servant, running on the spot as hard as ever, had nearly fallen over as his eyes flickered to the dildo, and she could see that his right hand was clenching and unclenching as he strove to keep it off his cock.

'*Faites attention*, Basile,' the Doctor whispered angrily, and Theodora saw the servant swallow and blink, dragging his eyes away from the dildo as it slid into her cunny. It was half-way up her now and Henri's other hand tapped her thighs. She heard him murmur, '*S'il vous plaît, mademoiselle*,' and adjusted her stance for him, allowing the dildo to slide yet deeper. She was already wondering what she was going to be ordered to do with it and her mouth was dry with excitement, her body shaking slightly with the pounding of her heart. But she could not understand how Basile fitted into her 'reward', as the Doctor had called it. Why was he running so hard on the spot? His face was crimson now with a combination of exercise, lust and chagrin at the Doctor's rebuke, and she could see threads of sweat trickling down his forehead, cheeks, upper lip and chin. His thick tongue came out, licking the sweat, and her cunny pulsed around the sliding dildo, longing for the tongue to be pressed to its sensitive folds, its more-than-sensitive cunny-horn.

But then the dildo had finished sliding inside her and Henri was testing it for firm insertion, shaking it a little, twisting it back and forth.

'*Est-il bien enraciné?*' came the Doctor's whisper. Henri slid back on his knees and stood up.

'*Oui, maître,*' he said. Theodora saw with a suppressed smile that he had a large bulge in his trousers too. The poor dears – to see her naked body, to stand so close to it, but to be unable to relieve their lust upon her!

'*Bien,*' whispered the Doctor. '*Voyez à les courroies.*'

Henri bent back to her, lifting the straps of the dildo, swinging them around her body to fasten them firmly around her bottom and waist. She could feel his fingers lingering unnecessarily on her buttocks and suppressed another smile. He could not help tormenting himself with her unattainable flesh! Or was it unattainable? What *was* the Doctor going to let her do? The Doctor was whispering something else now, but she didn't catch it. Something to do with Basile, who was – oh, had she spoken too soon? Basile had stopped running on the spot and, gasping from his exertions, had thrown his coat off and was beginning to unbutton his shirt.

'*Le pantalon*, Henri,' the Doctor whispered, and Henri bent to unbutton his fellow servant's trousers, then slid them carefully down, manoeuvring them around Basile's erection. *Is Basile going to fuck me?* Theodora wondered. His shirt was off now, dropped behind him on the grass as he stepped out of the trousers Henri had slid to his ankles, and Henri was working at the cord of his undergarments, ready to slide them down too. Theodora involuntarily licked at her

221

lips as she waited for his cock to spring into view. She could just imagine the length and thickness of it! And how it was ticking, almost throbbing, with the servant's vigorous young heartbeat. And his balls – they would be big too, sitting in a deliciously wrinkled and reddened ball-sack! She felt the dildo shift as her cunny-walls stirred and pulsed in tribute to the thought of it, gushing further cunny-juice.

'Théodora!' came the whisper, and she guiltily clutched at the dildo. It had begun to slide out a little, but how had the Doctor seen what it was doing? He was standing behind her still. But perhaps he had noticed her sway a little where she stood, knees weakening at the beauty of the young and muscular servant who was stripping in front of her. Yes, Henri was sliding his undergarments down now and his cock would – she frowned, grunting with disappointment. Basile's cock jerked into view, but it and his balls were looped with a strip of thick white cloth, almost mummified in it, concealing them from her eager gaze. The rest of him was naked now but for his cravat, which he was loosening with vigorous tugs, exposing the glistening, hair-coiled hollow of his right armpit.

Theodora's knees weakened again as she drew the scent of his sweat into her blood-inflamed nostrils. Such a fresh, strong, musky, masculine scent! She longed to have it smeared up the front of her body – breasts, belly, thighs – as Basile worked that long, thick cock slowly and soothingly in her cunny and Henri, whose bulge spoke of an equally splendid cock, smeared *his* sweat up her back and worked his cock slowly and soothingly in her bottom-hole.

Another whisper from the Doctor that she did not catch, and now Basile was stepping towards her. Was this it? Was he going to fuck her? But she still could not understand what the running-on-the-spot had been for. Ah. She tottered a little again, her knees loosening

222

beneath her as Basile stopped in front of her and the cloth-wrapped head of his cock brushed her flank.

'*Non*,' the Doctor whispered. '*Placez-vous à quatre-vingt-dix degrés.*'

And Basile turned himself to stand at ninety degrees to her, his cloth-swathed cock jutting out ahead of him in evident frustration. Theodora longed to drop to her knees in front of it, to tear the wrapping away, exposing the naked flesh of its huge head, cramming her mouth over it and seeing how much of its shaft she could swallow, till Basile's big bulging ball-sack was tight up against the fork of his thighs and he released its heavy load into her with a broken, sobbing groan of ecstasy, choking her with the thickness, saltiness and heat of his discharge . . . She shook her head, reluctantly emerging from the fantasy. The Doctor was whispering angrily again, and he was addressing her, not one of the servants.

'Pay attention, you little slut. I want you to smear yourself in Basile's sweat. Coat your hands in it and work it well into your body – every crevice, every hollow, *except* for your cunny and inner thighs. But keep your hands off his cock, do you hear? Henri will be attending to that.'

Theodora hesitated a moment. His sweat? She had to rub it into her body? But why? And it wasn't very . . .

'Théodora!'

The Doctor's whisper was low and venomous, implicit with threat.

'Get on with it, girl. Sweat – hands – rub. Now!'

She jerked guiltily and reached out for the solid, glowing male body in front of her, drawing in its rich masculine muskiness in a long, shuddering breath. It was fresh sweat, after all. Fresh sweat from fresh flesh. Basile grunted as her hands touched his body and she hid a smile. *I bet you're as sad I can't touch your cock as I am, poor boy*, she thought. Ah, how hot he was: she was almost burning her hands on him as she coated them in his sweat and then lifted them away to rub on her own skin. They flew almost against her will to her breasts and she closed her eyes with a grunt of her own as her palms, in which the heat of his body seemed to linger volcanically, pressed against her painfully peaked nipples. She rotated her hands on them, feeling her cunny pulse around the dildo inserted into it, releasing thick and burning juice to slide down her thighs.

Eyes still closed, sealing the richness of the smell and feel of him into her brain, she reached out for his body again, but her eyes flew open as she heard him grunt a moment before her hands touched him again. Ah, Henri had knelt in front of him, holding the cloth-swathed shaft of his cock steady in one hand as he began to unwrap the cloth with another. Her hands touched his flesh again, provoking another grunt, and she mischievously sent one sliding down his back to gather sweat on his lightly furred buttocks. She hid another smile: his cock had jerked as her hand touched his buttocks and she felt their muscles jerk and harden beneath her fingers. She was obeying the Doctor but fondling him at the same time.

But her hands flew back from his body prematurely: Henri had uncoiled a length of cloth with quick, sure movements and there, dripping with sweat, was the enormous head of Basile's cock. The sight of it made her cunny throb so powerfully on the dildo that she almost expected to hear a gastronomic lip-smack from below, and she had to have her hands on her breasts again, rubbing his sweat into her in tribute to the size and solidity of his organ. But what was Henri going to do? Was the Doctor going to make him *suck* Basile, like one of the 'nancy-boys' they had sometimes whispered about in the dorm? A wave of nausea struck her at the thought of it, but mixed with the nausea was a sharp, almost painful excitement. Imagine seeing one handsome boy sucking the cock of another handsome boy. And imagine the handsome boy swallowing the . . .

But no, so far the Doctor was saying nothing behind her and Henri's expression remained detached, almost clinical as he continued to unwrap Basile's enormous cock with one spiralling hand while the other held the unwrapped cloth beneath the droplets of sweat that poured off it. Would the whole cock have to be unwrapped before the Doctor ordered him to begin sucking? But why had the cock been wrapped anyway? She reached out again for Basile's body, feeling the ache in her nipples get even worse. Yes, she thought she'd be able to work an orgasm out of her nipples without putting a fingertip to her cunny, though she'd have to disguise it from the Doctor . . .

She jerked, almost crying out with fright. The Doctor's voice had sounded in her ear and she suddenly realised that he was standing right behind her.

'That's enough sweat on your tits, *chérie*. Elsewhere now, please. And do not tease Basile by fondling his buttocks under disguise of following my orders. You have harvested their sweat and are neglecting richer fields. His armpits, for example.'

She bit her lip in frustration, pulling her hand from Basile's buttocks, which she had been rubbing again. The Doctor walked to stand beside her and bent his head to sniff at her breasts. Henri had unwrapped half the length of Basile's cock now, still carefully catching the droplets of sweat that fell from it. Was that why the Doctor had moved forward? Was he ready to order Henri to begin sucking? She made a fist of one hand and pushed it at the dark curl of hair escaping from Basile's sealed nearer armpit. Still sniffing at her breasts, the Doctor whispered 'Basile' and the servant obediently lifted his arm for her.

She pushed her fist into the sopping nest of hair he thus exposed to her, rotating it, coating it in his sweat as her other hand roamed his flat, hard-muscled stomach. With a final sniff at her breasts, the Doctor raised his head.

'Good girl,' he whispered, watching as she withdrew her hands and began to rub the load of sweat they carried on her stomach. 'But your hands must stay well clear of your cunny, remember.'

'Very well, Doct—'.

A voice interrupted her.

'*Maître.*'

They both looked down and saw that Henri had finished unwrapping Basile's cock, pulling the length of cloth clear of it, but Basile's balls were still tightly swaddled in what must be a *separate* length of cloth. Theodora's cunny throbbed again and she had the sudden, glorious, searing hope that the Doctor would order Basile to take her from behind, ordering her to bend over and spread her buttocks for him, exposing the glistening pink –

'*Bien,*' whispered the Doctor. '*Épongez-lui et oindrez-la.*'

What was that? *Épongez* was 'sponge', wasn't it, but what was *oindrez?* Did it mean 'suck'? No, it couldn't be – Henri was to do it to *her*, not Basile. Her hands faltered on her stomach as she watched Henri rub the unwrapped length of cloth up and down his fellow-servant's cock, absorbing even more of the sweat that already soaked it. Then he lifted it away and a moment before she realised what he was going to do with it the Doctor was whispering again in her ear.

'*Oindrez* is "anoint", *chérie.*'

She gasped as Henri pressed the cloth, soaked with Basile's cock-sweat, to the dildo-shaft that jutted from her cunny and began to rub it up and down, making the other dildo-shaft move inside her cunny. But why was he doing this? What did the Doctor intend her to do? Breath touched her ear again and the Doctor whispered sharply.

'Sweat, *chérie*. Continue to rub yourself with Basile's sweat.'

She came out of her reverie, reaching for Basile's hot, solid flesh again, rubbing her hands on him, coating them in his sweat before bringing them back to her own body. Henri was mopping at Basile's cock again, gathering more sweat to rub into her dildo. But she still couldn't understand what all this was *for*. Why did the dildo have to have male sweat on it? Why did she have to rub Basile's sweat into her body? The Doctor was sniffing at her again, his head travelling up and down her flanks, confirming that Basile's sweat could be smelt on her skin. Apparently satisfied, he pulled his head back. She gathered two more palm-loads of sweat and rubbed them into her shoulders, then jerked with surprise. The Doctor's whisper was sounding again in her ear and he was pressing something into her hand.

'Take this, *chérie*. It will assist you to reach all parts of your back.'

Mechanically she took it, holding it up to see that it was a kind of back-scrubber, but with a head of soft absorbent cloth instead of bristles. Ah, she understood. She set the pseudo-scrubber to work on Basile's body. Her heart leapt for a moment as she rubbed the cloth-head over his nipples and he grunted with pleasure, his cock jerking even further from the horizontal. Would the Doctor rebuke her? She twitched guiltily as his voice sounded again, but he was speaking rapidly in French, issuing another order to Henri. She pulled the pseudo-scrubber back and began to rub it up and down her back, coating the silken knobbles of her spine in musky male sweat. Then, moments later, the scrubber was tugged briskly out of her hand and tossed aside. She felt her shoulders seized firmly by the Doctor, then felt his lips kiss her ear, lick at it. He whispered:

'*Es tu prête, ma* Théodora?'

Ready for what? she wondered, but she nodded,

feeling her stomach lurch with excitement around the fading glow of Basile's sweat, and replied, also whispering:

'*Oui, maître.*'

His strong hands tightened on her shoulders and she was turned to face downhill into that sun-bathing group of blind, deaf, green-skinned girls. Again the whisper came.

'*Es tu sûre que tu sois prête?*'

She swallowed, suddenly feeling sure that she *was* ready. This time she didn't whisper when she replied.

'*Oui, maître. Bien sûr.*'

The hands tightened even further, making her cry out softly for a moment with pain, and then released her with a sturdy push:

'*Alors, va-toi. Foutez-les. Foutez-les bien.*'

She had to run forward a few paces to keep from falling over, and began to look back over her shoulder, uncertain what the Doctor meant her to do. But his whisper reached her with hissing urgency:

'Go, *ma* Théodora. Fuck them. Fuck them all.'

She looked forward again and saw that one or two of the nearest girls seemed to have reacted to her approach: they had risen to their feet, opening their arms and beginning to swing and thrust their hips. But how did they know she was there? She took another step forward, and another. They must ... yes, they must be able to *smell* her – or rather, the male sweat that the Doctor had made her rub all over her body. Yes, they thought she was a man, and they wanted her to fuck them. She cried out softly again with pain: her nipples had hardened and throbbed with excitement as the realisation struck her. No, it was more than that: her nipples – and her cunny – were reacting not only to the thought that they wanted her to fuck them but also to the thought that she *could* fuck them. She had a cock, and by God she was going to use it.

Her faltering steps smoothed and lengthened, carrying her swiftly down on her prey, who were more and more aware of her presence. Almost all of the sunbathers were on their feet now, beckoning with blind, beautiful faces, wriggling or rotating their hips at her. Then their scent hit her: whether it had been there all along or was pouring fresh from their floral cunnies she was unable to decide later and did not care at the time. It was a delicious hot musk, so heart-racingly, so provokingly, so cock-stiffeningly female that she forgot that she herself was female, just as she had forgotten the three men who watched her from atop the slope. Her hand flew to the thick ivory-shaft that jutted from her loins and she rejoiced in the fact that her fingers could not close around it. Her whole body was tingling with the scent of the blind girls now and her heart was hammering in her chest like an engine. With a grunt of pure lust, she selected a target and sprang.

Looking back, she blushed at how clumsy she was as she tried to insert the dildo, though Winnie reminded her that it was hardly surprising: after all, she wasn't *really* a man and she had no idea how to use the great stiff piece of ivory between her thighs, and no instinct to come to her rescue either. But the orchid-girl knew exactly what to do: her slender arms, seemingly so fragile, so delicate, fastened like oak-roots on Theodora as the human girl's superior weight bore her down, and she expertly twisted and wriggled to lodge the head of the dildo in her cunny. Then, with a soft wheeze of that delicious flower-scent from her nose and mouth – there must have been air-spaces in her body, Theodora realised later – she impaled herself on the dildo's full length in one smooth movement, simultaneously swinging her slender legs around Theodora's waist.

Theodora, the breath driven out of her as those deceptively slender legs tightened on her like a vice, was caught between lust and panic now: for all her lightness, for all the softness of her body and the deliciousness of her scent, the orchid-girl was now in complete control, locking Theodora to her body and evidently ready to fuck like a maenad. Then the thrusts began, reported against Theodora's face in further soft wheezes of scent, and the human girl had the sudden conviction that the orchid-girl would have happily impaled herself on and thrust vigorously against a dildo twice as big. Her panic was subsiding now and her lust flaring up again to replace it: there was a perverse excitement in the contrast between the vigour of the orchid-girl's thrusts and the softness of her body, and particularly of the breasts that pressed against hers. As the orchid-girl began to fuck herself on the dildo, thrusting harder and harder, Theodora worried that she was going to bruise those soft flower-breasts, even cut into them, so stiff were the nipples she pressed against them.

But her worries for the orchid-girl's safety were lost in the next instant, for the excited crowd of other orchid-girls who surrounded the copulating pair now pounced. It seemed to have taken them a long time to react, Theodora thought bewilderedly at the time, but looking back she realised it could have been no more than one or two seconds. The speed and efficiency with which the first orchid-girl had impaled herself on the dildo had misled her, for no human girl could have accepted so much so swiftly. Be that as it might, even as she rolled with the first orchid-girl on the soft turf of the outdoor solarium, the other girls threw themselves into the fray, grappling indiscriminately with the penetratrix and the penetratee. Soft but exceedingly strong floral fingers, moist and faintly stinging with some aphrodisiac secretion, were suddenly prising her buttocks and the rear of her thighs apart, invading her bottom-hole and perineum and plucking and tugging at her dildo-splayed cunny-lips.

She couldn't decide on her own, then or later, whether the girls were trying to usurp or assist the sister who had impaled herself on the dildo. Perhaps it was both, or perhaps, she concluded after her first lecture about the orchid-girls from the Doctor, the whole situation was unnatural and could never have taken place in the wild. Perhaps orchid-girls spread themselves widely through their native jungle and never attempted to fuck a man in competition with another orchid-girl. But during a subsequent lecture from the Doctor she raised the topic and was told that the behaviour was entirely natural, though the number and unrelatedness of orchid-girls involved in *her* encounter was completely impossible in the wild. However, it often happened that a single *Megalophrys gynaecomorphica* seedling gave rise to two or more fully grown orchid-girls who could be regarded as identical twins, triplets, quadruplets or quintuplets. What was good for one was therefore good for all: by assisting a sister to copulate more effectively, a twin, triplet, quadruplet or quintuplet could assist the dispersal of her sister's genes, which were, of course, identical to her own.

Thus it was that the 'mobbing' Theodora had experienced had evolved to bring the penetrating male to even greater heights of ecstasy with his orchid partner, ensuring that he was thoroughly dusted with pollen; that he desired to penetrate her again; and finally, but by no means least, that his sperm flowed even more copiously into the orchid-girl's body. This sperm, the Doctor had discovered in his experiments, could and generally would later be shared with the orchid-girl's identical sisters in the form of a secretion from her breasts, almost as in human beings, and also, more exotically, from her shoulder-blades. Theodora's cunny had throbbed and moistened as she heard this, for she had pictured orchid-girls *suckling* an orchid-girl and her memories of the sexual 'scrum' in which she had been engulfed had returned in full strength.

But as the Doctor had explained, the 'scrum' she had experienced was both impossible in the wild, for never would so many orchid-girls be gathered in one place there, and wholly *unnatural*, in that the 'scrum' was composed of more or less unrelated orchid-girls, all striving to assist the penetratee by exciting the male penetrator (as they assumed her to be) to lengthier and more copious ejaculation. Theodora had nodded dreamily, feeling her thighs and bottom grow moist with reminiscence, and realising now that the scrum had not been the danger she thought it. If she had been dildoing a single orchid-girl she would been rolled and flung about as the Doctor had been during that first encounter of his in the brothel. Instead, she had been *cocooned*, as it were, by other orchid-girls, who had slowed and sweetened the frenzy of her partner's fucking. She shuffled where she sat on the Doctor's lap, remembering how their fingers had entered her bottom, tickling, stinging, provoking her, in conjunction with the knocking of the dildo in her cunny, to the first of her orgasms.

Ah. She sighed happily, counting off the orgasms she had had: seven at least, though towards the end she was laying extra orgasms on a single shuddering paroxysm that was almost frightening in its intensity. Indeed, it *had* begun to frighten her: she seemed to have whirled in the centre of a mass of soft and scented femininity for hours, buried 'to the balls' (she smiled, remembering how one of the soldiers had expressed it) in a cunny of astonishing muscularity and flexibility. No wonder the Doctor's cock had been so sore and inflamed after his first orchid-fuck! And how long, she wondered, would *her* first orchid-fuck have gone on? Now that the Doctor had confirmed the *unnaturalness* of the encounter, she thought it might have lasted for hours, till the pleasure of her orgasms had curdled and turned sour.

She had asked the Doctor at that point, groping beneath her bottom to learn whether his cock had stiffened again, and he had grunted and told her that she was right. It *would* have gone on for hours. That was why she had had to be 'hosed' free – after all, one of his male servants had nearly died of exhaustion during a similar experiment the previous year. Theodora nodded, feeling her cunny pulse luxuriantly, releasing another wave of hot juice as her groping hand reported that the Doctor's cock was indeed re-erecting. In another minute she would be on her knees before him, sucking, sucking, sucking. But she shivered momentarily too, remembering the 'hosing'. As she had rolled in increasing breathlessness in the middle of that 'scrum' of orchid-girls, streaming sweat in the scented heat created by her own body and the insulation of the rubbery orchidic bodies that pressed on her, she had suddenly felt an invasion of cold, and after a moment of shock had realised that icy – searingly icy – water was being sprayed on the 'scrum'.

The orchid-girl she had penetrated was still thrusting frenziedly against the ivory-dildo, but the 'scrum' around them was dwindling, as though blasted away by the streams of icy water. Now she caught glimpses of the men who were hosing her: it seemed to be the two servants, Henri and Basile, but they were dressed in strange, all-enveloping costumes that she later learnt were bee-keeper's outfits.

'Yes, *chérie*,' whispered the Doctor as, his cock fully erect again, he had pushed her gently off his lap and onto the floor for the fellatio to commence, 'it is dangerous, very dangerous, for a male of any age, but most especially a *young* male, to approach my orchid-girls unprotected. I positively believe – ah, *quel habilité!* – that they could rape a man to death, if allowed to work their wicked way with him undisturbed. That is why, *chérie – oui, oui, continue ainsi* – I have had those hoses installed near the orchid-girls' sun-bathing spot. Cold water is one of the simplest and most effective ways – *et les couilles, s'il le plaît* – of quieting *mes belles botaniques*, of making them relax their grip on a copulating couple. But the final girl, *la pénétrée*, well, as you remember yourself, it is difficult to make *her* relax her grip.'

Theodora had, with the Doctor's cock pushed almost to her throat, mischievously nodded and mumbled, experiencing a new sensation in her cunny: its present hot, oozing stickiness was overlaid strangely with a flesh-memory of the icy streams of water that had been directed between her thighs by Henri and Basile, as they tried to persuade the first orchid-girl to slide her own cunny off Theodora's ivory-dildo. It seemed a very long time that her cunny had been battered by the water, and when finally, the orchid-girl had slid reluctantly off and she herself had been able to rise shakily to her feet, she had fingered delicately at her cold-numbed cunny-lips and perineum, checking them for bruises as Henri, at the Doctor's whispered order, had begun to unstrap and slide forth the dildo.

Fourteen

'Pull!' Theodora shouted happily and Philippa, gagged and chained naked to an inverted wooden Y, was hauled aloft on a thick iron chain, able only to wiggle her wide-splayed feet to express her outrage.

'Pull!' Theodora shouted again, and an identically gagged, chained and naked Frances was hauled aloft too, feet wiggling with identical outrage.

'Pull! Pull!'

Theodora could not restrain her laughter now and it echoed between the iron walls of the shed as two more of Philippa's gagged, chained and naked lieutenants were hauled aloft to join their mistress. Knowing how it would increase Philippa's anger, she pretended to wipe tears from her eyes as she signalled to one of the Doctor's servants who had just hauled the girls aloft. He ran to a wall of the shed, picked up the wellingtons waiting there, and ran over to her.

'Slip them on me, there's an angel,' she said and the servant obediently knelt in front of her. She rested her hand lightly on his broad back as she looked up at the dangling quartet, who were twisting slowly back and forth on their chains, cunnies on full and humiliating display between their thighs, bellies bulging and chins still dripping with the water they had been forced to swallow, eyes wide above their gags, Philippa's in particular. Theodora grinned straight at her, then laughed again and really did have to wipe tears from her eyes this time. She signalled to another of the servants and he ran to fetch a small bull-horn for her. The wellingtons were on her feet as she accepted it with a murmur of thanks, incongruous beneath her elegant black riding outfit, and she stamped experimentally in them before nodding that the servants could pull the hessian mat away. As they ran to obey, she raised the bull-horn to her mouth and addressed the dangling girls, her voice distorted by her broad smile and echoing even more weirdly between the walls of the shed.

'Now, darlings, I know you're all dying to go – I'm sorry, getting ahead of myself there – I'm sure you're all dying to *know* just what all this is about and why you've all just been, ah, encouraged to drink so much water. The answer, darlings, is in the soil. Or rather, in the floor. Cast your eyes below you, darlings. See what those lovely big boys – and *aren't* they big, darlings? – are uncovering for you.'

The servants, whose trouser-bulges eloquently confirmed Theodora's words – had hauled away about half of the hessian mat now, revealing the huge disc of mottled metal that lay beneath it.

'Do you know what it is, darlings? No? Shall I give you a clue?'

She began to sing.

' "A sailor went to sea,

' "To see what he could see;

' "But all that he could see,

' "Was the bottom of the deep blue sea, sea, sea."

'Sea, darlings. Don't you see? Or rather . . .'

She traced a Cu in the air with her free hand, shook her head with a click of her tongue, and traced it again the other way around.

'Sorry, darlings. Forgot which way round it should be from your point of view. Now do you understand? Cu, darlings. Don't you see? Don't you . . .' She traced the

236

letters again. 'No? It's *copper*, darlings. And in a second or two, when those lovely big boys have finished exposing it for you, you're all going to be swung directly over it and you're going to dangle there till, well, I think I can express it best in song again:

' "Young Pippa swung to see,
' "To see what she could pee;
' "But all that she could pee,
' "Was pain for her poor cunny-ny-ny."

'Can you guess, darlings? Yes, that big copper thing is going to be *electrified* and you're all going to hang above it having drunk ever-so-much water at my gentle persuasion. That means, I'm afraid, that sooner or later, depending on how long you can restrain yourselves, one of you is going to . . .'

She raised her free hand and let it fall, twiddling her fingers to represent a stream of urine, then jerked it sharply up again to represent what was going to happen when the stream hit the electrified copper.

'And heavens, what a *noise* you will make as the stream of pee carries all those volts straight up to your cunny. Oh, yes, that reminds me. Basile, *les bâillons.*'

The mat was nearly off the copper disc now and Basile, trousers bulging even more from Theodora's description and mime of what was going to happen to the dangling girls, released the section he was holding and ran to a wall, where he picked up a long pole that had been lying there unnoticed. With a faint grunt he swung it into the air and carried it back beneath the dangling girls. One by one he tugged their gags down with the blunt hook at the end of the pole. Theodora shook her head at the noise that ensued as each began to shout at the top of her voice, Philippa issuing blood-curdling threats of what she was going to do when she got free, the other girls pleading with their tormentrix. Smiling, Theodora shook her head and raised the bull-horn to her mouth.

237

'Do shut your cake-holes, darlings. You might as well save your breath till you need it.'

The mat was fully off now and one of the other servants had run to the big vertical switch in the wall and was watching eagerly for her signal. Theodora strolled across the floor of the shed and onto the copper disc, which she stamped on in her wellingtons. Then she nodded to the waiting servant, who grinned and pulled the switch down with a loud *clack*. Now Theodora signalled to Basile, who was standing almost beneath the dangling quartet, pole resting on the floor of the shed as he waited for her signal. He nodded and brought the pole up again, having to work hard to control its full length. Theodora raised the bull-horn again.

'Now, girls, big Basile there is going to trundle you over to the pee-plate, as I think we can call it. If you look above you, you'll see that you're all attached to a kind of big wooden disc thingy that Basile will haul along a kind of roof-rail thingy – stop me if I'm getting too technical – until I'm satisfied you're all positioned perfectly over the pee-plate. Then the boys and I will sit and wait for the first cloud-burst, amusing ourselves as we see, well, as *I* see fit in the interim. But just in case' – she signalled to one of the servants again – 'any of you – and I'm thinking of you in particular, Philly – are planning to *burst* as soon as you get above me, well, as you shortly see, it won't do you any good. Thanks, darling.'

She had strolled to the edge of the copper disc as she had been speaking; now she took a furled umbrella from the servant who was standing cautiously on its border. Strolling back to the centre of the disc, she put the umbrella up and swung it above her head, then stood peering from beneath it, grinning with malicious glee, as Basile began to haul the dangling quarter of chained-and-splayed eighteen-year-olds towards her.

nexus

The leading publisher of fetish and adult fiction

TELL US WHAT YOU THINK!

Readers' ideas and opinions matter to us so please take a few
minutes to fill in the questionnaire below.

1. Sex: Are you male ☐ female ☐ a couple ☐?

2. Age: Under 21 ☐ 21–30 ☐ 31–40 ☐ 41–50 ☐ 51–60 ☐ over 60 ☐

3. Where do you buy your Nexus books from?
☐ A chain book shop. If so, which one(s)?

_____

☐ An independent book shop. If so, which one(s)?

_____

☐ A used book shop/charity shop
☐ Online book store. If so, which one(s)?

_____

4. How did you find out about Nexus books?
☐ Browsing in a book shop
☐ A review in a magazine
☐ Online
☐ Recommendation
☐ Other _____

5. In terms of settings, which do you prefer? (Tick as many as you like.)
☐ Down to earth and as realistic as possible
☐ Historical settings. If so, which period do you prefer?

_____

☐ Fantasy settings – barbarian worlds
☐ Completely escapist/surreal fantasy
☐ Institutional or secret academy

- ☐ Futuristic/sci fi
- ☐ Escapist but still believable
- ☐ Any settings you dislike?

_____

- ☐ Where would you like to see an adult novel set?

_____

6. In terms of storylines, would you prefer:

- ☐ Simple stories that concentrate on adult interests?
- ☐ More plot and character-driven stories with less explicit adult activity?
- ☐ We value your ideas, so give us your opinion of this book:

_____

_____

_____

7. In terms of your adult interests, what do you like to read about? (Tick as many as you like.)

- ☐ Traditional corporal punishment (CP)
- ☐ Modern corporal punishment
- ☐ Spanking
- ☐ Restraint/bondage
- ☐ Rope bondage
- ☐ Latex/rubber
- ☐ Leather
- ☐ Female domination and male submission
- ☐ Female domination and female submission
- ☐ Male domination and female submission
- ☐ Willing captivity
- ☐ Uniforms
- ☐ Lingerie/underwear/hosiery/footwear (boots and high heels)
- ☐ Sex rituals
- ☐ Vanilla sex
- ☐ Swinging
- ☐ Cross-dressing/TV
- ☐ Enforced feminisation

☐ Others – tell us what you don't see enough of in adult fiction:

_____

_____

_____

8. Would you prefer books with a more specialised approach to your interests, i.e. a novel specifically about uniforms? If so, which subject(s) would you like to read a Nexus novel about?

_____

_____

_____

9. Would you like to read true stories in Nexus books? For instance, the true story of a submissive woman, or a male slave? Tell us which true revelations you would most like to read about:

_____

_____

_____

10. What do you like best about Nexus books?

_____

_____

11. What do you like least about Nexus books?

_____

_____

12. Which are your favourite titles?

_____

_____

13. Who are your favourite authors?

_____

_____

14. Which covers do you prefer? Those featuring:
(Tick as many as you like.)

- ☐ Fetish outfits
- ☐ More nudity
- ☐ Two models
- ☐ Unusual models or settings
- ☐ Classic erotic photography
- ☐ More contemporary images and poses
- ☐ A blank/non-erotic cover
- ☐ What would your ideal cover look like?

_____

_____

15. Describe your ideal Nexus novel in the space provided:

_____

_____

_____

_____

16. Which celebrity would feature in one of your Nexus-style fantasies?
   We'll post the best suggestions on our website – anonymously!

_____

THANKS FOR YOUR TIME

Now simply write the title of this book in the space below and cut out the
questionnaire pages. Post to: Nexus, Marketing Dept., Thames Wharf Studios,
Rainville Rd, London W6 9HA

Book title: _____

NEXUS NEW BOOKS

To be published in July 2007

MOST BUXOM
Aishling Morgan

One thing rules Daniel's life, voyeurism. A desire far too strong to be denied, despite all the guilt it brings him. He knows the risks and is determined to give up his filthy habits. But when he finds himself as landlord to four voluptuous young female students the opportunities for peeping are far too good to resist. Unfortunately he has bitten off far more than he can chew.

Most Buxom should be a delight for all those who enjoy the female body in its full, opulent glory, while there is also plenty of the sort of kinky sex we have come to expect from Aishling Morgan, and even a splash of male submission.

£6.99   ISBN 978 0 352 34121 1

THE UPSKIRT EXHIBITIONIST
Ray Gordon

Mark and Anne have been tempted by the idea of wife swapping since their first shared sexual fantasies. They have the desire, the determination and a watertight relationship. Only thing missing has been the right couple to swing with.

But that small hurdle is overcome when they move next door to the sexy and exciting Johnny and Lisa. Their new neighbours are avid swappers and engaged in organising the season's largest swinging party.

As Mark and Anne take their first tentative steps into the waters of swapping they are soon immersed in a tidal wave of new experiences. The only thing left for them to discover is whether or not their relationship is truly watertight.

£6.99   ISBN 978 0 352 34122 8

If you would like more information about Nexus titles, please visit our website at www.nexus-books.com, or send a large stamped addressed envelope to:
Nexus, Thames Wharf Studios,
Rainville Road, London W6 9HA

NEXUS BOOKLIST

Information is correct at time of printing. To avoid disappointment, check availability before ordering. Go to www.nexus-books.co.uk.

All books are priced at £6.99 unless another price is given.

NEXUS

☐ ABANDONED ALICE	Adriana Arden	ISBN 978 0 352 33969 0
☐ ALICE IN CHAINS	Adriana Arden	ISBN 978 0 352 33908 9
☐ AQUA DOMINATION	William Doughty	ISBN 978 0 352 34020 7
☐ THE ART OF CORRECTION	Tara Black	ISBN 978 0 352 33895 2
☐ THE ART OF SURRENDER	Madeline Bastinado	ISBN 978 0 352 34013 9
☐ BEASTLY BEHAVIOUR	Aishling Morgan	ISBN 978 0 352 34095 5
☐ BEHIND THE CURTAIN	Primula Bond	ISBN 978 0 352 34111 2
☐ BELINDA BARES UP	Yolanda Celbridge	ISBN 978 0 352 33926 3
☐ BENCH-MARKS	Tara Black	ISBN 978 0 352 33797 9
☐ BIDDING TO SIN	Rosita Varón	ISBN 978 0 352 34063 4
☐ BINDING PROMISES	G.C. Scott	ISBN 978 0 352 34014 6
☐ THE BOOK OF PUNISHMENT	Cat Scarlett	ISBN 978 0 352 33975 1
☐ BRUSH STROKES	Penny Birch	ISBN 978 0 352 34072 6
☐ CALLED TO THE WILD	Angel Blake	ISBN 978 0 352 34067 2
☐ CAPTIVES OF CHEYNER CLOSE	Adriana Arden	ISBN 978 0 352 34028 3
☐ CARNAL POSSESSION	Yvonne Strickland	ISBN 978 0 352 34062 7
☐ CITY MAID	Amelia Evangeline	ISBN 978 0 352 34096 2
☐ COLLEGE GIRLS	Cat Scarlett	ISBN 978 0 352 33942 3
☐ COMPANY OF SLAVES	Christina Shelly	ISBN 978 0 352 33887 7

☐ EMMA'S SECRET DOMINATION	Hilary James	ISBN 978 0 352 34000 9
☐ EMMA'S SUBMISSION	Hilary James	ISBN 978 0 352 33906 5
☐ FAIRGROUND ATTRACTION	Lisette Ashton	ISBN 978 0 352 33927 0
☐ IN FOR A PENNY	Penny Birch	ISBN 978 0 352 34083 2
☐ THE INSTITUTE	Maria Del Rey	ISBN 978 0 352 33352 0
☐ NEW EROTICA 5	Various	ISBN 978 0 352 33956 0
☐ THE NEXUS LETTERS	Various	ISBN 978 0 352 33955 3
☐ PLAYTHING	Penny Birch	ISBN 978 0 352 33967 6
☐ PLEASING THEM	William Doughty	ISBN 978 0 352 34015 3
☐ RITES OF OBEDIENCE	Lindsay Gordon	ISBN 978 0 352 34005 4
☐ SERVING TIME	Sarah Veitch	ISBN 978 0 352 33509 8
☐ THE SUBMISSION GALLERY	Lindsay Gordon	ISBN 978 0 352 34026 9
☐ TIE AND TEASE	Penny Birch	ISBN 978 0 352 33987 4
☐ TIGHT WHITE COTTON	Penny Birch	ISBN 978 0 352 33970 6

NEXUS CONFESSIONS

☐ NEXUS CONFESSIONS: VOLUME ONE	Ed. Lindsay Gordon	ISBN 978 0 352 34093 1

NEXUS ENTHUSIAST

☐ BUSTY	Tom King	ISBN 978 0 352 34032 0
☐ DERRIÈRE	Julius Culdrose	ISBN 978 0 352 34024 5
☐ ENTHRALLED	Lance Porter	ISBN 978 0 352 34108 2
☐ LEG LOVER	L.G. Denier	ISBN 978 0 352 34016 0
☐ OVER THE KNEE	Fiona Locke	ISBN 978 0 352 34079 5
☐ RUBBER GIRL	William Doughty	ISBN 978 0 352 34087 0
☐ THE SECRET SELF	Christina Shelly	ISBN 978 0 352 34069 6
☐ UNDER MY MASTER'S WINGS	Lauren Wissot	ISBN 978 0 352 34042 9
☐ WIFE SWAP	Amber Leigh	ISBN 978 0 352 34097 9

NEXUS NON FICTION

☐ LESBIAN SEX SECRETS FOR MEN	Jamie Goddard and Kurt Brungard	ISBN 978 0 352 33724 5